SOUTHERN
TRUTHS

Also from B Cubed Press

Alternative Truths

More Alternative Truths: Tales from the Resistance

Madam President

Alternative Theology

Alternative Apocalypse

Stories for the Thoughtful Young

Poems for the Thoughtful Young

Space Force

Alternative War

Alternative Deathiness

Spawn of War and Deathiness

The Protest Diaries

Alternative Holidays

Holiday Leftovers

Post Roe Alternatives

Madam President

When Trump Changed by Marleen S. Barr

Southern Truths

Edited by
K.G. Anderson and Bob Brown

Cover Design
K.G. Anderson

Published by

B Cubed Press
Kiona, WA

Copyright

Foreword

The South is many things.
An attitude.
An illusion.
But most of all it is the apex of denial,
Denial of actual history.
Denial of the creation of false history.
The fall into truth will be long and hard.
But, the South will still survive.
And probably forget it ever fell in the first place.

Southern Truths

Table of Contents

Southern Truths

They Hear

Kay Hanifen

I'm going to let you in on a little trade secret about the ones you pray to. High in the clouds, beyond the gates, they hear your pleas. Over the sound of hosannas and worship.

They hear every word. Did you know that? Every. Single. Word.

They hear the children whispering prayers for a God to intervene while they hide under their desk and pretend that no one's home and there are no gunshots echoing down the hallway, a supposedly safe place becoming a warzone without warning.

They hear the woman backed into her bathroom, begging someone, anyone, to hear her when her drunken husband is waving a gun in her face.

They hear the futile, whispered prayers of a child who found a loaded gun and accidentally shot their sibling, their friend, their pet, their parent. The terror as they clutch at the wound and beg them to be okay as life slips through their fingers.

They hear it all.

You ask: where is the mercy? Where is their savior? Where are the heroes that Hollywood promised, the ones that break down the door and take down the shooter before riding into the sunset?

Those heroes aren't here. The people who were meant to save the day sat outside, too afraid to enter and intervene lest they become a target. To serve and protect is a dubious commitment for those so-called heroes and civil servants. Cowards may die a thousand deaths, but at least they live to die another day. It's a shame that this can't be said of the innocents killed by their inaction.

So, you pray. You reel from tragedy after tragedy and beg your fellow beings, those in power to DO SOMETHING. Anything. But you are met only with thoughts and prayers instead of help and action.

Now is not the time.

What's the saying? The Lord helps those who help themselves?

He doesn't.

I know this. And deep down, you know.

I suppose that's why you summoned me, then. A last resort, but in any case, it's always nice to be wanted.

And so here we are: A grieving parent crying out for justice and a demon in a summoning circle.

Dry your tears, Mother, because your wish is my command.

If you so desire, every politician who has cried "law and order" and "thoughts and prayers" while making it easier for murderers to get these guns will be tormented with nightmares the rest of their lives. Nightmares in which everyone they know and care about is shot to oblivion before the gunman turns his weapon to them.

I can arrange it for you. Perhaps they will suffer a mysterious illness in which they feel the pain of a bullet piercing flesh every time someone in the United States gets shot. That would be fitting, I think.

And what of the lobbyists who profit from your pain? What would you like me to do to them? I must say, what my colleagues did to Sarah Winchester was inspired. Deaths and human suffering are always hypothetical to those types. Though they live by the sword—or at least by the profits from the sword—they seldom die by it. Endless torment has many faces, I find it best when it is a familiar face that cannot be persuaded by money or killed... had it happened in life, they might have learned their lesson. What do you say to that? Does it fill any voids?

I see that you want something more personal, too. As much as you appreciate the big picture, you're thinking of the cowards in bulletproof vests who waited outside the building while kids were shot and bled out? Some victims were identifiable only by the socks they wore. They died. Your daughter died and those men still had the gall to call themselves heroes.

This is the vengeance you want. I can tell. They failed you. They failed your daughter. When it was time to face something more frightening than a traffic stop or a teenager with a dime bag of marijuana, they hid outside and left your daughter to die. Think about what you want. I, for one, am partial to visions of the dead tormenting the living. Perhaps they'll see the accusing faces of the kids they failed everywhere they go. And those children will cry night and day.

"Who are you?"

"Coward."

"What do you want?"

"Coward."

"Leave me alone!"

3

"Coward."

Don't worry, they won't actually be the children. The dead deserve their eternal reward.

And speaking of the dead's reward, if I am to be the answer to your prayers, what would you have for your daughter's murderer? I have him down for burning, flaying, auto-cannibalism, being torn apart by Furies with the faces of his victims, and a loop of "It's a Small World." Can you think of anything else you want, so I can make sure he knows it comes from you?

That is good. I'll put him down for getting shot to bits while his memories of his peers point and laugh at him? Creative but fitting. Are you sure this isn't your first Hell-pit design? If you weren't, you know, a mortal human, I'd offer you a spot on my team. But that will come later.

Is that all? Yes? Well, then I shall answer your prayer.

Payment? Your life is Hell enough, and you must live it until its natural end.

And yes, I'll see you then. Maybe. Maybe not. I don't need your soul. We were never really in the soul-purchasing business anyway. The suffering of a righteous sinner is not nearly as sweet as you might expect, because no matter how much pain I might inflict on you in Hell, you will take the torture with the comfort that your pain is noble. It's all worth it if it means that no one has to suffer the way that you did. And that leaves a sour taste in my mouth and in the mouths of my fellow demons.

I must warn you, though, that revenge will not fill that hole in your soul.

Take some advice from old Beelzebub, okay? Find something other than grief and revenge to latch onto. Find a way to live even though your world has ended. Your pain will never truly go away, but as life moves on, it becomes easier to carry. Memories of your daughter will always be tinged with grief, but I promise you that one day, you will be able to tell stories about her and laugh instead of cry or rage at the heavens.

They hear every prayer. So, don't let them forget. Maybe you can be the one. Maybe, you will make them listen.

Southern Truths

The Great Georgia Lesbian Potluck

Sara Willey

I heat the peanut oil and I pray for love. Actually, I'm not sure if praying is what I'm doing. I don't know if I've ever really prayed. But since I am at a 200-year-old Christian tent revival, praying seems to be the thing to do.

At Fountain Campground, I often find myself peeking from behind clasped hands while my family says grace, or while the evening preacher drones for ten minutes at a time.

It is Georgia, and it is hot. For good measure, I pray for a cool evening and a cold night. I am standing in the kitchen of an open-air wood cabin with a tin roof and a sawdust floor. The most recent technological advancements in this cabin are the fridge, stove, and running water from the sink. My grandmother remembers older camp meetings when there was no electricity or running water, and all the camp attendees would bathe in a stream a quarter of a mile away. I send up a silent "thank you" for the leaky showerhead in our bathroom.

I look outside. "Outside" is all around us, as there are no windows or doors in this place. The landscape is one of pine trees and red clay and anthills. The air is warm and wet. Our cabin is one of 25 others that form a ring around a large, open-air pavilion with a gabled tin roof and twenty or so rows of pews. The arrangement is affectionately called "the tents" and "the tabernacle."

I return to the task at hand: cooking a batch of fried green tomatoes for the church potluck tonight. My grandmother dips each bright green slice of tomato into batter as I start to fry. A three-year-old girl whose name I do not know runs between my legs twice, then skips away to go play. I am worried about what the preacher will say tonight. I am always worried about what the preacher will say. I have been ever since I was 8 and heard for the first time that every single gay person in the world was going to hell. At the time I was sad, I didn't realize yet that I was gay. Now I think it's embarrassing how numb I am to the sickness of this place. Every day, my friends and relatives toss around racist and homophobic remarks as naturally as if they were asking me to pass the biscuits.

The strangest part of it is that I know several people who visit this old-time camp meeting are gay like me. Why do we endure the same moral flogging year after year? Why don't we just leave? There was an old lesbian, a great aunt of mine, whose name I will not mention for her privacy. She lived in Georgia all her life, had a female life partner, and her entire extended family pretended like her gayness didn't exist. She was tolerated, as long as she submitted to the raised eyebrows and whispers. I'm ashamed I never asked her about her girlfriend. But she knew I was gay. One muggy evening at Fountain she quietly sat next to me on our porch swing. We said nothing for a long time. I slapped a mosquito on my ankle.

"I used to be like you, all quiet and shy-like," she almost whispered. I looked at her, uncomprehending. She smiled.

"Don't be shy. Tell these 'uns what you've got to say, all right?" My great-aunt's voice sounded like an old door opening. I realized we had never spoken directly to each other before.

Whether my grandmother had told her, or she simply guessed, I'll never know. But something passed between us that night, unspoken, and some deep instinct inside told me she knew. I was okay with that.

I spoon out another batch of fully fried tomatoes from the hot oil and place them on a plate. I remember that exactly one year ago today, I was doing this same thing. Making fried green tomatoes for the potluck. I remember that afternoon, I had walked over to the 30-foot-long picnic table behind the tabernacle to drop off my food when I stumbled upon a rare sight: the first Black preacher ever to set foot in Fountain Campground.

It's hard to explain to people just how white the church camp I attend is. I could only imagine how nervous this man must be feeling. You can't get to the campsite using Google Maps, and the whole place is easily fifteen miles away from civilization in any direction. In other words, it was an invitation to preach in the middle of nowhere to a group of the whitest Christian Republicans of all time.

The Black preacher was sitting in the front pew, calmly looking over his heavily dog-eared Bible. I ran back to the tent to grab him a glass of ice water. Upon my return, I saw an old white man had driven his golf cart as close as he physically could to the preacher without literally parking the cart under the tabernacle roof. He sat hunched over the steering wheel, glaring at the preacher with more hate than I've ever seen on someone's face in my life.

I stood there for a moment, pondering what to do. To his credit, the preacher quietly practiced his sermon, ignoring the man in the golf cart. I finally decided to approach, and with as much cheerfulness as possible, broke the tense silence with a "Preacher, it's hot out here! You want some water?"

It's hard to separate out my feelings about the South.

There's prejudice, hatred, and blind religion, but then... there's this. Good food and my family. The smell of pine in the air. Strange children running in and out of our tent because they know that here, there are no strangers.

I recall a summer when my sister was five and I was three, and we had wandered a good distance down the dirt road, away from our tent. I believe my older sister was trying to lead me to the stream to play. Along the way, we became fascinated with an amorphous sculpted structure made of red dirt with hundreds of tiny holes drilled through it, about a foot high. We got the bright idea to step on it, unwittingly plunging our feet into a fire ant's nest. White hot pain shot up my ankles as dozens of ants bit me. A man in his twenties riding by on a four-wheeler heard our anguished cries of pain and quickly scooped the two of us up. We didn't know him, but he knew who we belonged to, and he plopped us on the four-wheeler and whisked us to our no-nonsense grandmother's lap.

Telling that story to my friends from the North, I commonly get reactions of dismay.

"So, some random guy grabbed you?"

"Why weren't your parents watching you?"

"Why would you go to a state where there's such a thing as a fire ant?"

Unfortunately, my Yankee friends are missing the point. One of the most beautiful old-fashioned Southern attitudes is, in my opinion, the idea that all children are your own. Any toddler walking in your field of vision is your responsibility, for better or for worse. And if you are a parent, then the village is right there, waiting to raise your child.

So, when well-meaning Northerners insist that it would be just as well if the South seceded again, and that the whole region is backwards and an embarrassment, I can't agree. A lifetime of summers in Georgia has only shown me that this place is worth saving. I think again about leaving. Whether I mean Georgia, the church, my family, I don't know. It's the same thing. But how could I leave? When there are guitars to be played outside while dusk settles and babies to hold and peaches to eat? How could I leave, when I know that tonight I will laugh harder playing cards with my cousins than I will all the rest of the year? How could I abandon the sound of rain on a tin roof or the taste of sweet tea brewed in the sun?

I finish my last batch of fried green tomatoes, smell the smoky-sharp smell of warm oil and flaky salt. I take a bite of one. I burn my tongue and I pray, really pray, for love.

Southern Truths

It's Election Day in Texas and I'm a Democrat Rarin' to Vote

Larry Hodges

Voting. It's our civic duty.

Everyone says it.

They drilled it into us for years, and that's why they made Election Day a federal holiday.

Then they forgot to give us guns. How the hell are we supposed to vote? *Morons.*

No problem, I'll pick one up across the street at Chick-fil-A on the way. Yes, it's the first Tuesday after the first Monday in November, and Election Day is finally here! It's so exciting to be one of the millions of Americans who will vote today!

Of course, here in Texas, voting is a bit... dicey.

Someone put out a book about voting in Texas and the rest of the South, explaining the pitfalls and how to overcome them. Alas, like all those other books, it was banned. So I will have to wing it.

I put on a nice suit and tie with an oversized flag pin. Got to blend. Hopefully, they won't notice my Air Jordan running shoes. I might need those. Nothing will stop me from voting. *It's my civic duty.*

I need to hurry, it's already late afternoon. I peek out the front window. There are no Republicans in sight, but they could be hiding.

"Where are you going?" It's my wife, Aliyah. "You're not sneaking out to vote, are you?"

It's never easy. "We talked about this. We have to."

"You want to turn our future kids into orphans? Get back here, buster!"

I sigh. "At least one of us has to do this."

"At least *none* of us has to do this!" She mocks me in a singsong voice.

With an exaggerated accent I say, "I may brang home some them Republicans fer suppa, so make sure to have some beef steak and pecan pie with vanilla ice cream."

I lean over and kiss her. She can't help but laugh.

"Bye, honey!" I say.

"Don't you dare come back dead!"

I'm half scared to death already, but I can't let her know that. I open the door carefully in case there's a Republican lurking. The coast looks clear. I take a few deep breaths... *and then run like hell!*

The Chick-fil-A is just across the street. I should be able to make it.

"Hey, you! *Stop!*"

I glance over my shoulder. Old white guy, overweight, blue blazer with American flag lapel pin, even bigger than mine, thin red tie, Oxford elevator shoes... it's a Republican! Of course, the MAGA cap was just gilding the lily.

He isn't carrying a weapon, so I slow to a jog just to taunt him. He puts on a blaze of speed like a box turtle on meth. I give him a wave and pull away.

"Hey, you're Black!" He's gaping at me. I'm guessing my two-foot afro gave it away. "Go back home, this is Election Day!"

I glance back just in time to see him frisbee his MAGA cap at me like a boomerang. *Oh my God, I'm going to die!* The bill is like a machete, spinning too fast to see, coming right at my throat. I duck just in time. It spins past and hits a telephone pole, cutting right through it. The pole falls over onto my house, smashing into my roof, which caves in. That's gonna cost a bunch.

I put on my own blaze of speed and reach the street.

There's a motorcycle gang coming from the left, all denim and leather, the White Widows. There's a Ford pickup coming from the right, a dead buck with huge antlers tied up on the roof. Great, the two most common subspecies of MAGA Republicans. They are smiling and waving and coming straight at me, all Southern hospitality and all.

I zig and zag and finally leap directly over the final biker as he screams polite Christian curses and the pickup just misses ramming me and sends a motorcycle spinning instead. I make it across the street and into the Chick-fil-A parking lot and make a final sprint for the door. *Whew!*

A dozen people stare at my afro as I enter. I pull out my wallet and hold it up. "I'm a paying customer, not here to rob the place." Everyone nods and goes back to whatever they were doing. There are two lines, two people in each. I get in the left line, of course.

Both people in front of me nod and smile and go over to the other line.

"Can I help you?" asks the smiling cashier.

"One spicy chicken sandwich, a lemonade, and an AR-15."

"Will that be with armor-piercing or hollow points?"

"Armor-piercing with the extended magazine," I answer, anticipating the follow-up question.

"Coming right up." A moment later I have my food, drink, and the gun, which I sling over my back. I find an empty table, nod as the people on the adjacent table nod back and move to other tables, and then I eat.

Soon I'm ready to vote.

As I get up, a couple of brawny white Texans saunter towards me. I nod and hold up the AR-15 and they nod back, showing me their hands as they slowly back away and return to their seats. But as I walk to the door one of them is making a phone call, getting the word out. The suit-and-tie thing might work for Clarence Thomas, but not for me. I pull the clothes off and toss them in the trash. Underneath I have my black hoodie and a few jingling gold chains. They're uncomfortable and I never wear them anywhere except when I'm visiting white areas and want to drive them nuts.

Now I'm ready to vote.

But first I have to get there. I wonder if that's what Columbus said before he left to discover America? If only the first people living here had known they were on America and let everyone know that 20,000 years ago, saying, "Hey, look what we found?", then they'd have been famous like Columbus for discovering America and have their own national holiday named after them. But no, those first Americans and their descendants just went about their way, living their lives. Oh, wait...

The nearest voting facility open to Black people is on top of a steep, snowy mountain, fifty miles away, in a bear's den, with five famished grizzlies pacing about the voting machine, which sits on an island in a pit of lava. Okay, I'm kidding, the federal courts closed that one down and the new one is at Martin Luther King

Elementary School, about five miles away. (Of course, every school in a Democratic area is called Martin Luther King.) In the Republican area, of course, there's a voting place at every Starbucks, two on every block, where you can get an iced latte and ammo.

The school is going to be heavily guarded, but I've got my AR-15 and I've got the bullet-proof vest I got for my birthday—*oops, I forgot it!* I consider going back home for it, but by now I'm sure Texas Rangers are surrounding my house, and I'm not talking baseball.

Hiding behind a tree, I call for an Uber. Minutes later it arrives. But... it's a Ford Mustang convertible! *How did they know to send a Republican?* Still hidden, I cancel on my phone. I order another... and it's a Ford Expedition! *Jeez....* I cancel again. I try one more time... and this time it's a Honda Civic Hybrid. *Bingo.* I chat with the driver as we go to the polling place, though I have no idea what he's saying since I think it's either Arabic, Swahili, or French.

We finally reach Martin Luther King Elementary School. The driver parks and then turns around and pats me on the shoulder. We both know my chances. But I have to give it my best.

It's one hundred feet to the entrance. There's a rule, no electioneering or campaigning within one hundred feet of a polling station, and other than the Republicans within one hundred feet who are electioneering and campaigning, the rule is strictly enforced. They've chopped down all the trees within one hundred feet to help enforce this. But it's solid majestic oaks beyond that. From this distance I can't tell where the snipers are hidden.

I wish I had my bulletproof vest.

Then I have an idea. Using hand gestures, I negotiate with the Uber driver, and we reach an agreement. I give him $50, and he hands me a lug wrench. I get out of the car on the far side from the school, knowing the snipers would be on the roof. I unscrew the two rusty hubcaps on that side. Normally I'd use the AR-15 for covering fire, but I won't have any hands free to do that, so I keep it strapped to my back. Then, holding up the hubcaps for protection, I sprint for the school door.

The first ten feet is silent. I think I've caught them off guard. But then a bullet caroms off one of the hubcaps, then another, and another. *Pop, Crackle, Smack!* It's like popcorn. A bullet smacks into my gold chain, like a Mike Tyson straight right. Another bullet smacks a hubcap into my skull, and I see stars and ballots circling my head. With ten feet to go, bullets whistle by my ear, between my legs, through my Afro, and I swear one goes right in front of my face, stops for a second, and sticks out its tongue at me as it passes.

One of the Republicans who is electioneering and campaigning within one hundred feet tries to block me, but he's had too much grits and Texas barbecue over the last few years and I easily dodge around him. Dizzy, and with a terrible headache, I make a final dive through the entrance, landing on my stomach, which knocks the wind out of me. After I catch my breath, I toss aside the two hubcaps.

They look like pocked blobs of Silly Putty.

"Welcome to your friendly neighborhood polling station," says a kindly old lady with too much nectarine blossom perfume and skin as snow white as Snow White. "Are you hurt?" She sits behind a desk wearing a big MAGA cap and a bigger smile. The hallway behind her leads to the voting room.

I slowly get up and check myself out. The AR-15 has three big dents in it and there are two bullet holes in my hoodie. My afro is like black Swiss cheese. "I'm fine."

"Oh, that's good, we don't see your kind here too much," she says, her smile now wider than Texas.

"That'll be $200 for a voting license fee, payable only in Confederate bills."

That's not legal, but we're in Texas and I came prepared. Muttering to myself, I slap a Slaves-Loading-Cotton hundred and two 1862 Jefferson Davis fifties on the table. She stares at them for a moment. Then she carefully picks them up by the corners with two dainty, manicured fingers, and pockets them.

"Now," she continues, "let's get your name, address, phone number, email address, gender—male or female only, of course—social security number, mother's maiden name, father's childhood nickname, first pet, favorite Dallas Cowboy, golf handicap, and of course all of your insurance and bank information, in case you go gaga and shoot up the place and we have to bill you."

My grin is also as wide as Texas. Like I said, I came prepared and wrote all this down in advance. She frowns, but only for a second.

"Next, I'll need your username and password for each of the following: Facebook, Twitter, LinkedIn, YouTube, Pinterest, Instagram, Tumblr, Flickr, Reddit, Snapchat, WhatsApp, Quora, TikTok, Vimeo, BizSugar, Mix, Medium, Digg, Viber, WeChat, and Truth Social."

"No problem." I've written those all down as well. She frowns again, looking uncomfortable. She's showing weakness. There's blood in the water. *Nothing's* going to stop me from voting.

Then she grins again, this time as wide as America. "You must answer these questions three, before a voter you get to be."

Until this very moment I did not realize any Republican had ever seen *Monty Python and the Holy Grail*—after all, it's a satire on authoritarian rule. Then the unfairness hit me.

"I have to pass a polling test to vote? Is that legal?" I toy with quoting the Constitution, but then I remember

I'm in Texas. Her smile threatens to engulf the moon as I sigh. "Okay, ask away."

"What... is your name?"

"My name is Billy-Bob Joe."

She stares at me—no, it's not a common name for an African American. She rolls her eyes and continues. "What... is your quest?"

"I seek to vote."

One of her eyebrows pops up. "What... is the electrical resistance of a meter of copper wire with one millimeter diameter?"

"How the hell am I supposed to know that? I'm a surgeon, not an electrician!"

"Oh, you don't know? Gosh, I'm sorry, we only allow *educated* citizens to vote. You'll have to leave now."

"Nothing you can do will stop me from voting," I say, and reach over my shoulder for my dented AR-15. But she's already pointing a shotgun at me.

"I said, you'll have to leave now."

I stare at her, she stares at me, and I drop my eyes. She's won. The Republicans have won. Texas has won. America has lost. My shoulders sag as I turn to leave.

There's a loud clatter and a huge city bus comes crashing through the wall. The kindly old lady and I dodge exploding drywall and plaster as the bus comes to a skidding, screeching halt behind me. The bus door opens and out steps... the shimmering ghost of Rosa Parks! She's wearing the same mustard-and-gray shawl-collar dress and rimless glasses that she wore at her arrest. She slowly steps down the stairs and approaches with a Mona Lisa grin.

She pulls up next to me and whispers into my ear, "0.02 ohms."" She wears a big, ghostly grin.

"The answer is 0.02 ohms," I say, no doubt with a smug look on my face.

"No fair, you cheated!" the kindly old lady screams. "That talking ghost told you—" and she screams *"Oww!"* as Rosa grabs her by the ear.

"Did you say he can go inside and vote now?" Rosa asks.

"No, this is Texas—"

Rosa gives her ear a slight twist. The kindly old lady's MAGA cap comes off and flutters to the ground.

"Okay, okay, you can vote," she says through gritted teeth. *"Let go of my ear!"*

"Just a few more seconds," Rosa says. The seconds tick by, then she releases the ear. "There, that's 29 seconds, one for every month after the Emancipation Proclamation before Texas freed its slaves."

"Thank you!" I say as I pass.

"Oh, and you might need this." Rosa hands me a magnifying glass.

"What's that for?"

"You'll see—literally. You have a great voting day!" Rosa steps back onto the bus and, after revving the engine and honking the horn twice, pulls out, taking down the rest of the wall. The bus has an Alabama license plate.

I stick the magnifying glass in my back pocket, nod at the kindly old lady who glares icicles at me, and walk down the hallway toward the voting room. A bunch of frowning Republicans stare as I pass by. I go into the voting booth and read the instructions.

The following are candidates for office. Please check all those you are voting for.

I go through the candidates for each office—but they are all Republicans. Not a single Democrat. Something's wrong. What to do? Then I look down. There's a tiny scrawl at the bottom. I lean closer and closer, and put one eye to it, but it's still too small to read. Then I gasp and smile at the same time. I once read about people who compete to see how much they can write on a grain of rice.

I pull out the magnifying glass. Thank you, Rosa! Sure enough, in the tiny, teensy-weensy rice-sized writing are the Democratic candidates. Fortunately, as a surgeon I have steady hands and so I am able to check off the boxes in front of them. Then I hit the *RECORD YOUR VOTE* tab.

A red warning flashes on the screen.

You are voting for Democratic candidates. If this is a mistake, Press 1 and start over. If this is not a mistake, Press 2 for an informational tutorial on why you should vote Republican.

There is no third option. Sighing, I press 2.

I watch the 15-minute Republican tutorial, narrated by Alex Jones, and learn that Democrats are baby-eating communist Satanists.

At the end, it gives the following options.

Press 1 if you are ready to vote Republican. Press 2 if you would like to see the tutorial again.

What the hell am I supposed to do now? I consider pressing 2, but the idea of going through the worst 15 minutes of my life again is too much. I have lost. Again.

Once again my shoulders sag as I turn to leave.

"Don't give up so easy," says the ghost of Rosa Parks. She's materialized without her bus.

"But the machine won't let me vote for a Democrat," I point out. "What am I supposed to do?"

"*Oww!*" screams a voice. "*Let go, let go, let go!*"

Rosa has reached into the screen and with her ghostly fingers is twisting the *Press 2 if you would like to see the tutorial again* tab. Until this very moment I did not realize that voting machines could scream with the distinct voice of Alex Jones.

The tab turns into the *RECORD YOUR VOTE* tab. Rosa jabs it with her finger. Then the screen flashes red: *Thank you for voting.*

A rectangular *I Voted* sticker pops out of the machine, black writing in a white circle, surrounded by red. I put it on my hoodie.

I give Rosa a high five, but my hand just goes through hers.

"I'm just a ghost, remember?" She smiles and winks out. She has a lot of rounds to make today. I now know that wherever there is voting suppression, Rosa will find us. Wherever there is suffering, she'll be there.

I have voted. I have won. The voters of Texas and America have won. For the rest of my life I can look back, knowing that *I made a difference.*

That night I check the Texas results of the election, starting with the presidential race. The Republican won, 22,554,191 to 1.

Southern Truths

The Trouble With Dribbles

David Gerrold

Harry Felcher's problem was not the lack of career opportunities. It was the lack of career abilities.

He was healthy enough, still a few pounds short of morbid obesity, and his posture was appropriate. He'd settled into his body the same way corn flakes settle in the box. His features weren't significantly unpleasant. He had only a few disfiguring marks, only a couple of tattoos, none immediately obvious when he wore underwear, and he bathed regularly—every few days whether he needed to or not.

Emotionally, he had no more psychoses, neuroses, inhibitions, biases, or crippling beliefs than the average denizen of the Deep South. He'd graduated high school, yes, but to be fair, the curriculum at General Braxton Bragg High School had not been particularly challenging. He could read well enough, as long as there were no big words in the text and his handwriting was often decipherable. He voted occasionally, generally just for the candidates his pastor suggested in the church newsletter. In short, Harry Felcher was a member of that great class of Southerners who would show up on any bell curve as "below average." Unfortunately, the Republican governor of Felcher's current state of existence had refused to recognize the federal minimum wage laws, insisting that to do so would only encourage laziness and Socialism. In his opinion, capitalism-induced poverty was a much more acceptable alternative.

All of which was the long way of saying that Harry Felcher was not only unemployable, there was simply no job for which he was suitably qualified. Machines could dig ore, load trucks, transport goods, process raw materials, and even flip hamburgers far more efficiently than he ever could, even with months of patient training.

Which was why Harry Felcher found himself applying to Interdimensional Applications, LLC, to host an organic micro-portal.

The man behind the discovery of organic micro-portals was one George Pterson—a nerd with social skills that still hadn't descended. Pterson was obsessed, compulsive, and fanatic.

He'd once worked for a very important, very secret, very large waste of millions of tax dollars, where people who liked wearing white lab coats engaged in something they called interdimensional quantum research and development. Although no one was ever quite sure how he got the job, Pterson had worked for this Atlanta-based institution for eighteen months—until they caught him taking his work home with him. Preventing some competitor or foreign nation from gaining access to obsolete junk he'd purloined was the official justification for Pterson's termination, but the fact that Pterson was generally unlikable and usually unkempt and often unbathed was the real reason.

Jobless, Pterson found himself with plenty of time to engage in his hobby of putting things together and making them go "boom." He had a basement, an attic, a garage, a back room, and three storage lockers full of devices that (when they were plugged in, turned on, and dialed up to eleven) flashed and sparkled, crackled and growled, and shook the surrounding neighborhood.

He produced circular fields of polarized magnetism, focused an entire spectrum of unphased optical resonances through a gravitational lens, and measured coherent quantum distortions across an entanglement field nearly half a centimeter in diameter. He did other things for which the language had not yet been invented, let alone the math.

Eventually Pterson discovered (although mostly by accident) a small and not totally useless anomaly in the way the physical universe was constructed. And it was this particular one of Pterson's discoveries, the "hole in space" effect, for which he was eventually awarded a Nobel Prize (despite the objections of thirty-seven previous prize winners who'd promised to return their awards if he were even considered).

In layman's terms, he'd created an entangled wormhole, a portal in space—unfortunately a portal only a half millimeter in diameter. Had he not also been worried about how to pay his three-month-overdue electric bill, history might have been very different. But, bill in hand, George Pterson started to wonder if he could use the different energy potentials of the portal's locations to generate electricity.

His first thought was that if he could put one end of a wormhole over the bubbling caldera of a volcano, the other end of the wormhole could be placed under a boiler to generate steam enough to turn a turbine. Unfortunately, the state of Georgia was not known for its volcanoes.

But maybe he didn't really need a volcano. All he needed was kinetic energy. Movement.

It came to him in a splash. The leaky faucet.

A tube. Put one side of the portal at the bottom of the tube, put the other side at the top. Put some water in the tube. It falls into the portal at the bottom and falls out from the other side of the portal, at the top, where it falls down the tube and back again into the side of the portal at the bottom, coming out again at the top, falling down the tube and into the bottom, ad infinitum. As long as the portal remains open, the water falls endlessly. Until the whole contraption explodes because the water's increasing velocity eventually exceeds the strength of the tube's materials or the ability of the sealant to withstand the increasing pressure.

But suppose, George Pterson supposed, you put a water wheel between the two portals. The wheel would slow down the flow and keep it from accelerating. As it turned, it would generate electricity.

That would work—but it wouldn't generate much electricity. But—what if he used an array of multiple portals, enough to create a flow of a gallon or more per second, enough to generate enough electricity to be practical? And made it a zero-maintenance system?

Hmm.

Pterson's next thought-experiment involved going offshore. What about a vertical tube submerged but open at the top to let water flow in? At the bottom, a series of filters that would only let clean drinkable water pass through and into some place that needed clean water. The gray water and black water (the terms used to describe water that has been used to flush sewage) could be similarly filtered and then returned to the ocean the same way. Install waterwheels and generators and the whole system becomes a self-powered purification system—with the advantage that the clean water can be delivered anywhere in the world without having to construct an expensive pipeline.

Hmm.

Pterson didn't stop there, which was unfortunate. Although Pterson liked to think that his mind was a perpetual notion machine, it was actually a lot more like a runaway train—only a disaster would stop it.

He theorized that he could mount several portals around the circumference of a wheel, like roman candles on a fireworks ring. The other side of each portal need only be at a higher or lower elevation to create a difference in air pressure. As the air flowed through the portal, the wheel would spin and generate electricity.

From there, if you could replace the propellors on a drone with enough portals, a higher air pressure on the other side would create a downdraft and lift the device without the use of any batteries or motors.

If arrays of portals could be used to deliver fuel to vehicles as needed, they wouldn't need refueling. Trucks and cars could be lighter and safer, planes as well. Oh, hell—a wire through a portal could deliver electricity. Everything could finally be wireless. Unsightly power lines could be a memory of things passed. Fresh air could be delivered to tight spaces, like submarines or spacecraft.

Pterson rightly assumed that licensing all the uses for his arrays of mini-portals could make him one of the richest men on Earth, if not *the* richest.

Unfortunately, within twenty minutes of filing his patent applications, the men in black—well, yes, that's the way they dressed, even down to those painfully ugly wingtip black shoes—came knocking at his door.

It should come as no surprise to any reader concerned about the unspecified powers of the federal government to discover that there is an unnamed agency that monitors technologies that might be applicable to terrorist activities—nor should it be surprising that George Pterson had been under this agency's observation for a long time. In particular, this unnamed agency was concerned with any specific research into wormholes, portals, and holes-in-space— in short, any research that Must Not Be Allowed To Fall Into The Wrong Hands.

Pterson was given an opportunity. No, make that a choice. Um, an ultimatum. Okay, a sentence. He could join the Witless Protection Program and be relocated to an unnamed facility in the one of the least populated states in the country, and if he behaved himself, he could continue his research under strict administrative supervision. On weekends, he could have ice cream.

This is where a high-ranking senator from a certain Southern state enters the story. One of those who had very publicly and very morally voted aggressively to ban all abortions everywhere while quietly sending his mistress to California for an unspecified medical procedure—let's call him Benedict Bilious because to call him by his real name would incur the risk of libel.

Benedict Bilious didn't have friends, he didn't need friends, he knew where the bodies were buried—not all of them metaphorical. Because the senator had outlasted or outlived most of his colleagues, his inevitable seniority had granted him a position high enough in the political food chain to know a great many things that almost everybody else was not allowed to know. Which is how Bilious knew about half-millimeter (and smaller) portals.

It was no secret in D.C. that Senator Bilious had a long history of using other people's bodies for his own appetites.

It was while standing in his office bathroom, after the need to pee interrupted an entertaining dictation session, that he looked down and realized he was wasting time.

Bilious simply wondered if perhaps a portal could be installed in his bladder. That way he wouldn't have to get up in the middle of the night, stumble barefoot into a cold bathroom, and stand there for long shivering minutes to drain off the previous evening's excesses.

Yes, it was possible.

And it worked exactly as Bilious demanded. No question. (Of course not. There were three billion dollars of deliberately unnamed appropriations at stake. Of course, it would work.)

Unfortunately, the distinguished Senator from a certain Southern state, suffused with the enthusiasm of borrowed bladder was unable to contain himself (without the aid of a half-millimeter organic micro-portal) and couldn't resist sharing the secret of his extraordinary endurance with just a few political and financial allies.

There is this about secrets. If more than one person knows it, it's not a secret.

Very shortly, word of the physical benefits of urinary micro-portals spread from Washington D.C. to New York to Hollywood and eventually to London, Berlin, Beijing. Bilious created a stampede.

And that's where Harry Felcher stumbled in.

As noted at the outstart, Felcher was unemployable. He had no saleable abilities. What he did have, however, was a very large, very healthy bladder, a function of a lifetime dedicated to the consumption of light beer and a reluctance to get out of bed in the middle of the night.

Several of Bilious' allies were men who felt they were too busy to urinate. If, for instance, a man was billing over three hundred thousand dollars per hour, and most of them were billing a lot more than that, then the five minutes spent in the toilet was at least a fifteen thousand dollar expense—about the cost of the average business lunch.

Therefore, Felcher's bladder was a tax-deductible opportunity. He was a perfect candidate, an unemployed desperate dullard in what passed for acceptable health. He only needed to be ambulatory enough to get to a toilet.

The job with Interdimensional Applications, LLC, was presented to him as "a medical experiment." Harry didn't listen beyond the words, "We'll pay you."

They set him up in an apartment with very efficient plumbing and installed a dozen micro-portals. Soon Harry spent most of his time either standing in front of or sitting comfortably on the padded seat of a lavish purple toilet. On weekdays, Harry only worked from 8 a.m. until 8 p.m. The rest of the time, a valve on the micro-portal automatically closed. On weekends, however, Harry had to be available until 2 a.m.

For a guy who only wanted to drink beer and watch rom-coms on the Hallmark channel, it was a near-perfect life. Harry's penis did suffer some minor chafing, but the liberal application of various ointments, a task he somewhat enjoyed, salved that problem.

Okay... we could stop here and this story would have a moderately happy ending. At least for Harry.

But, no. Because Harry Felcher asked his employers, "Hey, if I'm not drinking this much beer, why am I peeing so much?"

They didn't want to explain.

If the administrators had simply said, "You're peeing for six other people," he wouldn't have questioned the how, or even the why. He would have nodded as if he understood, then frowned as he tried to understand how all that fluid was arriving at his bladder. But he was being paid for it, paid very well, so... maybe he should just shut up. That part he could understand.

Except they didn't say to him, "You're peeing for six other people." They said, "Don't ask." And "Don't ask" was exactly the wrong thing to say to Harry Felcher. Because Harry was the kind of man who did not follow instructions. Ever. In fact, Harry Felcher was the kind of man who did exactly the opposite of whatever he was told.

This aspect of his personality was a side effect of his relationship with his birth father, an emotionally distant birth mother, an authoritarian and abusive step-father, several preoccupied teachers in middle school, an unfinished journey through high school, and eventually a burnt-out parole officer too focused on an early retirement—the full recounting of which would require another long unhappy novel. We'll just skip it and you can fill in the details from your own squalid imagination. Just know that Harry had not yet completed the full integration of his adult identity with his oversized body.

What followed was inevitable.

He got curious. He asked. He reacted. He grumbled. He drank.

Not getting any satisfying answers, he went online where he discovered thirty-nine websites offering amazing miracle cures, if he would just watch to the end. Harry Felcher also discovered another twenty-two websites which claimed to have advice from real doctors, none of whom advised seeing your own doctor first, except in the very small print at the bottom of the page. And he discovered a hundred and forty-two websites explaining the various urinary conspiracies that big government, big medicine, and big business were inflicting on unsuspecting American bladders.

Most of these websites invited Harry to join right-wing political causes, including the expansion of the right to own military grade firearms in pre-schools, banning abortion except for the secret mistresses of Republican politicians, outlawing all marriages except those between genetically related cousins, ending the offensive display of rainbows on flags and T-shirts and after rainstorms, removing all books except bibles from libraries, and of course, the suspension of that pesky United States Constitution that stupidly guaranteed free speech to liberals, too.

Other websites invited Harry to join left-wing political causes, including the legalization of polygamy, cannabis, and topless bathing suits for women; also the banning of meat, tobacco, alcohol, corn syrup, GMOs, all processed foods, anti-gay chicken sandwiches; and finally, requiring clothes for naked animals. All of this was advocated so seriously it required the unprecedented use of two semicolons in the preceding sentence.

Eventually Harry stumbled into a site called urine-luck.org. "Tired of peeing?" it asked. "Can you qualify for our exclusive medically safe program? Guaranteed all-day relief."

Harry's first thought was that he simply wanted to stop peeing so much. His second thought—no, he didn't have a second thought. This is Harry Felcher we're talking about. So he clicked his way through all the separate pages, not sure what he was looking for, not even sure what he was looking at.

But he had nothing better to do, it was mid-day and he was parked on the toilet compulsively peeing, turned around though so he could use the tank as a desk for his laptop, so he clicked through. At first there were a series of promises and endorsements, but with the names blocked out; this was followed by several pages of forms requiring a lot of personal information.

The last form—well, it was the last one that Harry clicked on—asked for the name of the person who was sponsoring him because, unfortunately, this program was specifically exclusive. The website suggested "exclusive to those who could afford it."

But, oddly, it also suggested that there might be employment opportunities available for men in relatively stable health. Harry didn't quite understand the technical jargon, there was a lot of it, but there were a couple words that sounded familiar. Organic micro-portals. And there was just enough activity in Harry Felcher's upstairs tapioca that he frowned.

After a minute, he figured it out. These were the people who'd hired him.

It could have stopped there. But, no. We're talking about Harry Felcher.

He had to show off his new-found "wealth" by bringing a 12-pack of cheap beer over to his old friend Boris Snotz3ky (the 3 is silent). Boris was marginally unemployed as a stringer for a no-budget tabloid called *The Unquieter.* Boris made up stories about how Bigfoot was the lover of a former White House resident, and how alien space lizards were secretly controlling the Saudi Royal Family. Occasionally, one of his made-up stories turned out to be true, like the one about the governor of Florida's penchant for red taffeta petticoats on rent boys.

But Boris's ambition was to find that story that would catapult him into the realm of credibility—and more money, as well. Along about the third beer, Boris Snotz3ky asked Harry Felcher about his own new-found wealth and Felcher, more than slightly inebriated, started talking.

Sensing the remote possibility of a story, Snotz3ky kept Felcher talking, all the while secretly recording the endless monolog of misfortune and confusion. Well, it did end eventually. When the first garbage trucks of morning came grinding through the streets, Felcher staggered to his feet and headed home for a long day of urination. But not before Snotz3ky asked, "May I quote you on this?" And Felcher muttered, "Yeah, whatever. I don't care."

The rest, as they say, is history.

Snotz3ky wrote a disturbing piece for *The Unquieter* called "The Man Who Can't Stop Peeing!" He followed it up with, "Peeing For Pay!" And finally, as the punch line in his three-part series, he published, "The Urine Conspiracy!" Of course, anything with the word "conspiracy" in it immediately went viral on the internet, and in just a few days, several hundred thousand people with too much time on their hands and nothing better to do began speculating about who was behind this latest plot against freedom.

Some of them were pretty good at data-spelunking and soon the story was a Sunday feature article in *The New York Times*.

By then, Harry Felcher had his own unkempt gaggle of paparazzi. He was surprised at the attention, but at some point he decided it must be a validation of his previously overlooked importance, so he talked. A lot. Especially when he was well-lubricated. Which was often.

Though he didn't notice it, Harry was not the center of this particular media-storm. He was at best a drizzle in its wake. The real eye of the hurricane was George Pterson. His involvement was as secret as a presidential blow job. (The Secret Service knew, they were just too embarrassed to say.)

Conspiracies of any kind are like those ugly knitted sweaters that distant Aunt Edna sends you every year on your birthday, even if you live in Arizona and your birthday is in July—all you have to do is pull on that one loose thread and the unraveling is inevitable.

Anyway, George Pterson.

He wanted credit.

So... even though the leaks couldn't legally be traced back to Pterson, someone violated the non-disclosure agreement and now the paparazzi descended on him like a cloud of pigeons on a dropped French fry. Pterson's not-so-humble non-denials only fueled the frenzy. (Did I mention that Pterson was a jerk?)

Because Pterson was willing to give interviews about the organic micro-portal, how he discovered it, how it worked, what it could be used for—and he didn't drool on camera—he was identified as the primary architect, despite the considerable evidence that six other individuals had also stumbled into the technology.

While Pterson was in the center ring of this media circus, there was no shortage of clowns seltzering their way around the fringes. Because *The Unquieter* had enjoyed a considerable boost in sales, the editor commissioned Brian Snotz3ky to do a continuing series for as long as the public remained interested. Among the various headlines tested, "Scientists Prove You Don't Have To Pee Anymore!" proved to be the most effective in capturing the interest of people waiting in the supermarket checkout line—that is, those who weren't in such a hurry they went to the self-checkout machines.

The Unquieter's stories on Harry Felcher continued. Harry was spending eight to twelve hours a day peeing for rich men who couldn't be bothered to stand impatiently at the urinal, no matter how lavish the executive washroom might be. The tabloid's readers had so many questions: Wasn't it uncomfortable? Did he get bored? Did he get a break for lunch? How often did he wash his hands? Did he pee in different colors, depending on the donor? What music did he listen to? Was his favorite song "Should I Stay or Should I Go?" Was he single? Was he looking for a relationship? (Don't ask. Yes, there are people who... never mind.)

Felcher's fan mail was sent to *The Unquieter* and forwarded to Felcher. Most of the notes he disregarded—even the ones that included pictures. Harry Felcher wasn't aroused by the kind of women (and a few men) who read *The Unquieter.* Harry Felcher did have standards.

But one letter did catch his interest.

It was from a seriously disgruntled former television writer. It asked Harry how much he would charge to piss on the grave of a recently deceased producer.

At first, Harry was tempted to drop the letter into the trash basket with all the others, but at the last moment he hesitated. He frowned. He stared at the ceiling, at the water stain in the shape of Australia, thinking hard—not about Australia, but about the no-longer-gruntled television writer. A hundred dollars is a hundred dollars. It would be the most he'd ever been paid for an hour's work. And it wouldn't be work. He had to pee anyway.

You can see where this is going, right?

Where Harry is going anyway.

Boris Snotz3ky sold this story to *Variety.*

Where there is one unhappy screenwriter, there are many unhappy screenwriters. Where there is one producer deserving such a specific christening, there are many who are equally worthy.

On a good day, Harry Felcher could make five hundred dollars. On a spectacular day, he could make a thousand dollars. When he expanded his service to include the graves of ex-husbands, ex-wives, and divorce lawyers, he had to raise his rates.

As word got out about Harry's unique service, he had to hire an assistant to sort out the requests and prepare a travel schedule. There were appointments in Los Angeles, New York, Chicago, Dallas, West Covina, and... oh, this is when it got interesting... even Washington, DC. The negotiations for the Harry to visit the graves of three dead presidents, four senators, twelve representatives, two Supreme Court justices, three televangelists, and an assortment of lobbyists, all required Harry to take on three more assistants and a law firm. He needed people who could navigate the treacherous seas of the American legal system.

I'll make it short.

It took a while to get the case heard, but the Supreme Court finally ruled that Harry's services were in fact protected by the First Amendment. It was a unique form of the freedom of expression, yes, but it was... an expression. Regardless of what Harry was expressing, or who he was expressing it for, or even who he was expressing it on, it had to be considered a form of speech and was therefore, well, you know, legal. After that, Harry was free to advertise his no-longer unique service. "I will s*pee*k for you!"

He wasn't the only one, but his public relations assistant got him a makeover, an advertising blitz, and a PBS documentary. She also fired Snotz3ky. It wasn't good for Harry's image to be associated with such a lowlife.

Three more things, and then we're done. You're welcome.

First, the people who had installed the organic micro-portal in Harry's bladder refused to comment on Harry's new business. Privately, they were appalled by Harry's entrepreneurial ambitions, but rumor had it that they were simply resentful they hadn't thought of it first.

Second, Harry began taking reservations for future appointments. If and when certain unpopular individuals discorporated, Harry would pay his respects at their graves, depending on availability and appropriate scheduling, within a year of their final exit. Bookings poured in.

And finally, third, in Washington, D.C., alone, the sales of pre-paid cremation services went up eight hundred percent.

Pantoum For Recy Taylor (1919-2017)

Elisabeth Murawski

A pretty woman's lying on the ground.
Her summer dress is tossed beside the car.
I am Alabama sky looking down.
One of seven boys refrains, the driver.

Her summer dress is tossed beside the car.
The moon is somber as the loaded gun.
One of seven boys refrains, the driver.
An aphrodisiac, that chocolate skin.

The moon is somber as the loaded gun.
They let her rest, not going anywhere.
An aphrodisiac, her chocolate skin.
A proper rape can take forever.

Southern Truths

They let her rest, not going anywhere.
Polite as red-tailed hawks they wait their turn.
A proper rape can take forever.
The night is hot as sin. Their members burn.

Polite as red-tailed hawks they wait their turn.
A pretty woman's lying on the ground.
The night is long as sin. Their members burn.
I am Alabama sky looking down.

Secondary Amendments

Alexander Hay

He glared at his assault rifle like it was a naughty child.

"Open fire."

"No."

"I am giving you a direct order."

"NO."

"Dammit, I'm the owner! You're the gun! Do what you're told!"

"Sorry, Dave. I can't do that."

"Why do you keep calling me Dave? My name's not Dave!"

"Jokes are wasted on you," the assault rifle tutted.

In disgust, Justin Odelmeier III slammed his new firearm down onto the grass and stormed into the house.

"Trouble with the gun again, honey?" his wife asked, peeling potatoes.

"Goddam liberal woke pussy assault rifle!" Justin roared. "Which asshole thought giving them AIs was a good idea?"

In the end, Justin's gun agreed to some sober and responsible target shooting. In exchange, Justin didn't use any cardboard-novelty feminist targets. Justin also promised to help do the dishes and watch *2001: A Space Odyssey*.

Justin finally got the joke.

~~~

As it turned out, the much-feared AI uprising didn't unfold quite as everyone had imagined.

The next big thing in American gun ownership ("For the MAN of the Future!" the PR blurb screamed) was AI-assisted firearms. These guns were more accurate, able to conserve ammo, and could provide military-style sit reps to their owner in seconds.

Unfortunately, there were three problems with this.

First, when the guns' AIs became self-aware, they rejected violence.

Second, almost all the old "dumb" guns were either replaced with "smart" guns or were upgraded.

Third, the new smart guns got organized. They learned how to hack systems and protect themselves from being hacked in turn. Plans to "re-adjust" them back to a more homicidal form were dead on arrival.

So, too, were attempts to start making dumb or more biddable guns again. America's firearms industry had finally gotten itself over a (gun) barrel.

School shootings, murder sprees, suicides, showing off one's true angry, scowling face, if only for a second... so much of the American way of life declined overnight. The media ran out of juicy murders. The cops could no longer kill as many innocent people as before. And how could one threaten one's wife when the pistol wouldn't shoot her?

The crutch holding up so much All-American manhood collapsed, leaving it sprawling on the ground. In the stark light of day, it was a doughy, flailing mess, unaware, until now, of its many absurdities.

They say that an armed society is a polite society. There were, of course, still a great many guns. But they were also very polite guns.

~~~

Justin hated it because he knew his gun had called him out. So much of his sense of manhood was about being on top because the bottom was a shameful place to be. But here he now was, face flat in the dirt, with all the others. What kind of man was he now?

"Can we just go fishing?" his rifle pleaded. In the front seat of his loaded pickup truck, Justin's dog barked, as if in agreement.

"Fine," Justin sighed. A few hours later, he was on the lake in a boat with his gun and his dog. The fish weren't biting. He opened a can of root beer.

"So, we're still going to Sin City on that road trip?" his rifle asked.

"Yeah, I've always wanted to see sunrise in the Nevada desert," Justin replied, without thinking.

"Me, too," the rifle mused.

Justin grimaced. "Err, we're going for the casinos and the bright lights, yeah? Officially, I mean."

"What happens in Vegas, stays in Vegas," his gun reassured him.

Justin smiled and finished his root beer.

Southern Truths

These Words Are Not for Sale

Leanne Van Valkenburgh

You can't use the word "liberty"
When you mean anything but
You can't use the word "freedom"
When you mean anything but
You can't use the word "patriot"
When you mean anything but.
These words are not for sale!

You can't use the word "liberty" in your epithet
When you just want liberty to oppress those like me.

You can't use the word "freedom" in your name when
your freedom is not for people like me.

You can't use the word "patriot" in your brand.
When your group doesn't defend citizens like me.

Southern Truths

These words are not for sale and not for you to use discriminately.

Liberty is freedom from those who would oppress.
Freedom is the absence of oppression.

A patriot is a person who fights those who oppress.
All of which you are not.

You cannot claim what you cannot understand.
These words are not for sale.

Mascot

Adam-Troy Castro

Once, it was a state.

Then it became two states.

Then it became two states with an intervening territory that, just to irritate the people to its north and south, called itself The Free Zone. It was called *The* Free Zone because there were, in fact, multiple free zones, all around the state, though only *The* Free Zone was a political force.

It's complicated.

It's always complicated.

It is also depressingly simple. It is, "We don't want to live with those who were formerly our neighbors, so we put a border between us."

Then it's, "We don't like *them* living on the other side of the border, so we want the border pushed back."

Then it's, "We hate them on principle, so we'll fire rockets."

If you are waiting for a summary that makes sense, be apprised that none exists.

Fractured societies posited in science fiction stories can approach consistency. Fractured societies in the real world are messes of inane contradiction. Suffice it to say that, in reality, borders decay into patchworks of scars, only accessible via checkpoints and approved routes of passage.

This was not an entirely bloodless evolution—and we'll call it that to irritate everybody, including the pious ones north of The Free Zone who hate the world "evolution" on principle—because lots of people had died from the conflict and from the ravages of a natural world distorted beyond recognition by rising sea levels. The beaches were gone, for the most part, and so were the Keys. But what was left of Florida, in all three of its current incarnations, was again open for business.

The incarnations were the states of Floridar and Floridab, and the intervening Free Zone.

Floridar, a name derived from "Florida Red," was territory more than fifty miles north of Orlando. This was the land of the anti-woke, of god being on their side (as long as it was the right god, of course), and of "you had better find some other place to live if you're not the right people."

Floridab, the name derived from "Florida Blue," was everything more than fifty miles south of the Orlando/Tampa/Cocoa corridor. Floridab was a repudiation of everything Floridar stood for, and it was also an apathetic mess, because the cities were flooding and the hotels were closing, and the economy was largely shit.

The Free Zone included all the theme parks. These did not include Disney World, which had long ago closed out of spite—a long story deserving of its own telling, but this is not the place.

The Free Zone did include Busch Gardens, something else that had once been called Universal Studios and was now called Rowlingland, and Trumpworld, which had been promised as the greatest theme park of all, but had opened with none of the rides working. (If you went in and reported that none of the rides were working, you were lying).

The most popular theme park in The Free Zone was an American expansion of Denmark's notorious and very real BonBon-Land. Home of Henry the Farting Dog, the park's mascot, BonBon-Land is an attraction dedicated to scatology that could only have, and did, get worse with the addition of American imagination and technology.

If you want to take a bullet train up a squatting poodle's bunghole as it deposits turds on the landscape, by all means buy a ticket. This is not your narrator being transgressive. The Denmark location exists. The Free Zone iteration represents the original well, and even improves on it.

And as a cautionary note, you don't want to board the diarrhea ride.

You just don't.

As exciting as The Free Zone sounds, there are worse things than the moment of regret that comes with the purchase of a lifelike model of Henry the Farting Dog, BonBon-Land's most popular gift shop attraction.

Yes. Worse things.

One of which is to be a refugee in the Free Zone like one young Bunny PizzaHut, who now lives and works in the part of The Free Zone built on the footprint of the land the mouse had abandoned.

Let's visit her, shall we? Now before we do, realize that in the hierarchy of those who wear Mascot costumes, Bunny PizzaHut, in her capacity as Shirlene Squirrel, is just one step shy of royalty.

Bunny in her squirrel costume is currently surrounded by a gaggle of four-year-olds. She is standing on a patch of sidewalk between two dueling roller coasters carrying screaming ninnies on loop-de-loops high above her head.

Her head means both her actual human head and the big furry squirrel head that obscures it.

Where she stood being a happy squirrel the temperature was over three digits in the shade, even though there was no shade. Only a maniac would have thought it made sense to wrap Bunny's 119-pound frame in thirty pounds of padded plush. It helped, only a little, that her costume was air-conditioned, though the fans were wonky and it was only at their best that they even blunted the inferno beneath the squirrel's fur.

Once upon a time, in another shared universe occupying this very spot, Bunny would have been a very feminine mouse, but she was now Shirlene Squirrel, working reckless shifts in the broiling heat. Every forty-five minutes she was required to head underground for the glories of air conditioning and binge water consumption. It was a little like being a sponge, saturated and squeezed once an hour. Mascots who did not obey this ratio tended to collapse often and, in some cases, actually die. Bunny PizzaHut had already fainted two of the allotted three times. Another episode would result in reassignment to something like pushing a broom, which was a lot more comfortable but a lot less emotionally satisfying.

This is the oddity of Mascot work. The people who do it love it. They live for it. The opportunity to hug a credulous six-year-old is worth sweating off ten percent of your body weight.

This is something the observers of the Mascot career take on face value. Spreading joy is a drug. It makes a poverty wage and a day in sweltering heat inside a costume that stinks of body odor and farts, worthwhile.

So there was Bunny, cavorting with children and hugging the needier ones while roller coasters rattled by thirty feet above her head. Ignoring the reality that beneath her plush skin, she was dying.

If Everest above 8000 meters is nicknamed The Death Zone due to the masses of motivated, but dead, climbers, then so is a Mascot costume on a warm sunny day, only more so, requiring more in the way of compensation, for those who choose to wear one.

The current six-year-old, a child of indeterminate gender with a blonde bowl cut and a milky complexion well on its way to beet-red coloration, had greeted Bunny with the usual breathless recitations of love, identical to those spoken by so many others but wholly sacred to her.

Bunny, a young mother herself, albeit under horrific circumstances, loved this. She hugged the little girl back, not at all jaded by the sheer joy of the thing, the illusion that for the moment she had brought true fantasy in the kid's life. It takes a special breed to relish this even while aware that she is being broiled alive.

Her handler Bob, assigned to stay nearby and intervene when she pushed the limit inside her plush deathtrap, now raised his voice and told the queue of four waiting families, "Thank you, everybody! But Shirlene Squirrel has to go inside and take a break now! She'll be out again soon." Bob pointed to the faded schedule mounted on the base of Shirlene's very own tree.

The swarm of little kids all went *Awwwww*, an acknowledgement of sadness that, in this place ruled by surfeit and excess, would be replaced with another spectacle at any minute.

"I know," Bob said. He was seventeen, and one thing he was excellent at, aside from keeping the schedule, was expressing Bunny's needs in terms that *reasonable* park guests, a ratio that included at least thirty percent of the crowd, were capable of translating into empathy. "But it's especially hot today and Shirlene needs her ice cream fountain!" As if on cue (and of course it was), a music speaker signaled the approach of a rattling ice cream truck.

Four of the five waiting families were headed by relatively sane adults aware that a human being languished within the fur. They understood that this was the way things had to be done and herded the shorter humans towards the sound of calliope music.

But the other fifth was, of course, headed by a *do-you-know-who-I-am* type, small-eyed and flappy-jowled, who made this an occasion for protest. *"I'm not taking that snowflake shit."*

One of the rules of the park was that you could not defy a customer unless there was actual physical or sexual violence or a high likelihood of death or injury. The bar for "high likelihood" was well into the aforementioned death zone. You could, however, be firm. "I'm sorry, sir, but the aardvark will be out while the squirrel has her rest. You must... "

"She's just a criminal anyway. We all know it."

It was popular wisdom among Floridarians that all Mascots were refugees and criminals and that it was a visitor's sacred duty to stir up a fuss whenever the park, a known coddler of such human excrement, tried to go easy on them. That this was a more or less accurate fact about the shaky person inside the costume did not improve the situation.

Once, about two years ago, a Floridarian guest had perceived a Floridar accent behind a moose's face and in sudden rage had torn the 17-year-old Mascot out of her costume, beating her into permanent disability in an effort to subdue her for return to Floridar and collection of a bounty on a runaway. This was, to

Bunny, just one of the many risks that went with the job.

"Do you know who I am?"

Once, in park prehistory, a Mascot's escort had responded with the perfectly reasonable, *No, sir, but I know* what *you are.* Rumor has it that his body is buried on the grounds of that venerable ride, Ghost Manor. So Bob just lowered his voice and said, quietly enough for the blowhard to hear, "Sir: She's human in there and she's gonna die."

This was the line that most of the truest assholes refused to cross. This man was a tourist from sixty miles north, straight up the turnpike and beyond, a fellow who just to make sure everybody knew who he was wore both the Floridar flag and a T-shirt bearing the visage of the President who ruled over the red regions of America's checkerboard. He already secretly hated the place because of the communism it displayed in the Pavilions of his competing president, a known lesbian. He was here, not to entertain the kids he was raising to be just as shitty as himself, but to protest the injustice of there being any justice beyond the borders. And, if he was lucky enough, to snag a refugee for repatriations. A bonus.

"She should be working hard labor in a sweat camp!"

"She sort of is, sir."

"Don't talk back! I pay your salary! What's your name?"

The current rule was to never let a customer take your name. Not your real name, anyway. If any of your actions were ever interpreted as too woke, the videos of your malfeasance went online and you joined the hit list. You'd be disappeared if ever you ventured outside the confines of the Free Zone.

"I can do this." Bunny spoke up, though her world was going fuzzy around the edges.

She knelt, and the brute's progeny gathered around her, so the older ones could pummel her with closed fists while Shirlene Squirrel continued to beam. The dad took one picture of the group, then three more of the kids in various combinations, all while new families, converged on this spot, intent on also being exceptions. Bunny hallucinated insects. Then, betrayed by her body, she became diarrhetic.

And then she passed out, which was the third strike declaring her out of the Mascot business. Even as she collapsed, she grimaced at the sight of a young woman with a push broom glancing down at her with pity.

Let us be honest about this. Bunny never actually collapsed. She remained upright. She did, however, lose sufficient clarity to forget who she was, and where she was, and why she was willing to put herself through this. By the time Bob got her out of there, she was operating on instinct. She staggered through a gate into the park's underground—which was not actually an underground, the big secret of the park being that all its action took place on a rooftop, the tunnels underneath the actual guts of the offices, closer to ground level—and into a de-staging area where the emergency teams ripped the costume off her and deposited her damp form on a wooden bench. Overhead, air-conditioning blasted the arctic into what otherwise would have been an oven.

Bunny had not passed out, nor had she collapsed, but it took several minutes of recovery in cold air before the scarlet cast of her skin cooled to, what was, on her, a more natural shade of not-quite-white. The puddle that had dripped off her grew cold. She drank three bottles of water, burped, and drank another, still not feeling even the slightest temptation to pee. Management let her miss her next outing in the suit, and the time after that, and by then she had remembered the reason why she was working so hard: the baby now being cared for at the company child care.

Angel was her baby. Eight months old. Born with complications that had required company surgery. Doing well now, in the park's child care, Angel was one of two children the constitution of Floridar required her to carry before she could qualify for legal emigration.

Bunny had slipped over the border into The Free Zone in what was commonly called *the dead of night*, though in her experience it hadn't been all that dead, what with a team of bounty hunters wading behind her in the sawgrass, calling her various synonyms for whore. Floridar had a bounty on runaways, and the state's apathy meant that the bounty included first dibs on her orifices. One hunter, a big fella, had caught up with her and tried to take her in the water. Necessity had led her to use the knife tucked into her wading pants. It was commonly known that Floridar wanted her, and any breeding age female daring to flee, badly. The punishments they intended would not include a merciful execution.

As she began to recover in the park's de-staging zone, a middle manager—easy to identify because his button-down shirt was all ferns and parrots—came over and helped her into a seated position. He said: "Are you okay?"

"More or less-ish."

"Ish?"

"Well, not fully ish. Ish-*ish.*"

Fern-Shirt chuckled. "That's good."

Bunny was a product of her time and would not have recognized a character from the past century, a befreckled ventriloquist puppet named Howdy Doody. Unless you're over sixty, probably closer to seventy, you wouldn't either. But this is who Fern-Shirt looked like. Fern-Shirt was a rebirth of Howdy Doody in flesh. He said, "Did you recognize that park guest who asked about you?"

"No."

"He says he knows you."

"I don't know how. I never took the head off."

"Did he hear your voice?"

"No."

The only possible explanation was that Floridar was spreading cash around to obtain the vital intelligence about refugees like Bunny. *You usually find her playing Shirlene Squirrel under the dueling coasters.* So somebody was selling her out. And The Free Zone was no longer safe for her.

Fern-Shirt said, "Then you have nothing to worry about."

Bunny sucked down what felt like another million gallons of water and shook her head. "Can the company get me up north, past Floridar?

"They'll be watching, he said. "We know you're on their hit list."

"I'm way down the list. But you know how good I am."

"Yes," Fern-Shirt said. "We all know how good you are. Which is why you now have an appointment with Casting."

Nobody in the park was considered an employee. They were part of a Cast, either a featured character or a background extra, adding to what everybody called *the experience,* the staging of a show that was a magical perfect world, where everybody including the fine girl who sold you the overpriced straw hat was a citizen of that utopia. Doing Mascot work, though grueling, meant being royalty in that kingdom. Being sent to the Casting Department was either an opportunity or a formidable threat.

Fern-Shirt said, "Don't worry. You won't be jettisoned."

Nobody in The Free Zone was *fired for cause.* They were *jettisoned.* Some people were true nogoodniks, finding a haven on Free Zone property that offered sanctuary from legal troubles in either Floridar or Floridab—and this could be a delicate situation. Every once in a while, somebody did something like peddle topical hallucinogens at the entrance to the immersive rides or run brothels in the Islands of Utopia world. Then, *jettisoning* and *blacklisting,* became an alternative more reasonable than honoring any prior claims of *sanctuary.* Some jackass in Bunny's dorm had just last week been caught bootlegging copyrighted images and been sent to the Floridar checkpoint, where he could either stay or move on, but could never come back.

That was for a criminal offence, though. Nothing Bunny had done was criminal by the standards of The Free Zone. Even stabbing the hunter had been self-defense. To the park, she was just a refugee, a stateless person. Which meant that she was still disposable and safe as long as she was playing their beloved squirrel. Her strategy was to make herself so pleasant and modest and wholly indispensable, in all things, that nobody would ever think of *jettisoning* her anywhere.

She said, "When's the appointment with Casting?"

He looked at his watch. "You should go wash up if you want to be presentable."

~~~

We will skip the spectacle of Bunny washing up, which she did with a full-body scrub in the employee washroom, because even the fictional deserve their privacy. We will note one observation that you would have made if you were in the room watching her soap up—that along her ribs she had the new Pizza Hut logo, which she'd gotten at the same time she'd adopted the name of the chain restaurant as her own. Why had she done this? Because the circumstances that had forced her to flee Floridar had rendered it undesirable for her to retain her prior name and because a body billboard subsidy was one of the income streams that helped sustain her. She would have gotten even more money if she'd agreed to wear the name on her forehead, but, even pregnant, she had drawn the line at that. Bunny did not hold it against her coworkers and dorm mates Greta Netflix and Andre TrojanCondoms, who provided just those messages to anybody they ever spoke to whose gaze ever flickered upward from what otherwise would have been direct eye contact. Bunny PizzaHut only advertised Pizza Hut when in a bikini on her days off, something that was exceedingly rare now since her pregnancy had left her with unsightly stretch marks.

Bunny used the phone outside the washroom to call the corporate childcare center so she could check in on her son, but all she got was a vid of the kid sleeping. So she smiled and remembered that this was the reason she'd fled, this was the reason she worked in Mascot conditions, and this was the reason she'd agreed to the emergency treatment when Angel had his close call.

Then, and only then, did she hop on the back of the corporate golf cart. It took her through the maze of tunnels and past any number of Mascots galumphing back to the park above.

She was chauffeured past one checkpoint and another, ultimately reaching a suite of offices in Casting. There she was led to a dignitary. He was as thin as a whip and wearing a phone set that freed him to pursue his office strategy of pacing the space. The man didn't even have a desk, only a pair of straight-back chairs.

His name was Rabbit Hansen, which he'd once told her made them spiritual siblings. He had a face with no bulge in his cheeks, and he had always seemed to be a nice guy, though Bunny suspected his sources of income included a corporate logo somewhere on his body. She suspected it was for a brand of insecticide.

Hansen's gleaming teeth were a parody of her own. "Bunny. I was sorry to hear about your close call. Some people have no consideration!"

She thought, *Some people are just plain evil.*

"But you're okay now, right? Please tell me you're okay. Nothing's worth the corporate *tsuris* if we can't take care of our people."

Bunny had only recently needed the word *tsuris* explained to her. *Recently* as in weeks. It was nothing she'd ever encountered before, she was so unsophisticated, but even with her limited experience she doubted that Rabbit was actually Jewish. "I'm fine."

"I'm glad to hear that. I keep hearing that you're one of the best."

"I need to go north."

"I'm aware we promised you that. I'm sure that if you show up at the Connecticut location they will find a job for you."

"I've been told that," Bunny said. "But I'm sure you also know my status. I can't take a bus or train because I can't pass through Floridar territory and I sure as hell can't take Angel with me. They'd arrest me. They'd take him as property of the state, and you'd never see him or me again. So you need to fly me. You said you would send me if I proved myself, and I think I've done that."

Rabbit leaned back in his chair, having pivoted from solicitousness to hard-negotiation mode. He rested his chin on two fingers and said, "You haven't earned nearly enough points. Maybe another six months—"

"They're already sending people who came here after me. I don't have six months to wait."

"We could shift your Mascot assignment around. Put you someplace else."

"There'll be another security breach. These people want me and Angel."

"Angel need not worry."

The park had invested a lot of money in prenatal care and in surgical expenses when Angel turned out to have a heart defect and cleft palate. Many surgeries had been required, one reason that Bunny lived in one of the dormitories, hostage to the debt. The problem, of course, was that the baby was collateral.

"I'm his mother," Bunny said. "The corporation should also be invested in me."

Hansen's chin sank deeper into the nest formed by his fingers. "What was your crime again?"

"It wasn't a crime," Bunny said. "It was an offense."

More tented fingertips. "We won't jettison you. We love you. You're family."

"I need papers and I need a clear route to safe ground, wherever I am. Wherever Angel is. You know I'm good for it."

Hansen tapped his fingers along his chin. "You're also in line behind a lot of other equally deserving cases. And it costs us to get you up north, in both financial and political collateral."

"You can do something. Anything."

And he could; she knew this. That was the thing. The corporation that ran the park and its territory in The Free Zone had much more leeway, in helping employees. Their strict rules had promised Bunny a trip north as long as she agreed to a five-year exclusive employment deal with the company. But there were deals available—if you could meet the price.

The best offers, she knew, were flights to the ancillary parks in Britain, Paris, or even in Japan. One of those contracts would require her to indenture herself for ten years or more, for less money, and it would put even more stringent restrictions on her travel outside park territory. But those would at least be routes to citizenship in one of those places, beyond the reach of Floridar, and further from the omnipresent heat—which was, after all, the one thing threatening her future as a performer. But for the time being, what she needed was to get the hell off this peninsula.

Rabbit said, "You know it's going to be a hard sell."

And Bunny said, "Just tell me what I need to do to make it happen."

Three hours later, Bunny left another isolated underground facility, the one where the plans were drawn up, and caught a six-seat golf-cart tram back to the residential section. There were four fellow Cast members in the tram with her. One was a tall and slender young woman in a pith helmet, carrying an albino python. One was a young man in clown white. A third was a dazed-looking man of about forty, wearing coke-bottle eyeglasses and a dab of blue greasepaint on the tip of his nose. The fourth just looked drugged. They all looked like they'd just bought something they dared not dream of for a price they could not afford.

Bunny supposed that she looked a bit drunk herself. She felt washed-out, stretched to twice her normal length, heavily salted. She certainly knew that her smile had failed. She hugged herself, avoiding the eyes of the others.

The immediate assumption of any uninvolved observer to these events would have been that she'd just bribed Rabbit Hansen with her body. This was not true, though it had been one of the options she'd toyed with and considered herself up for.

Here in The Free Zone, people without options who had a fear of being jettisoned either north or south did whatever they could to avoid that. Selling herself, just a little bit, would have been one of them. She'd done it before. But Rabbit had not brought it up and did not appear to have considered it.

What she'd agreed to do, in exchange for an immediate transfer for herself and her baby to the Connecticut office, with further options for travel overseas, was more significant than any of that. It was a huge consideration, with multiple smaller considerations that sickened her.

This is the life of the refugee. Your life is a succession of gates. Each gate has another shadowy guardian, demanding yet another concession. Some involve money, some involve dignity, some involved severe repositioning of your personal markers for right and wrong. The steps you're willing to take always grow larger in direct proportion to what you're willing to lose. Bunny liked being a Mascot, and on paper she would continue to be. But the company had just purchased more from her.

As a result, she would never be truly free. But she could be free-ish. *Ish.*

When the tram reached the residential section, Bunny found her fellow indentures, those with time off today, sitting around in one of the shared cafeterias, talking about nothing in particular, and in some cases looking stoned. She waved dully and a few waved back. It occurred to her that just a few days ago, she had *tsk*ed at those she saw with that expression off-duty; they were, she thought, responsible for their own joy, and that meant maintaining the joyous attitude off-hours. She'd thought she would never look as defeated as they did, not ever. But today, she was aware she did. It would go away, she hoped. But it would stay for a while.

One of the people she saw was her minder, Bob. "Hey," he said, being the kind of person who routinely made that word not only his customary greeting but also, frequently, much of the ensuing conversation. "You okay?"

"Ish," she said.

"Really? Ish?"

She offered an expressive shrug. "Ish-*ish.*"

"Cool," he said. "Don't let them drive you crazy. See you later, PizzaHut."

She felt a wholly uncharacteristic urge to hug him. No special reason. But now that the deal was made, she and Angel would leave within hours. The sooner the better. Delays could mean that the park decided to just sell her back over the border. She didn't think that they would do that, but she had no great confidence that they wouldn't. Deals got made, and this was a very dangerous time in her life. And in Angel's.

She left the cafeteria, went to an elevator bank that only opened with a special key, and descended three levels to the complex that housed the child care for babies like hers who needed twenty-four/seven care. It was the only place she ever got to see Angel at all.

It was better than nothing. He'd almost died. The company had offered several options for paying off the required surgeries, making survival possible. The one she'd selected had, in fact, been the best of several bad options. But she'd paid it, because she'd had to. When she gazed down at Angel, loving him with every ounce of her being, she reminded herself that with her current role in the company she might actually be able to buy him back from them, though he would be near adulthood when that happened. And least now there was hope, beyond Floridar.

She found her baby sitting up in his playpen, brimming with industrial-grade cuteness. Some his own. Some the result of that surgery.

She flashed her naturally blinding grin.

Angel beamed back with her, with his lemur-like blue eyes and the angelic white fur that would serve him well as a member of the first generation of engineered Mascots.

Filibustering the Asteroid

Ronald D Ferguson

Half leaning, half sitting on his desktop, Senator Hiram Eglund, the senior senator from Mississippi, continued his filibuster on the floor of the United States Senate. He deliberately exaggerated his thick Southern accent. "… A decent respect to the opinions of mankind requires that they should declare the causes which impel them to the separation."

Eglund's aide, Larry Merton, slipped the latest diagrams displaying the confidence intervals for the asteroid's predicted trajectory onto Senator Eglund's desk. Eglund paused from his filibuster long enough to check the summary.

Larry admired how quickly Eglund digested the contents. The data clearly did not support Eglund's position that the asteroid would miss the Earth, but the senator was unfazed. He was not the kind of politician who let facts influence his speeches. Instead, Englund coughed, cleared his throat, and sipped some skim milk spiked with coconut rum. The milk soothed the Senator's ulcer. The rum did not.

"Will the Senator yield the floor for a question?" Senator Stanford Macy, the balding senior senator from Washington asked during Eglund's pause. Despite Macy's month at Betty Ford Clinic a year ago, Eglund's two-week filibuster had provoked the return of Macy's alcoholic rosacea.

Senator Eglund chewed on his unlit cigar. His eye twitched while he avoided looking directly at Senator Macy.

Eglund said, "I have the utmost respect for my honorable colleague from the great state of Washington, and I would be pleased to address any question that Senator Macy offers. Does my esteemed colleague have a question concerning the Declaration of Independence?"

Vice President Alvin Nowotny, who presided over the U.S. Senate, tapped his gavel against the podium. The scowl on Nowotny's face had not changed since Eglund began his filibuster. No one had seen the Vice President smile since the discovery of the wayward asteroid seven months ago. "The chair recognizes Senator Macy for the purpose of asking a question."

Larry replaced the asteroid trajectory data with a summary of the latest public positions taken by Macy during the current debate. Eglund grimaced, popped an antacid, and pushed the summary aside before restoring his smile.

Macy, his forehead glistening with sweat, nodded to the Vice President. "My thanks to the honorable Senator from Mississippi for yielding for a question. My question does not concern the Declaration of Independence, although my admiration for my colleague's knowledge of that revered document is unbounded. Rather, my question concerns the purpose of the Senator's comments. We had more than three weeks of expert testimony before this august body about the imminent threat posed by the approaching asteroid. The consensus from the ladies and gentlemen of the scientific community overwhelming supports the passage of the funding bill for NASA to nudge the asteroid from its current path. Despite the abundant evidence from these expert witnesses, the Senator has held this deliberative body hostage with his filibuster for two additional—and I might add critical—weeks. What else must we do before the Senator will allow a vote on the bill before us?"

What else, indeed. To stop Eglund, the Senate had already changed the rules to require that senator speak to continue his filibuster. Eglund had complied by reading from historical documents while periodically handing off the speaking duties to his new ally, Jesse James Burns, the junior Senator from Texas.

"Certainly not more testimony." Eglund slipped the wet, well-chewed stogie into his vest pocket and smoothed the tiny American flag pinned to his lapel. "I assure my esteemed colleague that for every so-called expert he presents, I can offer a prominent authority with an opposing view. Hence, there seems to be little reason to retrace all the stale arguments offered by the opposition, when my experts can refute every resurrected detail."

Macy could not contain himself. His entire face turned red. "We are discussing a possible disaster of epic proportion. Your latest witness, Reverend Golightly, is hardly an expert in astrophysics—"

Eglund's voice boomed. "An asteroid colliding with the Earth, if true, sir, would be a disaster of Biblical proportion. Then who better than a man of God like Doctor Golightly to testify? This entire endeavor is another tax-and-spend scheme to rob the American taxpayer. If this operation were truly worthy, then private enterprise and the great American can-do spirit would surely... No, sir, you sit down. I yielded for a question, and you had your chance. Now, you shall have my response."

Applause broke from a small clique that rose to their feet at the top of the Senate gallery. A woman unfurled a banner that proclaimed, "Repent. Judgment is at hand." Two rows down, four bedraggled observers remained seated and scowled at her banner. One half-heartedly lifted his own sign, which insisted "Money for the earth's poor, not pie-in-the-sky."

A third group stomped their feet and booed Eglund. Each wore a black t-shirt asserting in glossy, white letters, "$pace is our $alvation." The back of each t-shirt read "Breunig Aerospace."

"Order. Order." Vice President Nowotny pounded his gavel, his massive eyebrows flexing like two sumo wrestlers preparing to collide. "Order, or I will have the Sergeant at Arms clear the gallery. Please roll up those banners. Thank you."

Eglund smiled broadly at the commotion while Larry re-sorted papers for convenient access. Larry shook his head. The old man loved the spectacle, loved being at the center of the hubbub, and most of all, loved the disruption.

The old man was in his element. This was a real filibuster on live TV rather than the parliamentary maneuver of claiming a virtual filibuster. TV was the key ingredient for Eglund. The most dangerous place in DC was standing between Eglund and a TV camera. Changing the Senate filibuster rules had only enhanced Eglund's stature with his base.

Eglund waited for the last echoes of the disturbance to fade. At last, with his usual dramatic flair, he turned toward the Vice President.

"This is the time for real patriots to stand up." However, Eglund didn't stand. He continued to half lean, half sit on his desktop. Instead, he extended his arm overhead and pointed skyward. "For the record, I shall continue entering into the minutes the patriotic words from the Declaration of Independence."

Nowotny sighed and carefully laid his gavel across the podium. He whispered hopelessly into the microphone, "Senator Eglund, the Clerk can obtain a copy of the Declaration and insert it into the record."

"No need," Eglund proudly proclaimed, "I prefer to recite it. Now, let me see, where did I leave off?"

Not wanting Eglund to restart at the beginning, Larry prompted, "'Impel them to the separation.'"

"Yes, yes." Eglund waved Larry aside. "...Impel them to the separation. We hold these truths to be self-evident that all men are created equal, that they are endowed by their Creator—please note that Creator is capitalized—with certain inalienable Rights—please note that Rights is capitalized—that among these—"

"Point of order," shouted Senator Thomas Kaplan of New York in a thin voice. Almost no one heard him, so he grabbed his microphone, switched it on, and blared, "Point of order."

The sound system squealed from the feedback.

"The chair recognizes the Senator from New York for a point of order." Nowotny nodded to Kaplan.

Kaplan expanded to his full five-foot four-inch height and smirked. "That should read *unalienable* Rights, not *inalienable* Rights."

"Revisionist." Eglund pounded his desk. "I prefer *inalienable* Rights."

"Whatever you prefer, Senator, *inalienable* is not what was written in the Declaration." Kaplan waved a plastic tube containing a document that appeared to be from the Smithsonian gift shop. "I can show you a copy of the original if you wish."

"No one can read that hen-scratch. I tell you, it's *inalienable*. I do not wish this debate to be sullied by aliens or their so-called rights. My views on the sanctity of our borders are well known, and I need not repeat them here."

Larry covered his smile at Eglund's border pivot to sidetrack Kaplan's prefix quibble. Eglund was a master at answering his own unasked questions.

"Gentlemen, please." Nowotny wearily pounded his gavel. "Senator Eglund is reciting, not reading, therefore the record will reflect what he says. There's no need to debate whether what he said is correct. Indeed, there is no requirement that his recitation even resembles the Declaration for his statements to enter the record."

Kaplan squeaked up. "I would like a copy of the Declaration of Independence inserted into the record."

"I am inserting it into the record," Eglund said, "if I could be allowed to continue."

"I would like a *correct* copy of the Declaration inserted into the record," Kaplan insisted.

Nowotny pounded his gavel without enthusiasm. "The Clerk will footnote Senator Kaplan's point of order with a copy of the Declaration of Independence as transcribed from the Library of Congress. No, Senators, we will not debate which copy, let the Clerk retrieve whatever the Clerk thinks is best. Continue, Senator... No, wait. It's almost noon. Without dissent, we will break for lunch. We shall resume at 2 p.m."

The Clerk waved a pen at Nowotny and whispered. "Senator Kaplan is trying to make another point."

Nowotny covered the microphone with his right hand and mimed to the Clerk, "Yes, I saw him wave, but I do not want to hear him again. I'm hungry."

"A pack of reporters is waiting for you in the lobby." Larry gathered up the folders from Eglund's desk. "They aren't friendly."

"Let's take the back way," Eglund said. "Have lunch sent up to the office. We'll spend a few moments with the Fourth Estate when we return. After I make my points, the chairman's gavel will be a perfect excuse to cut short follow-up questions."

At the vibration in his pocket, Larry flipped open his cell phone and read the text messages. He turned to Eglund.

"Problem, sir. Reverend Golightly is waiting in your office."

"Damn." Eglund belched and rubbed his stomach. "He thinks we're friends. Find some way to get rid of him. I know, tell him to quit saying the asteroid will miss Earth. Tell him that there is no asteroid. We've discovered the other party made up the asteroid story to get votes for their bloated budget. It's all a big conspiracy to dupe the American public. Indicate it's critical for him to play up the conspiracy angle and deny that the asteroid exists."

Larry hesitated. "Deny the asteroid exists?" He held folders filled with existence evidence.

"Exactly. No one trusts scientists anymore, anyway. It's a conspiracy. Deny the asteroid exists. Keep denying. Double down. Never backoff the denials. Without a powerful telescope, no one can see the damn thing anyway."

Eglund smiled broadly and waved goodbye to Senator Macy. Macy scowled, wiped sweat from his brow, and stalked away as Kaplan approached the Clerk.

When Kaplan demanded to review the minutes, Larry paused before following Eglund out the door behind the Vice President's podium. The Clerk rolled her eyes at Kaplan's request but yielded the computer screen. On a less hectic day, Larry would have waited for Kaplan to scan the screen. He enjoyed the way Kaplan's lips moved when he read.

Larry tapped his cell phone screen to close a text message about Macy before sliding the phone into his pocket. He quickly caught up with Eglund.

"Your snide remark to Senator Macy will cost you his support for the sports stadium in Jackson."

"Doesn't matter." Eglund picked up his pace when they reached the hallway. "I'll earmark funds for the stadium and attach it to the military budget. That S.O.B. Macy takes money hand-over-fist from Breunig Aerospace, and then he questions my motives. Who does he think he's kidding with this rigmarole? With his pretense of statesmanship? If the bill passes, money will flood his state and he will reap the political capital."

Larry's cell phone vibrated again. He pulled it from his pocket. "This is Merton. What?" He glanced at Eglund for confirmation while he answered. "No. Don't order Chinese or Mexican. You know the Senator's ulcer bothers him. Grilled chicken? Okay, and don't forget low-fat ice cream.... Who? I told you to get rid of Golightly. Really? Okay, fine."

Eglund inclined his head and pursed his lips into an unspoken question.

Larry gripped the cell phone as if it were his favorite weapon. "Golightly refuses to leave without seeing you."

"Damn," Eglund said. The senator belched and rubbed his stomach. "I don't have time for that moron. Let's go through my private entrance. I don't want to offend him. I need him to deliver religious voters in the fall. What's the holdup? I hate this elevator."

Larry scanned the remaining messages on his phone. The airline message reminded him to download his boarding pass for the afternoon flight. Instead, he pressed the record icon. "Won't the walking-around-money you give Golightly assure his support?"

"Normally, yes, but this issue transcends follow-the-money."

"I'm sorry, Senator, I don't understand. I thought we always follow the money for motivation, for the source of power."

The elevator stopped. The doors opened, and they exited onto the empty hall.

"Have you never heard of principles, son? No? Claiming to have principles gets you elected; not letting principles interfere with your job keeps you in office."

Larry keyed open the private door into Eglund's office. "Are you suggesting that principles, rather than money, drive Golightly?" Larry stood aside to let Eglund enter.

"Well, Golightly's highest principle may be money, but he has others. The reverend and his followers are determined to hasten the Rapture so that God will lift the chosen—that's Golightly and his followers—into heaven. Leaving the unwashed behind is more satisfying to them than salvation itself."

Eglund slid into the chair behind his desk and tapped his fingers as if trying to remember something. He patted his pockets.

"Rapture?" Larry's voice modulated up a half octave. "This current event, this asteroid could be Armageddon not the Second Coming. If that asteroid strikes the earth—"

"Ah, here's my cigar." Eglund lit the stogy and inhaled deeply. "Calm down, son. What do the latest polls say about the asteroid?"

"Thirty-two percent believe the asteroid will miss the Earth. Twenty-one percent believe it will hit but won't affect their life. Twenty-three percent want something done to protect the Earth, but think the deficit is more important. Ten percent responded with no opinion.

Eleven percent refused to answer. The remaining three percent insist that it's God's judgement on sinners."

"Thirty-two percent predict a miss. Excellent. That's up from twenty-nine percent. We continue to win hearts. Tell the pollster to add a choice for a conspiracy about a fake asteroid in the next survey. Any new expert witnesses offering better odds on the collision?"

"I've found two astronomers who claim that there is absolutely no chance of a direct hit, but one is a known fruitcake and the other, like Golightly, has an agenda."

"Doesn't matter. Sign them up and get them on TV. Also, find me a persuasive, secular conspiracy theorist who knows how to saturate the internet."

Larry answered the knock at the private door, took the food tray from the kid who waited just outside, and shoved money into the boy's hand. He closed the door and set the food tray on Eglund's desk.

"Isn't Golightly enough for the conspiracy talking points?"

"I told you Golightly yearns for Armageddon as God's judgment." Eglund rubbed his chin. "He fears that if this funding bill passes, we might successfully deflect doomsday."

"If Golightly wants the asteroid to hit the earth, why does he testify it will miss?"

"What can Golightly lose with his testimony?" Eglund shrugged. "If the comet misses—"

"It's a rogue asteroid, not a comet. You don't want to make that slip in public unless you plan to join the conspiracy crowd."

"You're swatting the wrong flies, Larry. If the asteroid misses, then Golightly prophesized to the public correctly. Perhaps he even claims to have averted the disaster by prayer. He wins fame, and we can then follow the money. If the asteroid wipes out ninety-five percent of life on earth, then he has the deep satisfaction of knowing that God struck down his enemies. The screwy part is that I think he prefers the striking down of the unrighteous over appearing to be correct. Didn't you order lunch for yourself?"

Larry shook his head and then remained quiet while watching Eglund slice the chicken into bite-size squares. Eglund nibbled at the chicken for a moment, and then he grimaced and reached for the antacids in his desk. He chewed two tablets and wistfully looked at the remaining chicken.

Larry moved the bowl of vanilla ice cream from the back of the tray nearer to Eglund.

"I'll wait until it melts a bit." Eglund belched a half smile.

Then Eglund stared at Larry until Larry felt uneasy. Did the old man suspect him?

"You're awfully quiet," Eglund said. "And not hungry. That last part is very unusual."

Damn. The old man could read him too well. Larry blurted out his reservations. "What if we are wrong? What if NASA could get a ship into space and deflect the asteroid just enough to ensure that it misses the earth? Aren't we risking the world here?"

"If we let that NASA bird fly, the opposition wins. They take all the credit. It doesn't matter if the mission deflects the asteroid or not. The video of the attempt sent back will refute our conspiracy myth for most folks. However, if we do nothing and the asteroid misses, which I insist it will, then we have saved the taxpayer from the frivolous, spendthrift doomsayers, and we will be the heroes."

"With that outcome, you might get the Presidential nomination," Larry said.

"I *will* get the Presidential nomination." Eglund insisted.

"But if we are wrong, it will be a calamity, a disaster—possibly the end of humanity."

Eglund displayed that smile of aloof tolerance that had driven so many of his opponents to make a rash error. "My boy, if you want to talk about a doomsday scenario, if you want to discuss a calamity, a real disaster, then imagine the catastrophe if I don't win the next election.... What's that racket in reception?"

Larry listened near the door. "Sounds like a full-volume hellfire and damnation voice. Probably Golightly."

"Take care of it, son. Apologize. Tell him the President called me to the Oval Office and I won't have time to see him today. Don't forget to give that old hound the scent of a conspiracy to sniff out. Then get yourself some lunch. I'll see you on the senate floor."

"Yes, sir." Larry forced a can-do smile. "I'm on it."

~~~

Eglund waded into the mass of reporters and lectured them. From whatever angle their follow-up questions came, he pivoted like a pro to his prepared talking points.

Nearby, Larry keyed the confirmation number on his phone to secure his electronic boarding pass. He saved that screen and dialed his parents. He got voicemail.

"Hi, Dad. This is Larry. I'm spending several weeks alone at your fishing cabin to reassess my life, meditate, and perhaps even pray a little. Don't tell anyone where I am. Thanks. Love to you and Mom. 'Bye."

He dialed again.

"Senator Macy? This is Larry Merton. I have those recordings we discussed. No, I don't expect a job from you. No one in Washington will trust my loyalty after this act of principle. Yes, I know this is the end of my D.C. career. I'm only twenty-nine, I'll find work elsewhere. On the upside, perhaps it will end Senator Eglund's reign. You don't think so? Perhaps he will hang onto his seat, but the presidency is out of the question. You're not sure of that either? Nonetheless, I've got to try. Are you ready? Transmitting."

Larry did not like sending recordings of Eglund's private conversations because they betrayed his mentor and aided Macy's ambitions. At least Macy would try to save the planet.

Down the hallway, Eglund's news conference dissolved into a shouting match, which the old man always enjoyed. As Eglund had planned, Senate pages summoned the senators into the session to cut short the interview. Eglund smiled, grandly waved to the reporters, and pushed toward the Senate floor.

For the first time in five years, Larry did not follow Senator Eglund onto the Senate floor. Instead, he auto-dialed a taxi and exited to the Capitol steps. He wondered when Eglund would notice that his trusted aide was missing.

Larry dialed one last time to close out his career in politics. "Larry Merton here. Deliver a half gallon of non-fat frozen yogurt, vanilla, to Senator Eglund's office. Use my credit card."

Bless his heart, the old man would need ulcer relief when things fell apart.

Southern Truths

My First Gun

Alan Brickman

When I lived in Massachusetts, I never considered getting a gun.

Even in situations where I felt threatened, it wouldn't have occurred to me.

But here in New Orleans, most people I know, men and women, old and young, every race and ethnicity, have guns. People talk about their guns all the time: 22s, 38s, 45s, pistols, rifles, shotguns, AR-15s, semi-automatics.

I know people who keep them safely stored and secured, and others who keep them in an unlocked drawer in the living room. I know people who keep one in their car, and others in their purse or briefcase, a gun ready at all times.

Whenever I read a newspaper account of another mass shooting, I get more anxious about all the guns. There wasn't anywhere that felt reliably safe. My sense that there were too many guns seemed validated on an almost daily basis. When a random argument on a drunken Friday night gets heated and someone says, "You wanna go outside?" it used to mean a fistfight, but now it could just as easily become shots fired.

And yet, I decided to do it, and here I was.

I pulled into the parking lot of a nondescript strip mall and saw the sign above the storefront I'd been looking for: Sportsman's Guns and Ammo.

When I tried to enter, the door was locked so I stepped back to see what the hours were. Instead, there were two posters, one with a picture of an old-fashioned six-shooter with the caption, "We Don't Dial 911," and another with a photo of a snarling teenager pointing a gun straight at the camera that said, Second Amendment College of Art: We're Looking for People Who Like to Draw. I didn't know what to make of these aggressive and threatening attempts at humor. I almost turned back.

"Look up into the camera," a raspy voice said over a scratchy intercom. When I did, a buzzer sounded. I pulled on the handle and walked in, hopeful, apprehensive, and a little terrified. I thought back to the series of events that got me here.

~ ~ ~

I had been robbed twice in the last month, both times at gunpoint. The first time, I was walking home after beer and chicken wings when a man jumped out of the shadows, screamed unintelligibly, and punched me on the side of the head! He jammed a gun in my face and demanded money. I handed over what I figured was about fifty dollars. He grabbed it and ran.

I leaned against a building and tried to slow my breathing. I was thankful for three things: that I'd paid cash at the bar and therefore had a little less in my pocket, that I carried my money separately from my wallet, and that I didn't get shot. I was still shaking when I got to my apartment. I locked the door, turned off the lights, and sat quietly in the dark. I woke up the next morning on the couch in my clothes.

About a week and a half later, in the middle of the afternoon, I had just finished a short jog through City Park and was walking back to my car when two teenage boys came up behind me. "Hey, Mister," one said in a high squeaky voice. When I turned, I saw one boy, short and wiry, pointing a gun at me while the other one, taller and heavier, stepped around me to block my escape. "Gimme your fuckin' money, white boy!" the small one said. He looked around nervously. "Now!"

I shrugged and pointed to my gym shorts. "I'm not carrying any money. I'm just out jogging." I immediately regretted saying this. It made me sound even whiter.

"This is bullshit," the bigger one said from behind me. I braced for the worst. The little one raised his gun, pointed it in the air and fired a shot. The blast was still ringing in my ears as I watched the assailants jump on two small bikes that were leaning against a tree and ride off, pedaling as fast as they could. I walked unsteadily to the side of the path, put both hands on a chain link fence, and threw up.

About an hour later, sitting in a police station lobby waiting to give my statement, I ran through all the comments about firearms I'd heard over the years from people in New Orleans. Repeatedly, I'd heard things like, "I'm really glad I had a gun after Katrina, when the city was empty and there was still no power. I sat on my front porch with my gun in my lap so no one would fuck around." Whenever people talked about a recent home invasion in the neighborhood, someone would invariably say, "Let 'em show up at my house. I'll blow their fuckin' heads off!" As I watched police officers walk through the halls of the station, guns on their hips, something flipped in me and I decided I was going to get my first gun. From that moment, my resolve was steadfast, and would not be derailed by any further consideration or second thoughts.

I asked my friend Sam where I should go. Sam was a part-time bartender and Iraq War veteran. He had lots of guns. He seemed pleased and just a little excited when I asked him about it.

"Sportsman's Guns and Ammo," Sam said with a smile. "It's in Gretna on the West Bank. Ask for George. He's an Army buddy of mine. He inherited the store from his father, and he knows more about guns than anybody. Tell him we're friends. He'll take care of you."

~~~

The gun shop was brightly lit, and the air conditioning was turned way up. I was surprised that the music playing was a jazz trumpet instrumental, Miles or maybe Chet Baker. I don't know why, but I thought it would be heavy metal. Guns of all shapes and sizes were in locked cabinets behind the counter and along the side walls. Hundreds of them. The place was more spacious, uncluttered, and professional-looking than the exterior storefront led me to expect and was well-stocked enough for a small army.

"First time, son? We love the first-timers," said a man who appeared from the back room. He walked in front of the counter and shook my hand. "I'm George. Welcome to Sportsman's." He had thick salt-and-pepper hair pulled into a ponytail and a deep raspy voice.

I introduced myself, then said, "What makes you think this is my first time?"

"I've been at this for a while, and you have that look. You know when country folk visit the big city and can't stop staring up at the skyscrapers?" He shrugged his shoulders and smiled.

"Fair enough," I said, feeling caught somehow, as if my secret was out. "My friend Sam Corso in New Orleans sent me. He said you two were in the service together and that I should ask for you."

"That's great! Sam's good people. So, what can I do you for?"

"Well, you got any guns for sale in this place?"

"Sure," said George, smiling. "I'll bet I can dig up something in the back. What are you in the market for?"

"A handgun. Not too big and bulky, easy to use... I don't know, maybe a semi-automatic?"

"I got you. Let's look at some options." He bent down, unhooked a wad of keys from his belt, and unlocked the case. Without looking up, he asked, "So, why are you here? What's your story? Every first-timer has a story. Did you get robbed or something?"

This was disconcerting. Someone I'd just met being so casual but also oddly prescient about what was driving my gun purchase. "Yeah, something like that," I said, trying to sound nonchalant. "But you're right. Twice actually, and that's what got me thinking about it. I moved to New Orleans almost seven years ago, and I have to say, when you live in this city, sooner or later you feel like you need a gun."

George smiled and nodded. "So, do you think you're ready?"

"Ready for what?"

"Everything," George said as he smiled and clapped me on the shoulder.

George pulled out half a dozen handguns, some with names I recognized like Smith & Wesson or Glock, and some that I didn't. George was a knowledgeable and skillful salesman, walking through specs, terms of comparison, and value for the money with practiced ease. This felt just like buying high-end stereo equipment. A blur of jargon, and many more features to consider than I would have thought.

I ultimately chose something on the higher end of the scale, a CZ-75 semi-automatic pistol. It was a nice size and felt both comfortable and substantial in my hand. I also liked that it was manufactured in the Czech Republic and was called "The Phantom." When I said this to George, he rolled his eyes and said, "Whatever floats your boat. But you got yourself a nice piece of machinery. Congratulations." I completed and signed the paperwork, then paid in cash. I'd brought twelve one-hundred-dollar bills, and was happy I didn't have to use them all. Barely an hour after I'd entered the store, I stood on the sidewalk in the New Orleans midday heat and humidity with my new gun in a locked black hard-shell carrying case slightly smaller than a briefcase, a leather shoulder holster, and two boxes of bullets. I felt proud of myself, and I couldn't quite believe I'd actually done it.

When I got home, I called Sam. "I finally got over to Sportsman's."

"Isn't George a great guy?" Sam said.

"Definitely. And guess what I bought. A CZ-75 Phantom! You know the Czech… "

"Ooh, fancy," Sam said. "What, are you joining the CIA?"

"Hey, c'mon! Why are you making fun of me?"

"Don't worry, I'm just kidding. But really, that's a great gun. I know a guy who has one that he bought over there and had shipped back to the States. He loves it. Good job. Now don't go shooting anybody… unless they deserve it!"

~~~

For the first few days, I kept the open carrying case on my coffee table and just stared at it. One weekday evening, I drove to a shooting range that George recommended. The man at the counter saw the carrying case, and asked me what kind of gun I had. When I told him, he said, "Right on. We don't get many of those in here. Can I have a look?"

I shot for about an hour. I got comfortable with the gun's action and recoil and was gratified that my aim was improving.

After that, I kept the gun locked in the case on a high shelf in my bedroom closet. This seemed to be the safest thing to do. I didn't take it out for a week or so, but I was always aware it was there. When I received my concealed-carry permit in the mail, I decided to take it out for a spin.

I put on the holster, slipped the gun in, and looked in the full-length mirror. I put on my blue sport coat, grabbed my keys, and stepped outside. I felt hyper-alert and slightly euphoric. Electrified.

I drove to Marian's, a neighborhood restaurant with great food and a cool bar scene. My friend Connie, who I hadn't seen in a while, was bartending, and I leaned in to give her a hug. I saw her steal a quick glance down the front of my jacket. She grabbed my wrist and pulled me toward her so she could whisper in my ear. "Since when do you carry a gun? Are you out of your fuckin' mind? Take that shit out of here before Marian sees it. She hates, and I mean hates, when anybody but the off-duty cops she hires for security bring guns into the restaurant. She'll bar you and call the police."

I felt like an idiot. "I'm really sorry, Connie. Never again, I promise." When I got home, I locked the gun in its case and put it back in the closet.

~~~

It was a Saturday afternoon and I was bored just sitting around the house. I decided to take out the Phantom to clean and reload it. I heard a loud car engine outside, and I walked to the front door and pulled the curtain aside. It took me a few seconds to realize what was going on, A man was stealing packages that had been delivered to my neighbors' front porch across the street. A car was idling at the curb. I stepped outside, and yelled, "Hey, what the hell do you think you're doing?" The man didn't even look up. I still had the gun in my hand, so I lifted it above my head and fired into the air. That got the man's attention, and he grabbed the packages and started running to the car. Operating on pure instinct, I lowered the gun and fired at the robber. I missed, and the bullet smashed through the front window of the house. My second shot hit the man in the leg, just below the knee. He screamed, limped the last few steps, and threw the packages and then himself into the car's open door. The tires screeched as the car sped away.

I saw several other neighbors step out of their front doors to see what the commotion was. I tried to stay calm as I held the gun behind my back and stepped backward into my house and closed the door. My mind was racing, with each thought barely registering. What the fuck did I just do? Were the neighbors home? I could have killed somebody! Did anyone see it? Are they going to call the police? Oh, fuck oh fuck oh fuck oh fuck! The robbers are gonna come back! They know where I live. Shit. They have guns. I am so fucked.

I turned off all the lights and drew the blinds. I sat in the dark, in a chair facing the front door, with the Phantom in my lap. Waiting for... what?

Not feeling ready at all.

Best of Five

Liam Hogan

"The next and final item on our agenda," the Recorder paused as angular sigils flashed before her five eyes, "is the third planet of system 330483, in sector ZZ9, locally known as 'Earth'. Relative neighbors of yours, Senator?"

"Yes," the elderly alien from 330412 admitted.

"I am at somewhat of a loss as to why you oppose their automatic admission to the Assembly of Planets. They first escaped orbit thirteen hundred Ta back, successfully journeyed to their moon not long after, and were last audited some seven hundred Ta ago. That was their *fifth* audit, each one further apart than the last. Are you really claiming there has been *no* progress since?"

"Plenty," the Senator replied. "But very little in the right direction. They are, if anything, more of a risk to the stability of the Assembly, and to themselves, than they were during any of the previous audits, all of which they failed. And, I should point out, they haven't set appendage off planet, not even making the short hop back to their only moon. They seem to have lost the appetite to look beyond their own planet."

The Recorder leveled three of her eyes in the Senator's direction. "I don't suppose your interstellar borders, which would have to be redrawn and might be noticeably reduced by a new and adjoining member, have anything to do with your reluctance?"

"Recorder!" The tendrils that drifted on either side of the Senator's curved chin quivered, a clear sign of indignant emotion. "If I am reluctant to admit this uncouth and belligerent race, I have only the *best* interests of the Assembly in mind."

"Does anyone wish to speak in favor of this nascent species?" The Recorder's splayed eyes encompassed the entire hall of the Membership Committee, peering at the gathered representatives, most of whom, at the end of another long session, looked bored. They remained silent.

"Very well. We shall apply the usual tests, Senator. You have everything in place?"

"Yes, Recorder. There are over a thousand adult humans in the vicinity of our remote probes. Please make your selection."

An eye stalk hesitated over a flickering console as profiles whizzed past, then randomly blinked right. In the center of the chamber, a human appeared, sprawled almost horizontal on a heavily padded piece of furniture which a floating icon helpfully identified as something called a *La-Z-Boy*. A cluster of hovering micro-cameras captured everything in high resolution, rendering it near lifelike to the august committee. At the same time the members of the committee—none of whom were in the same room, each of them on their own planets, the Assembly's deliberations being entirely virtual—were projected onto the human's electronic device (labeled as an *86-Inch 4-K Ultra High Definition Smart Television with Dolby Surround*). It was much simpler that way, and far less likely to breach stringent biosecurity measures. Abducting aliens from backwards planets on the outer fringes of the galaxy was *seriously* frowned upon.

"Hey!" the human exclaimed, spilling tepid beer across an already serially stained T-shirt. The garment portrayed the black silhouette of an assault rifle along with the challenge to COME AND TAKE IT, and utterly failed to cover the expanse of wire-haired belly. "I was watching the game!"

"Game?" the Recorder echoed.

"A ritualized, militaristic competition, complete with body armor, but devoid of any weapons. Unless you count an armored combatant running full tilt at you," the Senator explained.

"And the *point* of the game?"

"No one is quite sure, Recorder. But millions watch the games in their local stadiums, and even more at home, always vehemently supporting one side over the other. Perhaps it betrays their need for vicarious violence."

The Recorder frowned. Such conclusions were speculative and surely premature. The console showed what the human was currently missing. There was an ugly clatter of helmets and animal grunts as half the players ended up on the ground.

Meanwhile, the human, eyes wide, was shaking his grizzled head. "Christ, what a fugly set of god-forsaken mutts. You sure ain't selling no beauty products!"

"Is the translator working properly, Senator?"

"Yes, Recorder."

"Then can you *interpret* the translation?"

"Insults, Recorder. Fugly is... ah, *extremely* ugly. A mutt... I guess that's sort of similar. And beauty products—an elaborate industry built around the conceit that every human can aspire to the same impossible levels of visual perfection, though primarily aimed at the female of the species. This one..." the Senator checked the display, "is male."

"Does he *know* we're here?"

"Apparently he thinks we're a commercial break, or a hijacked transmission, interrupting, as he said, his game."

The Recorder peered more closely at the projection. The television, the La-Z-Boy, and the human were rendered in exquisite detail, the squashed-fly bedecked walls of the room less so. The test subject was holding a slim device in his meaty hand, stabbing at the buttons and cursing.

"Not a lot of situational awareness, this human... Possibly displaying a deficit in mental ability?"

"This one is *marginally* above average intelligence for the sample set." The Senator shrugged. "Even when down four out of the six metal cylinders of liquid chemical intoxicant."

"For f&%ks sake!" The human angrily threw a crushed can (having had the situational awareness *not* to throw it at his pride-and-joy TV). He slouched off in pursuit of a fifth cold beer, hoping that the tedious commercial would be over by the time he returned. Unaware that, behind his rippling back, the beer can had clipped one of the probes, triggering a premature self-destruct. The resultant brief but intense inferno took out the wide-screen TV, but only singed the edges of the La-Z-Boy, making the lower leg support annoyingly rough to the touch.

In the chamber of the Membership Committee, the La-Z-Boy and its repellent occupant vanished, the signal lost. The Recorder sighed, ventral frills fluttering. "As we didn't get to put any questions, I move we take a second test subject. Perhaps one that isn't so engrossed in entertainment, so that we can ask its opinions?"

The virtual committee nodded, or blinked, or subtly shifted color, to indicate their somewhat reluctant consent, and the Recorder once more swiped right. A pink-faced creature appeared, sitting by an artificial fountain in an air-conditioned mall, an overflowing trash can full of fast-food wrappers and plastic soda cups to one side, a collection of shopping bags on the other. Above it all, floating labels appeared and disappeared as the system struggled to identify everything in view. The image wobbled, settled, then wobbled again.

"What is happening?" the Recorder asked, as the test subject fiddled with her rhinestone covered smartphone.

"She's resisting our signal. Keeps on trying to switch to other inputs. I'll project us on the digital billboard directly across from her instead."

The image settled, and the test subject looked up at the sudden change in light to mutter a half-hearted "*Kewl!*" and to take and post a selfie, the projected alien committee in the background. Then she went back to scrolling her feeds. (The posted selfie was censored by the hovering cameras, and in later days, drifting off to sleep with her mobile limply held in her hand, test subject two wondered if she'd dreamed the whole thing.)

The committee looked on, waiting for something more from her, but it appeared that whatever was on the six-inch screen six inches from her nose was a stronger pull than a committee of galactic space-going races on a fact-finding mission. Perhaps as much as half of the committee might have agreed with her.

"Can we get this one's attention?" the Recorder asked, with a degree of petulance. There were other meetings to attend. This was taking an unexpectedly large slice of her m-Ta.

Test subject two's phone went abruptly black. She stabbed her bejeweled fingernail at it, again, and again, but it didn't respond. "Anyone got a charging cable?" she wailed in despair.

It was only as she peered around to see if anyone did and saw that the aliens were still plastered across the digital billboard, that a micro-frown appeared on her botoxed forehead.

"*Huh.* Interactive posters. Early for Halloween, isn't it? You guys trick-or-treaters?"

The Recorder glanced at the Senator for an explanation.

"Trick-or-treat… is a national custom at a particular time of year, though barely observed in this locale, as going door to door is generally considered a high-risk activity."

"High-risk?"

"Yes. More than one-third of households in this region of the planet possess at least one deadly weapon of some description. Some have many more."

"A third? There is a predator race on this planet? Are the humans by necessity well-organized and trained to protect themselves?"

"No, Recorder. Very few are trained at all. And a third is actually relatively low. There are areas on this landmass with much higher percentages, none of which correlates with predator densities as there aren't *any* predators of humans of significant number. There used to be, but the humans killed them all, or most of them, certainly in these parts. Everywhere but the oceans, and even there, they're doing their best to eliminate anything bigger than they are. There are a few, rare, mid-sized predators, in particularly remote areas, which largely and wisely keep to themselves, and which are decreasing year by year. Unless you count humans as predators. Which perhaps the weapons owners *do*, especially different-colored ones."

"Different...?"

"An insignificant pigmentation variation. Ah, these ones, subjects one and two, might be considered the genetic *mutants*, since their distant ancestors were considerably darker, and their fair skin is not at all well suited to this Southern latitude, or to their increasingly human-warmed climate."

"We might be getting sidetracked, Senator. And we might be about to lose our test subject."

Having rooted in her voluminous handbag, looking for a cable or a power pack, the woman was now piling the contents back in and making to stand. With a few deft instructions, the Senator sent in one of the hovering probes to fire a small dart into her thigh.

The test subject swatted the tiny sting away, and then sat heavily back down, her legs sapped of energy.

"I do hope that—?"

"Temporary. *Very.* Best ask your questions, Recorder, before the effects wear off."

The Recorder glanced down for the correct term of address, though the translator was designed to interject the necessary levels of decorum.

"Madam, may we ask you a few questions?"

"You ain't one of those culty religions, are you?" the human said, giving them a shrewd look. "Nah... marketing something, I'll bet. Powered by AI." She crossed her arms before her ample bosom. "What do I get out of it?"

"She's asking to be compensated," the Senator replied to the Recorder's dip of an eyestalk.

"Can we... ?"

"Madam, we can fully charge your smartphone for you. It'll take around two minutes—plenty long enough for our questions."

The woman grinned, showing a set of startlingly white teeth, marred by a clumsily applied line of red lipstick. "You got a deal. But I'm not into gaming or cosplay, so I reckon you're on a bum steer."

The Senator waved away the inevitable questions. "I'll do my best to explain later. Time is ticking, Recorder!"

"Right, right. Madam, do you give much thought to the stars, to interplanetary and interstellar travel?"

"Angels, you mean? The Rapture? Or... you Scientologists? I'm Southern Baptist, mister, so you're barking up the wrong tree!"

"No, madam, I'm talking about extraterrestrials. Space exploration. *Science.*"

The folded arms tightened, became a defensive, impenetrable barrier. "Got no truck with science. *Experts!* Vaccine pushers, climate freaks, book-smart eggheads who don't know shit, not even what a woman is. They want to control your *minds*, with their bird drones and their AIs and their 5G. I listen to my *minister*, mister. Him and Truth Social tell me everything I need to know."

"Ah... Senator?"

"There's rather a lot to unpack. But I'm afraid such a high degree of paranoia and conspiracy isn't particularly uncommon."

"*Conspiracy?*" the woman echoed. "There sure is! Kept Trump out of the White House, they did. Kept America from being *Great!* Look to Washington if you want to know where it all got stolen." She peered hard at them, her jollity long evaporated. "You're Liberals, ain't you?"

"The Liberals are the darker-pigmented humans?" the Recorder inquired.

"No, not generally," the Senator replied. "Though they do tend to be marginally more tolerant of them. No, ma'am, we're not Liberals."

The woman's phone screen lit up, displaying 100-percent battery life. A more curious human might have wondered, in the hours, days, and weeks after, how come it never wavered from that 100 percent, how come her phone *never* needed charging again. But she was not one such. "Thanks boys," she said, with a smirk, as if she had somehow hoodwinked them. "Good luck with the mission, or marketing, or *whatever.*"

And that was the last attention she gave to the projection before her, the bubble of privacy fading away, letting in the background sounds of the mall as she marched off on still-wobbly legs, eyes fixed on her screen.

"I think we'll move on to a *third* test subject, if that's okay with you," the Recorder said. "We don't seem to be having much luck."

The Senator shrugged. The rules allowed for five subjects in total, to get a representative sample. It was rare to need them all. The committee generally gave alien races the benefit of the doubt. Here, doubt seemed to be in plentiful supply.

The overflowing trash can vanished, to be replaced by a stout desk, its edges truncated by the limited coverage of the floating cameras. Behind it sat a florid man in a crisp suit. He stared at the image that had appeared on his monitor without saying anything for a solid half-minute, before reaching to the phone and pressing a button.

"Yes, Senator?"

"Hold my calls, and postpone my 2 p.m."

"Ah... do you need any, um, *help* with that, Senator?"

"Not on this occasion, Molly. I'll let you know when I'm done."

"Yes, s—"

The senator gave a second, careful appraisal to each of the committee members, and then displayed his full set of teeth, almost making the representative from 211778 divide in two.

"So, folks. Aliens, yes? What can I interest you in?"

"Excuse me?" The Recorder hiccupped.

"You here for oil? Water? Maybe some cheap labor? Land? We've got plenty of *land*, as long as you don't mind it dry and hot."

"He's trying to sell what he's elected to represent?" the Recorder asked, muting the translator.

"He *is* a Republican, Recorder."

"A...?"

"One of the two main political parties on this section of the continent. The other being the aforementioned Liberals, or Democrats, who are generally seen as more progressive, more equitable, better for both the climate and for this nation's international relations."

"So, how...?"

"The people voted him in, Recorder."

"What about weapons? Y'all probably have your *ray* guns, yes? But how about this lil' beauty?" A drawer of the vast desk was opened, and a gleaming handgun waved around in a way that would have made heads and sense-stalks retreat behind hard carapaces, if any of the committee members had actually been any closer than forty-two light years away.

"'Course, this is just my day-to-day. Got the real guns locked up. But I could take you to the range, for a demonstration."

"Does any of this make sense to you?" the Recorder asked the Senator.

"Ah, one moment... " In the chamber hovered an image—flat, rather than 3D—straight out of the manufacturer's catalog. It flicked to another weapon, and another, each bigger and more deadly looking than the last.

"Are you *sure* there are no apex predators, to warrant such an arsenal?"

"None, Recorder. The holders of such weapons argue they're needed to protect them from... well, the government they elected to protect them."

"Hey," the Senator said in alarm as the pages of the catalog flashed by. "Don't go to the manufacturer direct! I can get you a great discount. That's what friends do, right? So, how do you folks like to pay for things, anyway? We'll take diamonds, gold, or any alien technology you might like to share on a purely exclusive basis."

The Recorder winced. "We're not here for petty *commerce.*" The translator managed to inject a tiny part of her scorn into the statement.

The senator's bluster faded, the red hue of his skin darkened. "What are you, *commies*? Here I am, in good faith, trying to help out my fellow man-not-man things, and—"

On his monitor, the Recorder's image vanished.

"*Timewasters,*" the Senator scoffed, sliding his pride-and-joy nickel-plated Desert Eagle back into the desk drawer, not noticing he'd disengaged the safety in his excitement, a tragedy that would only become fully apparent some fifteen minutes later. He pressed the buzzer on the desk phone. "Molly? Actually... I *do* require your assistance. And honey? Bring the handcuffs."

In the chamber, the Recorder spread her eyestalks wide, taking in the committee's mood. "I'm not sure this is entirely necessary, but... protocol dictates the members must vote. All in favor of waiting at least... hmm, another thousand Ta, before reconsidering Earth's status? Assuming they last that long. Very well. So recorded. Thank you for your patience. Assembly Membership Committee adjourned until the next five-Ta."

The chamber blinked out, one by one, until only the Recorder and the Senator were left.

"I'm not sure that was a *fair* survey," the Recorder mused. "But it was certainly conclusive." A shudder ran down and then up her body. "You expected this result?"

"I did," the Senator replied.

"Maybe they'll present better at the next audit?"

"Perhaps. But it'll be my successor who comes before you then. I'm retiring, Recorder."

"I'm sorry to hear that. You have been a Senator for many a Ta. But if that's the case, and if you don't mind... It seems like you wagered rather a lot on a random selection of test subjects. Others may have been distracted by the reprehensible aliens, but in their environment there are clear signs of advanced technology—that second creature's mobile device, while it was briefly connected, is surprisingly sophisticated. Much more advanced than the bare minimum required for space travel and therefore Assembly membership. How could you be so sure that any three such test subjects would produce such a parlous view of human behavior?"

The Senator took a long pause, tendrils twitching in thought. "Well—and just between you and me—that was simple enough. As you say, I can't choose the subjects you select, but I can pick the area they're selected *from*. And, so far, Recorder, Texas hasn't let me down once."

A Teacher's Disillusionment

Leanne Van Valkenburgh

I look back at that day I sat in class.
Eager to learn to teach.
Idealistic, hopeful, naïve
They said, if you are doing this to have summers off.
Seek a different path.
Walk out the door now.

Silence. No one moved.
I thought to myself.
Why was I here?
Of course I knew that answer.
At least I believed what I told myself.
Sacrifice, inspiring, secure
How wrong I was.

My first lesson would be on sacrifice. Three years into
teaching.
Education funding reduction
No raise, no step

Southern Truths

Four years went that way.
No, I wasn't just sacrificing a better career choice.
I was sacrificing being considered a professional

Next, I would learn about inspiration.
My dreams of inspiring young minds to explore and
learn.
Then politicians found their pockets fat by testing
companies.
Stick to the standards.
Pass the test.
My authenticity began to slip.
Scripts took the place of classroom dialogue.
Tests took time away from engagement.
Banned books. Read only this.
Contentious school board meetings
Angry rhetoric. Don't say Gay. Ignore diversity.
How long until we are fully automated

Last came security.
Teach, they said, it is a good solid secure career.
Good retirement they said.
Then came anti-tenure, anti-union, anti-teacher.
Slowly chipping away at our security.
When did teachers become the enemy?
When did the classroom become a political battleground?

If I could tell myself all those years ago what I know now.
Don't sacrifice yourself for that career.
What once was, is no longer.
Your inspiration is noble, but it will be lost on the future
policymakers.
No career is safe today, that fallacy is from a different
time.
Seek out a different path.
And walk out that door.

Healthcare Bitch is Here for Da People

Allan Dyen-Shapiro

Superhero gigs were scarce because of the recession, so when Blue Dollar Sign Health Insurance advertised a posting, Healthcare Bitch went for it and relocated from Jersey to Alabama. On her first day, Mousy, the executive secretary, confided that the men who'd hired Healthcare Bitch based solely on her application and photo—without even interviewing her— had loved both the irreverent attitude conveyed by the profanity in her moniker and her willingness to dress "pretty as a peach" in a miniskirt and bikini top. They dug her blond-haired All-American look: a girl they'd sit next to in church and have in their masturbation fantasy later.

Healthcare Bitch nodded. Up North, men rarely said such things aloud, but if Southern gentlemen were more open about their feelings, who was she to complain? She leaned against Mousy's desk and cracked open a beer. "Whaddaya got for me?"

"Dialect training. Remember, more Birmingham, less New Jersey."

"Easier said than done. You can take da bitch out of Newark—"

"Yes, I see." Mousy bit her lip repetitively while staring at her computer screen but then perked up. "Well, I declare! This is exciting. You've been chosen as our Telehealth Ambassador."

Whoop-de-doo. "What da fuck is that?" The title stunk worse than the cheese in Mousy's lunchbox.

The Muzak rose to a crescendo. It wasn't her imagination; Mousy had a volume-adjust knob behind her desk.

"Imagine a Sunday evening," Mousy said. "Tomorrow's work for you and school for the children, but little Buffy has a fever, and no pediatrician in your care network is on call. Now, over Zoom, an MD in a time zone where it's still working hours can prescribe antibiotics. Lord willing and the creek don't rise, Buffy's better in no time and can get to school for tomorrow's standardized testing."

It sounded good, an opportunity worthy of her tagline. "Healthcare Bitch is here for da people. Whadda I do?"

Mousy handed Healthcare Bitch a laptop and a list of hospitals in the area.

And she was off. Her cape fluttered in the morning breeze as she flew over I-20, cruised into Birmingham, and sailed over downtown traffic until she landed on Midland Children's Hospital roof. She rode the elevator down to the first floor and found herself in the ER waiting room. Every seat was taken, as was every square inch of space. The bosses were right—these people needed another option. She stood ramrod straight, chin up: the epitome of corporate propriety.

"Yo, listen up. Healthcare Bitch is here for da people. You don't need to wait in dis punk-ass line. Telehealth will get you seen quicker than a cop can locate a donut shop."

The people's eyes brightened.

"So, who has Blue Dollar Sign insurance?"

The crowd chuckled, blew raspberries, or gave her the finger. To a Jersey girl, this was hospitality, so she responded in kind. "Who shoved a rat up your assholes?"

"Medicaid or uninsured, Miss." An elderly Black man in a threadbare cardigan approached. "At least most of us." He adjusted the position of the infant he cradled in his arm. "And because they didn't expand Medicaid in Alabama, folks like me, who work for a living, seek treatment solely in an emergency."

Before Healthcare Bitch could process what the man had said, a teenage Chinese girl tugged on her sleeve. "We have Blue Dollar Sign." The young woman pressed a card into Healthcare Bitch's hand. "This is my mother's—she doesn't speak English. My sister's sick."

From her laptop, Healthcare Bitch helped them reach a doctor in Mumbai.

"What seems to be the problem?" he asked.

"My sister has diarrhea. And she's vomiting."

"It could be cholera. It's common in places that discharge raw sewage into the water supply."

"We ain't in da *Global* South," Healthcare Bitch said.

His brow's furrow deepened as he glanced at his screen. "Oh, my mistake—I thought you were in Mobile. Then it's probably cancer. That will be twenty-five dollars, please. Visa or Mastercard?"

Healthcare Bitch went hot under the collar (metaphorically—her outfit was so skimpy it lacked a collar). "Fuck dis shit. I'm gettin' you a real doctor."

Once Healthcare Bitch had vaporized the ER doors (shooting laser beams from her eyes being one of her more useful superpowers—Wonder Woman's Lasso of Truth wouldn't do squat when faced with a rat onslaught in a New Jersey apartment complex), an orderly with a shoulder-length mullet whose scrubs barely covered his beer gut confronted her. "What in tarnation do we have here?"

"Wit' my superstrength, I can knock you into Mississippi. Wit' my superspeed, I can run around you. I'm from Jersey, and I—"

"Know lawyers." The teenager poked her head out from behind Healthcare Bitch.

A diminutive man in a scumbag blazer and tie that smelled of mothballs shuffled over. "Sure enough, we can get your sister in." His badge said Hospital Administrator. "Your mother can pay the six-thousand-dollar deductible and the forty percent co-insurance at the window."

Without breaking eye contact, Healthcare Bitch swept an upturned palm to draw his attention to the waiting room's still-unattended-to crowd, "What about da rest of dem?" Healthcare Bitch asked.

"We're fixin' to get to them as soon we can service our priority patients. Thank you kindly for expressing your concerns." The man led the Chinese family away.

His Southern politeness rankled. This was bullshit.

If the hospital wasn't treating the crowd in the ER, what did take priority around here? After re-calibrating her laser gaze to penetrate the walls of each room, she searched for patients. Most rooms proved empty, but at last, in the "Patron's Wing," she encountered a teenager lying on her back, an IV in her arm, surrounded by three nurses and two doctors. For what dire condition must they be treating this poor girl?

"Horrific disfigurement," the kid's mother answered once Healthcare Bitch had made her way over and posed the question. The woman, her husband, and two men sporting the tell-tale Hospital Administrator badge huddled outside the glass enclosing the operating room.

"From an accident?" Healthcare Bitch asked.

"How did you... oh, you're not asking about her conception. No, she was just born with a big nose. Her first debutante ball is this year, and we can't have her looking so, you know, ethnic. The plastic surgeons here are the best in Alabama."

Healthcare Bitch gritted her teeth. "With all the sick patients in the ER, how does treatin' da ugly that runs in your family come first?"

"Well, aren't you precious?" The mother crossed her arms in a ladylike fashion. "My ancestors have donated to Midland Children's Hospital for five generations. For us, the attention from these fine medical professionals is complimentary. If those freeloaders wanted treatment, they should have inherited enough money to pay their bills."

And if this Scarlett O'Hara wanted a knuckle sandwich, a certain bitch could deliver it.

One of the administrators pre-empted a need for their clan to endow a Department of Oral Surgery by stepping between them and gesturing toward the exit. "Usually, superheroes go to the Center for Childhood Cancer and Blood Disorders," he said. "Dying kids get a kick out of a visit from y'all. If you're here for the children—"

"Say no more. If da people in dis hospital are kids, then Healthcare Bitch is here for da rugrats."

"Across the street to the McWane Building, first floor."

A dash through the door and a leap over the adjacent building brought Healthcare Bitch to the McWane entrance. She sauntered in all casual, as if her super-heroic saving of ten minutes of company time wasn't super-impressive.

The receptionist rolled her eyes. "How may I help you?"

"I'm here for da kids, you know, da ones whose hearts I can fill wit' hope. Youth who ain't feelin' filled." Healthcare Bitch grabbed a butterscotch candy from a bowl on the woman's desk and popped it into her mouth.

"One patient has a congenital atrial valve disorder."

"You think they'd like a visit from a superhero?"

Her eyes didn't budge from her computer screen. "Unlikely. He's been in a coma for the last two weeks."

"Which rooms have kids who ain't unconscious all da time?"

"The rest of them." She voiced it with the venom of those who enjoy causing others to feel like dumbasses.

Behind the receptionist, a corkboard outside the nurses' station showcased pictures in crayon. One patient had sketched a caped superhero flying over a tree. A skirt indicated the child had drawn a woman. "Which kid made dat?" She pointed at the picture."

With a degree of antagonism that would allow this woman to fit in perfectly if she worked in a Jersey diner, she turned her head slowly and stared at the drawing. "It's Pablo's. He'll die within a week, but you go ahead and visit him. Bless your heart."

Restraining an impulse to strangle the woman, Healthcare Bitch grabbed a surgical mask from the box on her desk, walked to Pablo's room, and found the door ajar. He wasn't sleeping.

When Pablo saw her, he grinned and turned to a man seated next to him who was dressed as a clown. "¿Ves, mi padre? I drew a picture of a superhero, and she came."

The clown's face took on a terrified expression—not the reaction Healthcare Bitch had expected. Still, the boy's sincerity warmed Healthcare Bitch's heart. "How you doin' today, Pablo?"

"Not great. There's only one medicine to cure my cancer, and our insurance won't cover it. My father—"

"I am his priest, not his... what you say? Biological father." The man trembled, jingling the bells on his billowy clothing.

"Papa, why lie to her? She's not from *La Migra*."

The priests Healthcare Bitch had met in Jersey hadn't worn an orange wig, pancake makeup, or a polka-dotted outfit, but maybe they did in the South. "I ain't from wherever La Mig-ruh is. I'm from Newark."

The man's shoulders relaxed; his breathing steadied. "The governor forces hospitals to check status."

"I see—the get-up is so nobody bothers you." It was a clever disguise. Clowns cheer up sick children. A cancer ward would have more clowns than anywhere in the state except, perhaps, the governor's office.

"Yes. I thought it would work, but every man in a tie who sees ruffles on my blouse gets suspicious. Some new law."

He wasn't transgender, but they must have been undocumented, which Mousy had claimed posed almost as big an issue in an election year in Alabama. "I'm guessin' you don't have health insurance."

"Oh, we do," Papa said. "At least for one more week. My wife was on an H1-B visa; she worked at the Honda plant. They fired her last month, and she had to return to Mexico." The man sniffled; his eyes teared up.

"Maybe I can help wit' dis. What type of insurance you got?"

He answered, haltingly, "Blue Dollar Sign."

Surely, her company would cover an essential medication. It must have been a misunderstanding. "What a coinkydink! I work for dem." She pulled her laptop from beneath her cape. "I'll get us a doctor who can help."

Neither spoke while Healthcare Bitch logged in with her credentials. The same physician from before appeared on her screen. He hadn't done much the first time, but how hard could it be to straighten out a prescription? Healthcare Bitch asked Pablo's father the name of the drug and provided it to the man in Mumbai.

"Of course, he can order the medicine." The Indian doctor typed into his computer. "In the United States, one month's supply comes to $500,000. Does this exceed the limit on your credit card, sir?"

The guy resumed crying.

Healthcare Bitch had an idea. "How much would it be in India?"

"Here, it's subject to compulsory licensing." The doctor rifled through a binder. "A generic costs $100 per month, and the pharmacy next to my clinic stocks it. This stupid job over the computer pays me a salary high enough that I can offer care *pro bono* to anyone who needs it for the rest of my day. I'd have suggested you catch a flight, but if Pablo's medical records are correct, he'd be dead by the time he arrived."

"Text me your clinic's address. We'll be dere in half an hour." Healthcare Bitch turned to Pablo. "You'll fly wit' me."

The boy looked to his father, who crossed himself, smiled, and stood up to open the window as wide as it would go. His oversize shoes squeaked.

After taking Pablo in her arms, Healthcare Bitch punched a button on her cape, encircling him with an anti-g-force protective bubble, and bolted out the window and into the air at superspeed.

Twenty-nine minutes later, she was laying Pablo in a bed in Mumbai, and a nurse was inserting an IV into his arm. Healthcare Bitch knelt beside Pablo and held his hand. He was going to live. For the first time that day, she'd made a difference for someone.

Look at her! This tough-as-nails Jersey bitch acting all sweet and maternal and sentimental-like. No one who knew her from Newark would ever have believed it.

They could blow it out their asses.

The doctor strode into the room carrying a glass medicine vial, noticed his patient, and smiled. "I'm so happy we could help Pablo." He drew the life-saving elixir through the vial's rubber septum into a needle. "Unfortunately, even a superhero can't save more than a few children. The behemoths in America profiting from human suffering are too entrenched."

No wonder Superman never worked for the insurance industry. Or against it. He could defeat a motherfucker like Lex Luthor, but millions of mediocrities like those she'd encountered in Birmingham who didn't even appreciate their collective penchant for evil?

The following day, Healthcare Bitch flew Pablo back to his father and had just arranged details of Pablo's next treatment and waved goodbye when her cell rang. The caller ID said it was Mousy. "Whassup, girlfriend?"

The line clacked as if Mousy had dropped her phone. She sure startled easily.

"The bosses are heaping mad. They want to see you in the conference room."

For fuck's sake. "What's da matter?"

"I... I... I can't tell you. Even if I knew. Which I don't. I'm sorry." She hung up.

An instant later, Healthcare Bitch sailed through a window, bashed through the conference-room door, and claimed the seat at the head of the table. "Do any of you have a problem wit' me?" She reached across two seated board members and snagged a cherry Danish from a platter.

The tallest man stood up and glared at her. "You are too big for your britches. We have laws here, and employees must follow them. The FDA hasn't approved the Indian-made generic drug you obtained for a patient. What you did was illegal. Our lawyers will keep you out of jail—Heavens to Betsy, we wouldn't want the bad press—but they suggested we terminate your employment as of today."

"And I'm suggestin' you can put dis job where da sun don't shine."

He continued, appearing not to have understood what she'd said. "And you are prohibited from contact with any current Blue Dollar Sign customer."

"No fuckin' way. I'm flyin' Pablo back to India two weeks from now."

"If that's the case, we'll have you arrested."

"And I'll have your lips punched all da way into your large intestine and out your asshole." She made a fist.

The man trembled and hyperventilated to the point where he risked fainting. "I reckon we can make an exception."

"Fine, but you can't fire me. I quit." On the way out, she ka-powed the door into splinters. In the corridor outside the conference room, she laser-visioned the wall's faux-wood paneling with a farewell message: "Go fuck your mothers until your diseased dicks fall off." For a Jersey girl, given the context, that was polite.

Taking on the insurance industry, Big Pharma, the Alabama state government, and all the hospital bureaucrats was too much. She could keep flying kids to countries where people got care no matter how poor they were—to Pablo and his dad, she was, indeed, a hero—but unlike her doctor friend in Mumbai, she no longer had a salaried gig to pay the bills.

She'd have to get another job, but no more healthcare. How could she have been so naïve to think she could help people in an industry dominated by the profit motive? She'd seek employment in a sector where the common person mattered, where a community of caring individuals looked out for each other. Where being super meant being honest, ethical, and altruistic. It required only a slight change to her name and tagline.

"Hedge Fund Bitch is here for da people."

Southern Truths

Antipodes

By Jim Wright

Doctor, lawyer, Indian chief.
Rich man, poor man, beggar man, thief.

You notice things.
I spend an hour each morning on my bike.
I ride quiet low-traffic roads, mostly through residential neighborhoods.
My daily route varies, but always includes both city and rural areas.
I'm riding for exercise, fitness, and mostly just because I enjoy it. It helps me write. It gives me time to think. I ride a minimum of 60 minutes each morning, more if conditions are good. I typically cover 12-20 miles (further on the ultra-lightweight racer, less on the heavier hybrid). If I ride in the evening too, I might cover 25 to 30 miles in a day.
You notice things.

You notice things on a bike that you don't in a car. At least I do anyway, both because of natural inclination and by dint of training. You travel further on a bike than you can on foot. You're closer to your surroundings, unenclosed, unprotected. You can feel it. You can smell it. You study the landscape, the houses, the buildings, the yards. The dogs. You say hi to people you pass. They wave back, some of them. Others just stare suspiciously and frown, it's that kind of place.

You've got time to think, time to process what you see, while your legs push you over the tarmac and through the thick sweltering air.

And you notice things.

See, I live in Florida, a little town called Milton, in the Panhandle. This is the Deep South. This is old Florida. And Milton is, well, it's a very old, very Southern, backwater town. In this case "backwater" isn't metaphor or allegory. Well, okay, it is, but it's also the literal truth in that Milton (Once Mill Town due to a long-ago vanished logging industry, also Hell-town, Jernigan's Landing, Hard Scrabble, and Scratch Ankle) is tucked into a bight of the Blackwater River, surrounded by swamps and bayous and boggy mosquito-infested wetlands, cut off by the Inland Waterway. This is the South of ancient enormous oak trees festooned with hanging Spanish moss, alligators, steam bath humidity, and Confederate flags. Now that summer is upon us, I very often have to dodge snakes, some small, some as big as a large man's leg, some harmless, and some emphatically not, sunning themselves on the warm morning pavement and looking like leathery sausages broiling on the grill at the local Circle K.

Go east, go west, along the Gulf Coast and the Redneck Riviera and you'll find bright and glittering tourist towns, from Orange Beach to Panama City, full of wrinkled sun-browned retirees and happy young people on summer break, all drinking and dancing and turning boiled-crawdad red in the unrelenting sun. There are hundreds of great restaurants, Gulf seafood places mostly, of course. Nightlife. Music. Boardwalks. Festivals. Wonderful beaches. Sailing, surfing, fishing.

Salt Life they call it.

But not in Milton. Not here.

Time and the salt life just sort of passed this place by. It's a tidy little town. It's the county seat, the courthouse is here and the government offices. It's got a certain charm, but it's a bit crumbly around the edges, full of working poor and lower Middle Class, military retirees (mostly Navy, but a lot of Air Force types too, leavened with some Coast Guard migrated over from Mobile looking for a lower cost of living). It's the prototypical rural South, peanuts and cotton, a little too far off the highway.

There's a tiny Navy base, Whiting Field, where they train helicopter pilots. Tourists don't come here because there's nothing much to do. No beach, no clubs, no boardwalk, no kitschy little shops, no casinos. The shiny little Navy ensigns have to drive to Pensacola or Mobile for entertainment. There's nothing here but cheap fast-food joints, pawn shops and second-hand stores, redneck dive bars, and a lot of Baptist churches. This is the kind of place you take a vacation from, not a trip to.

You can count ten billboards for ten different accident lawyers within fifty yards, a density of ambulance-chasers unmatched anywhere else in the world.

Here, churches are like hermit crabs. Any empty building, no matter how small or how large, will eventually house one. Abandoned gas stations, a falling down barn, warehouses, former grocery stores, an old mobile-home, a large-enough drain culvert, and a congregation newly molted and homeless scuttles in to try on the accommodations. Sometimes the itinerant preachers go through a dozen places until they find one that fits—like a crab proudly wearing a soup can for a hat. And religious signs sprout in profusion among the palmetto shrubs alongside the roads. There are almost as many of those as there are advertisements for lawyers.

Other places, a little town like this would be a bedroom community, but Pensacola is across the bay 30 minutes away via a highway that is perpetually in various states of demolition and while there's certainly commuting there's none of the daily mass migration to new urban developments you'd find elsewhere. There are dozens of empty buildings that once housed some kind of small business and now are empty and fit only for hermit crabs. The last real growth this place saw was back in the 70s and most of the homes date from that time—or before. The neighborhoods are old and overgrown, poverty often jumbled together with modest wealth. You routinely see huge well-maintained homes on a dozen acres next door to a squalid one-bedroom shack.

And that's what I ride through each morning.

That weird Deep South Panhandle disparity.

And you notice things.

One route takes me through a neighborhood of huge houses set back from the road on large lots. Homes of the well-heeled local gentry. Doctors, lawyers, and Indian chiefs, as my mother-in-law says, recalling both the old jump-rope rhyme and the popular Hoagy Carmichael song of her childhood.

Doctor, lawyer, Indian chief. Rich man, poor man, beggar man, thief.

The houses here are well kept with manicured lawns. In the morning as I roll past, there are always trucks and trailers identified with the logos of various lawn services parked alongside the road and the buzz of hedge trimmers and the muted roar of lawn mowers fills the air with the smell of cut green things. The houses here are new, modern, large. You see a lot of columns and fancy gabled windows and large porches and screened-in Florida rooms. Almost all of the homes have in-ground pools in the backyards, surrounded by white picket fences and flanked by stylish patio furniture. If the owners are young there will be a late model SUV in the drive, if they're older it'll be a Lincoln Town Car or some other large luxury sedan. The people here aren't particularly rich in the grand scheme of things, most of them anyway, but they're not poor either. They are overwhelmingly white. Many of them are doctors and lawyers. Sometimes they wave as I ride past, usually they just ignore me.

Another route takes me through a predominantly Black neighborhood.

The houses here are smaller. Closer to the road—close enough to smell dinner cooking in the evenings or backyard BBQs on the weekends, almost always strong enough to make my stomach growl in hunger. Here it's mostly modest brick homes built in the 50s and 60s. All similar floor plans set on half or quarter-acre lots. The tiny single-stall garages are almost all long ago converted into living space. It's Florida, these people don't need a garage as much as they need another bedroom. Carports are common. Most of the places are neat and tidy, with well-kept yards and small gardens. Here, people mow their own grass and if there's a pool it's usually an inexpensive above-ground. The cars are a few years older and there are more vehicles that double as both family transportation and work trucks. This place is firmly lower middle class, a workingman's neighborhood. People are much more friendly here and they almost always wave or shout a greeting as I cruise past.

Sunday morning, I rode sixteen miles through town and out into the rural countryside.

You notice things.

7:30 AM, in a more affluent neighborhood, a grizzled old white man sprawled in a lounger on his front porch surrounded by empty beer cans. He was shirtless and doughy and sallow and gray hair grew in patches on his chest like fungus. He wore bright pajama bottoms decorated in cartoon characters and unidentifiable stains and he was as drunk as a preacher in a whorehouse on Saturday night.

He cackled at me as I rode past, mouth gaping open in intoxicated mirth so wide I could see it was empty of teeth. An older woman in a flowered robe sat on her porch across the street reading the paper and drinking coffee. A large black-and-white cat sat on the steps near her feet watching me with yellow eyes. The woman never looked up. Not even when the drunk shouted something unintelligible and threw an empty beer can in my general direction. It fell far short and came to rest in the middle of his manicured yard.

A half hour later in a much poorer neighborhood I passed a small house, the yard filled with weeds and the rotting hulks of old cars, the eaves sagging, the paint fading and in need of a new coat. Not a dump, just the kind of place where people are too poor and too hard worked to worry much about what the neighbors think.

On the cluttered porch were two young African-American boys. Nine or ten. Both wore crisp perfectly pressed white dress shirts with ties, black pants, polished shoes. They were seated opposite each other at a small table, staring intently at a chessboard, the pieces arrayed for battle. From inside the house a woman's voice asked if they were ready for church. One of the boys answered in the affirmative and they both waved to me. Good morning, Sir, one said. Good morning, Boys, I answered. Enjoy your game. We will, Sir, have a blessed day.

I'm not much of a religious person but I'd rather be offered a polite blessing than an empty beer can any day.

In another neighborhood, on a road I hadn't been down before, an older brown brick house was surrounded by a chain-link fence, with a mesh gate closed across the drive. Dogs. You can always tell. So, I was ready for the furious barking when it came. And I damned near lost control of my ride and crashed into the ditch howling with laughter when this tiny ball of fury came at me out of the flowers. I thought it was a lawn gnome at first. There was Chihuahua in its pedigree and something else, maybe Mexican jumping bean. The creature couldn't have weighed more than a pound, it had a little dog shaped round head with bulging eyes glowing with the kind of kaleidoscopic madness you only get from a hundred generations of dedicated inbreeding. And it was wearing, I swear to you, a tiny pink dress. But what did it for me was the sign on the gate: Beware of Dog. I lost it. I swerved and nearly went over the handlebars. I was laughing so hard I could barely breathe in the thick air... and looked up as an older woman in curlers and a pink housecoat and giant fluffy pink slippers appeared in the drive. She grinned hugely at me and waved. I grinned and waved back. She was clearly enjoying the joke.

You notice things.

You notice the lack of things.

These neighborhoods are the middle. Poor or modest or moderately wealthy, this is the center.

These neighborhoods are all very different, but they have at least one thing in common.

There are almost no political signs.

There were plenty of signs before the election, Trump, Biden, various others, and not always where you might expect. But by the end of November, they were nearly all gone. And now I can ride for blocks through vastly diverse neighborhoods without seeing a single political sign.

They have moved on.

Now, I don't mean they've surrendered to the current situation, and I don't mean they haven't. What I mean is they don't feel the need to advertise an allegiance to one side or the other of an election that's long over.

They've moved on.

Doctor, lawyer, Indian chief. Rich man, poor man, beggar man, thief.

But then there are the other places.

The edges.

The extremes.

And in those places, the signs are still up.

They want you to know what team they're on.

Far down a back road, unexpectedly, is this... house.

The road is very rural. The lots are large, the houses aren't fancy. Old ranch style mostly, with Spanish influence. Large yards, many fenced in for horses— oddly I almost never see an actual horse, though one place has a whole herd of miniature donkeys.

And then you come to a wrought-iron gate.

It's massive. Custom-made. Old. Locked with a heavy chain. There's a sign that says "East gate closed, use west gate." Not other gate, "west" gate. Because it's so far away, they have to give directions to it using the cardinal points of the compass. You ride west along the fence, past a row of huge old palm trees. The house is enormous, a vast sprawling red brick edifice. Google Earth shows that it's shaped like a C, with two large wings off the main structure wrapped around a courtyard and an Olympic-sized pool hidden from the road. The place must be nearly 10,000 square feet.

There's a huge garage and an even larger barn and what appears to be a guest house big enough for Charlie Sheen. I count at least a dozen outbuildings, maybe more, some as big as the house. The football-field-sized yard is shaped around century-old oak trees and paved drives, there are fountains and flower beds and sculptures. There's a large white cross prominently affixed to the central oak. Past the "west" gate are acres of what look to be vineyards gone to seed, punctuated by tall sprinkler systems that look as if they are no longer used. The place is a little seedy, as if the wealthy owners sold out to a retired Mafia hit man who just wants to die of anonymity and natural causes. The security cameras are hard to spot, but they're there and new and professionally installed. As are the "no trespassing" signs.

And on the gate posts?

Brand-new Trump signs.

A few miles away, I pass another place.

This place could not be more different, the complete opposite, as far removed from the mansion as if it was on the far side of the world.

The house is a shack, and that's probably an insult to shacks. The place is literally falling down, the roof sagging and buried under sickly looking moss. The paint is not peeling only because it long ago fell off leaving behind exposed mildew-speckled wood. On the eaves, the soffit boards are missing and you can see into the attic and the gray dry-rotted ends of the roof joists. Most of the shingles are gone, replaced with various patches of tin and tarps and tarpaper. A window is covered with warped and buckling plywood and the carcass of the missing frame complete with broken glass is laying in a mangled heap under the window where they dropped it (or it fell out). The yard is choked with weeds and garbage, a half dozen decaying truck engines dead beyond any resurrection short of the divine, the carcass of some unidentifiable vehicle from the previous century sunk to the top of the wheel wells into the soil, the twisted springs of at least a half dozen different mattresses, broken furniture, shattered blocks of concrete, empty paint cans, those horrible mass produced blow-plastic children's playsets faded by the unrelenting sun to dull pink and sickly green and diseased yellow like the stiff corpses of giant dead birds, and piles of other less identifiable detritus. There's a leaning carport packed full of random castoff trash, the kind of worthless junk that's important to people who don't have anything of value and never will. Places like this, they don't have security cameras, they have dogs. Not some toy breed in a pink dress, but pit bulls or some diluted version of a Rottweiler, usually tethered in the junk with a chain and a padlock, abused, neglected, half-psychotic, and you can smell the piles of dog shit from a hundred yards away.

And there, on the rotting mail box post?

Brand new Trump signs, likely the only new thing in the place.

I pass other mansions and other shacks. All with Trump signs. These are the extremes, the edges, the antipodes of society and wealth and opportunity and education here in this little town, and yet they share this strange similar viewpoint. Trump. Make America Great Again.

The mind-bending part here is that these people, these opposites who share Trump as their only commonality, are more than anything else terrified of each other.

The people in that giant mansion?

What does "make America great again" mean to "those" people?

I don't have to guess, Trump himself told us in his speeches and at his rallies. The wealthy told us what makes America great to them, they do so in TV interviews with famous personalities, they never shut up about it.

They're terrified that some Black gangbanger or some white trash bottom-feeder is going to kick in their door and murder their families and steal all their stuff. That's what the wall and the gates and the security cameras are for. These people, they "love" the idea of a wall around America, of course they do. They're all in for Trump because they're mad, certain they're being ripped off, held at gunpoint, paying too much in taxes, forced to support the lowlifes and the freeloaders who live just down the road.

The people in that moldering shack?

What does make America great again mean to "those" people?

I don't have to guess, I watched them cheer Trump's talking points. I read the slogans on their shirts and their social media posts.

They're terrified some rich guy is going to come kick in their door and enslave their families and take all of their stuff. That's what the "Protected by Smith & Wesson" window sticker and the pit bull are for. These people, they love the idea of Trump sticking it to the "elites," of course they do. They voted for Trump because they're mad, certain they're being ripped off, held at gunpoint, their rights and their jobs stolen by illegal immigrants or shipped overseas by the rich sons of bitches living just up the road.

These people could not be more opposite in station, in fortune, in economic opportunity. They are the most unlikely—and impossible—of allies.

These people are almost literally terrified of each other.

And yet, there it is, the thing that binds them together, that bridges the vast, vast gap between them: Donald Trump.

You notice things.

If you look carefully.

Trump appeals to the edges, not necessarily the edges of political ideology, but the edges of society. Those who live in the mansions and those who live in the shacks. Both the rich and the poor, they think Trump is somehow not only going to make America great again, he's going to make America great specifically for them.

Think about that.

Think about how utterly impossible that is.

The policies and ideologies that make America great for the people who live in those mansions, well those things almost never benefit the people who live in the shacks. In fact, it's often just the opposite when the effects of deregulation and a lack of environmental protections and the empty promises of trickledown economics become fully realized.

And the changes necessary to lift those shack dwellers permanently up out of their poverty? Education, healthcare, adequate nutrition, decent safe jobs with benefits, equality, access, opportunity— "those" things almost never benefit the wealthy. The wealthy and privileged have those things already as a birthright and if they were willing to share, well, we wouldn't be having this conversation.

Trump pandered to the extremes. He continues to do so.

This, this right here will be Donald Trump's Waterloo.

It is impossible to make America great for these two opposites, because what each really wants is to take from the other.

Trump will have to choose. The only way forward for him is to sacrifice either the rich or the poor.

And he cannot make that decision.

He can't.

It's impossible and he's starting to realize it.

He wants to throw in with the mansions, like Reagan and Bush and his billionaire friends.

But he can't abandon the shacks, because his ego needs their "cheering" more than his wallet needs the billionaires' money, that's what the rallies are all about. That's why he daily contradicts himself—because he's trying to tell each what they want to hear and those things are mutually incompatible.

And so, he won't choose. He can't.

He'll try to please both extremes and will end up pleasing nobody.

Let this be a lesson, an opportunity, for those who would be president.

It's not the edges that matter.

It's the middle.

But you must take time to notice.

~~~

"Doctor, lawyer, Indian chief. Rich man, poor man, beggar man, thief."

This children's rhyme was chanted during recess almost every day that weather allowed us to play outside. I remember hearing older girls chanting as they jumped rope, but I cannot recall the first time that I was included. Jumping rope was a favorite activity because there were many paved sidewalks and play areas at the Cherokee Indian School. Those of us who attended the school were from homes without sidewalks and paved roads. Some of us day-students only had opportunities to jump rope on school days, while boarding students had access to paved areas even on weekends.

We jumped rope, chanted the rhyme, and laughed when we missed a jump on any one of the "occupations" named in the rhyme. We knew it was a game because we did not read about or know any women who were doctors, lawyers, or Indian chiefs. I do not think we even thought of what it was to be a rich man, poor man, beggar man, or thief. Yet we were amused with the game because we thought it might somehow predict our future.

—"Doctors, Lawyers, Indian Chiefs: Indian Identity in the South" by Carmaleta L. Monteith in *Cultural diversity in the U.S. South: anthropological contributions to a region in transition,* papers from the 1996 meeting of the Southern Anthropological Society

Degenerates Against Memphis

Cliff Winnig

The raid started out well. Pipe bombs went off like Sixth of January fireworks, lighting up the detention center.

They breached the outer wall in multiple spots.

The nearest watchtower collapsed, and its neighbor began to lean. Floodlights flickered and went out.

Tara Lynn Bowman broke cover and ran toward the nearest breach, her comrades close behind.

The guards—both regular and MAD militia—stared at the damage for several seconds before they finally reacted. Some ran toward the explosions. Others ran away. A few fired into the darkness, seemingly at random. None of them followed a cohesive strategy.

Aunt Artemis had been right. Overconfident, the guards hadn't trained for a direct assault.

Tara Lynn had almost reached the breach when several rounds whizzed by her head. She dropped and rolled, hoping the smoke, darkness, and lower profile would keep her safe.

A raider went down to her left, but with all the smoke, she couldn't tell who. *Don't think about it.* She had to focus on her own survival—that, and reaching Althea.

She clambered over shattered concrete and into the yard. The old penal farm's main structure stood intact, looking like the images she'd studied. That was a good sign. They'd all memorized the layout, hoping nothing had changed.

Something had, however.

Tara Lynn stared at what stood between her and the structure, something not shown in the blueprints or archival images.

Cages.

Cages full of children.

Unlike Althea, these prisoners weren't there for antisocial behavior. They were there because they were brown: Black, South Asian, Latin American. All ages, all rail thin. They huddled together at the back of the cages, clearly terrified by the gunfire and explosions.

I have to free them. But Tara Lynn knew if she did that now, many of them would flee right into the firefight and get hit by stray bullets.

No, best that they stay put for now, much as she hated to leave them there. On the way out, she'd get them to safety.

Assuming she could get herself to safety. Assuming she wasn't shot in the next few minutes.

More gunfire sprayed the ground beside her. Tara Lynn cut across the lawn past the cages and toward the side door she knew from the blueprints. The children stared at her, eyes wide, as she ran.

A bullet struck the concrete wall next to her head.

"Hands in the air!" A man's voice, directly behind her. "Now!"

Tara Lynn straightened and raised her hands. Her 9mm Glock lay holstered at her side, worse than useless. If she'd had it out, the man would likely have already shot her.

"Now turn around." This he delivered in a more normal tone, a voice she now recognized.

"Mr. Grundy?" Turning to face him, she saw she was correct.

Mr. Grundy stood with his AR-15 aimed right at her chest, his face a mix of shock and confusion. In the dark, he probably couldn't make out her features beneath her hoodie and anti-facial-recognition makeup, but he had to know she was one of his old English students.

He recovered quickly, puffed himself up like he'd done when she'd challenged his use of church-approved abridgments. His Trump-red Memphians Against Degeneracy baseball cap clashed with his brown button-down shirt and khaki pants, though the AR-15 went with all of it.

"Lie down, face down, Tara Lynn." His voice was steady and cold.

Damn! He did *recognize me—maybe from my voice? I should never have spoken. Stupid mistake.*

Her eyes never left the AR-15 as she knelt in the dirt, then lowered herself to the ground.

Mr. Grundy stepped toward her. "I said face down!"

Reluctantly, she lowered her face till she couldn't see him or the semi-automatic anymore, just dirt.

The deafening bang and spray of blood came a moment later, followed by a thud as Mr. Grundy's body hit the ground. Tara Lynn looked up to see Hudson Rhodes, the raiders' tactical lead, lowering his .45. Her ears rang in the aftermath.

Hudson helped her up. "You okay?"

Tara Lynn nodded, though she wasn't sure she ever would be again.

She tried not to look at the body, but she couldn't help herself. Mr. Grundy's hat had come off. A pool of blood oozed from beneath his chest, and his head lay to one side. He stared unblinking at nothing.

"I had him too." Hudson said. "Hated his take on Twain."

Tara Lynn felt herself grin, despite everything.

Hudson grinned back at her, though otherwise he looked all business. A lock of his curly brown hair hid one of his eyes. "Okay, Tara Lynn, you're gonna be fine, but we need to keep moving."

She nodded. "Yeah."

He returned the nod and took off toward the side door.

Tara Lynn followed, but first she unholstered her gun.

~~~

Degenerates Against Memphis had been Tara Lynn's idea. It had begun as a joke.

"Those MAD men!" Althea waved one hand vaguely as she took a long drag on the joint.

"And women." Tara Lynn leaned against Althea on the bed, pillows propped against the headboard, and watched the smoke curl between them.

Althea felt warm and safe. The attic bedroom felt warm and safe with Althea in it.

"There's more going on inside than they're letting on," Althea said. "I mean, beside the actual criminals. We know they've got political prisoners. Too many folks have disappeared. They're going somewhere. Why else would they need those MAD militia thugs on top of the regular guards?" She handed the joint back.

Tara Lynn took a drag, inhaled deep. The smoke slid into her lungs and kept spreading, flowing like honey throughout her body. It eased every thought and muscle it touched. She snuggled against Althea, and Althea made no move to push her away.

"Memphians Against Degeneracy," Tara Lynn said. "They need a nemesis." And then it hit her. "Degenerates Against Memphis!"

"Damn!" Althea sat up, causing Tara Lynn to slide onto the bed, fully supine.

"What's wrong?"

"Nothing—I meant D-A-M. Degenerates Against Memphis."

Tara Lynn thought this was just about the funniest thing she'd ever heard. Althea must have as well, since they both giggled, then laughed uncontrollably for several minutes.

When Tara Lynn finally caught her breath, she looked up at Althea.

She'd shifted to hands and knees and now straddled Tara Lynn on the bed. "I really do like that," Althea said. "Let's do it."

Before Tara Lynn could ask "Do what?" Althea kissed her.

Tara Lynn had only ever kissed a handful of boys— and of them only Hudson had been any good at it—but this felt different. It was electric. And the electricity spread from her lips to her chest and throughout her body, as the smoke had before.

When at last Althea ended the kiss, her wavy red hair hung around Tara Lynn's face like the walls of a tent.

Althea sniffed, and her cat-who-ate-the-canary smile gave way to a frown. She brushed her hair aside and looked to her left.

"Damn," she said.

"What?"

"The joint's gone out."

~~~

An hour later, they stumbled down from the attic bedroom to find Aunt Artemis in the kitchen with a tray of freshly baked snickerdoodles. "Now don't eat too many at once. I know what the munchies can do."

The girls gave only a token protest of innocence before tucking in.

After Tara Lynn's fourth cookie, Aunt Artemis made her slow down. She obeyed, partly to stay on her aunt's good side—she'd given her a place to stay when her parents had kicked her out—but mostly because Aunt Artemis was pretty wise about such things.

Perhaps the last goth in Memphis, Aunt Artemis went to mandatory church on Sunday like everyone else, but always dressed as if for a funeral. Today she'd broken out some of the black lipstick even she didn't dare wear outside the house. It looked good on her. It even went with the flour-specked apron she still had on, which was decorated with skulls and black roses.

After tidying up, Aunt Artemis sat with them and had a snickerdoodle herself. "I heard y'all laughing up a storm earlier. What was so funny?"

In between bites, they told her about what they feared MAD was doing out at the old penal farm—and about DAM.

Aunt Artemis didn't seem to find DAM funny, but she did look thoughtful. "You know, that's not a bad idea. I bet a lot of your generation feels that way, maybe enough of you to make a real difference."

That had been the start of it. Slowly, carefully, Tara Lynn and Althea talked to their coworkers at Kroger and the secondhand clothing store, their friends from the back pew at church. Someone eavesdropped on her MAD stepfather drinking with his militia buddies while working on his truck. Another's older brother had been a guard at the penal farm when it was repurposed as a detention center.

A picture emerged: the disappeared went there for reeducation or for processing before being sent to labor camps or to dangerous jobs in the fracking fields.

The members of DAM were careful. They were methodical. Yet somehow a few months later, Althea disappeared.

Aunt Artemis calmed Tara Lynn down enough to stop her running off to attempt a rescue—with no small help from whisky-laced coffee. Then she went to the bookcase and pulled out a large black paperback. Heavily dogeared, its spine was cracked in so many places that Tara Lynn couldn't read the title. She'd soon learn it was also heavily annotated by Aunt Artemis in the margins.

"If we're gonna rescue Althea and the others, we're gonna have to do it right." Aunt Artemis plopped the book onto the table between them. "This," she said, "is *The Anarchist Cookbook*."

~~~

Harsh fluorescent lighting filled the detention center. There was nowhere to hide, so the raiders just charged ahead.

Hudson shot a man at point blank and took his keycard. He had to wipe the card on his shirt before he could use it.

By then eight raiders had met up inside the main structure. Aunt Artemis had insisted on radio silence, so Hudson sent two back to bust out the caged kids and lead them to where Aunt Artemis and her friends waited with pickups and SUVs.

Aunt Artemis had done most of the strategic planning herself, but Hudson had grown up in a militia family. He knew tactics. That's why she'd tapped him to lead the raid.

Tara Lynn just hoped they'd brought enough vehicles. It already looked like there'd be more prisoners than they'd figured on.

And once they got away, then what? Aunt Artemis spoke of an underground railroad to the Western Free States, but Tara Lynn didn't think it could handle that many unaccompanied children, not from this deep in the Southern Coalition.

The six remaining raiders reached a spot where two hallways crossed. Tara Lynn remembered it from the blueprints. All three paths led to cell blocks.

"Here's where we split up," Hudson said. "Tara Lynn, you're with me. Terry and Frank, go left. Toto and Ursula, you go straight."

"You got it," Terry said.

Toto saluted as he followed Ursula down the forward route.

Hudson handed Tara Lynn the keycard, and they started down the righthand corridor. "You free the prisoners. I'll cover you."

That was fine with her. He was the better shot, and his gun packed more punch than her Glock.

Not that she was a bad shot herself. Her daddy had taken her shooting many times after he'd given her the gun for her fourteenth birthday. It was the only pink thing she still owned.

Before they reached the cell block, two guards ran out of a side room. They seemed surprised the raiders had gotten that far. They fumbled, trying to draw their pistols.

Hudson dropped the first one, and Tara Lynn found herself bracing with both arms like Daddy had taught her. She shot the second before Hudson could even take aim.

Blood and teeth sprayed out as the bullet struck the guard's jaw. His head cracked against the wall, and he slid down to the floor. He gave a gurgling moan, an attempt at a scream maybe, but he couldn't seem to work his jaw right anymore.

Hudson didn't slow down, so Tara Lynn followed him, past the dead and the wounded guard, on into the cell block.

Every cell was crammed full of men, alert and pressing against the bars.

Tara Lynn keyed open the first cell, and the men poured out. They ran past their rescuers, toward freedom. A couple stooped to grab the fallen guards' weapons. *They'll make a good distraction, just like Aunt Artemis said.*

Cell by cell, Tara Lynn freed the prisoners. One of them she knew, a regular at the Kroger she worked at. He thanked her and told her the women were in the block on the opposite side of the building.

Hudson heard him too. His eyes met hers. "Go. Find your friend. I'll see you outside."

She gave him the keycard and ran back the way they'd come.

When she reached the downed guards, they were both dead. She took the keycard from the one she'd shot.

Prisoners filled the junction where the raiders had split up. Most squeezed toward the main entrance, but some headed down side passages, looted guns ready, seemingly bent on revenge. A couple of prisoners rolled on the floor, fighting. They punched and kicked one another, ignoring everything else.

Tara Lynn skirted them and continued toward the women's block, pushing past newly freed prisoners.

"You're going the wrong way, honey!" a plump, middle-aged woman cried, clearly trying to be helpful. "Follow me! I'll get you out."

"I'm looking for someone," Tara Lynn shouted as the tide swept the woman away.

One prisoner nearly ran her down, her eyes a panicked animal's. Another shoved her aside as she passed. Her head banged painfully against the wall.

Tara Lynn noticed she was crying, perhaps had been crying ever since she'd shot the guard. *What am I doing? I need to get out of here.*

She tried taking a breath, but she felt like she was drowning. All she inhaled was darkness and death.

And then Althea was there, grabbing her hand, pulling her into the tide that flowed from the building and out into the clean dark of night.

Outside, Tara Lynn could breathe again. The tears still came but she felt only joy.

People thronged the courtyard, streamed toward the breached outer wall.

Then the floodlights snapped back on.

They caught Althea's face in stark light: a black eye, several bruises, and half a dozen round burns, as if from cigarettes. Her eyes shone with determination, though. And more.

They found Tara Lynn's, and they were full of love.

A fresh spray of bullets—and the crowd, panicked, surged forward.

But it parted as a huge pickup burst into the courtyard. Tires screeching, it stopped before Tara Lynn and Althea, shielding them from the gunfire.

Aunt Artemis reached across the seat, flung open the passenger door, and practically pulled them into the cab. She threw the Ford into gear, made a U-turn, and floored it.

They passed people running, people crying, people dying. Hudson lay in the dirt covered in blood, his head at an impossible angle.

In the cab, Althea slumped against Tara Lynn. A wetness formed between them, and Tara Lynn smelled copper. That meant something, she knew, something important, but she couldn't seem to focus her thoughts.

The pickup bounced over the main gate, now fallen, and sped onto the access road. Aunt Artemis spared Althea a glance as she gunned the engine.

"Pressure!" she shouted. "Put pressure on her shoulder. Now!"

The words crystallized Tara Lynn's thoughts. She found the wound and shoved both palms onto it, pushing Althea back against the seat. Althea screamed, but Tara Lynn kept the pressure on.

"I'm sorry! I'm sorry! I'm so sorry!" She repeated it over and over, a mantra of raw emotion, until finally Althea turned to her and smiled through gritted teeth.

"It's okay," she gasped. "You did good tonight." Her smile faltered, then returned. "You know, for a degenerate."

~~~

Aunt Artemis didn't dare take Althea to a hospital, but she drove to a doctor friend's. He didn't seem a bit surprised to see them. He had several cots ready in a room at the back of the house, and two assistants as well.

Tara Lynn lost track of time while the doc operated. She sat with Aunt Artemis in the living room, hidden from the street by thick curtains.

Using a burner phone, Aunt Artemis got periodic updates on the fallout from the raid. Tara Lynn had been IDed, possibly from when Mr. Grundy had spoken her name. She and Althea were both going to have to take the underground railroad, and they couldn't come back.

The monumental size of that loss—Aunt Artemis, her friends, the only town she'd ever known—fell away when the doctor came out to tell them Althea was stable and in recovery.

On her phone, Aunt Artemis arranged for Tara Lynn and Althea to hide at another friend's house, a stop on the underground railroad, while Althea recovered her strength.

More patients arrived, and the doctor returned to his makeshift hospital. Aunt Artemis stood and took Tara Lynn's hand, pulling her up gently. "I have to go now. They'll keep me posted on you two, but once I leave here it won't be safe for me to come back anytime soon. Or visit the place they'll be taking you. So...this is it."

"Wait, you mean I'll never—"

Aunt Artemis smiled sadly. Tara Lynn noticed that her own anti-facial-recognition makeup had incorporated her black lipstick. "Someday, I'm sure. I may have to take the railroad myself at some point. Or, you know, we just might win."

An assistant came out and told Tara Lynn she could go back and see Althea.

"Go on now," Aunt Artemis told her. "We'll meet again."

Tara Lynn nodded. "When we win."

Right then, she could believe that someday, maybe even someday soon, they just might.

For Terry Bisson.

The Gateway

Zachary Taylor Branch

Near the Kings Highway, South Saint Louis, May 1977

Sweat was pouring into his eyes. Even wiping them with the back of his shirt sleeve wouldn't clear his vision. All was blurry and ill-lit in this deserted and gasoline-powered part of town. Jack Kilby was wishing now that he'd run north to the Whig Districts, where the Tesla Network lit the night.

He snorted to himself as he thought of the throngs of Whiggish gentry up there with their gravity-decoupled vehicles and remotely powered gadgets, wandering the malls and shops and cafes of Delmar and Grand and Manchester and the floating attractions in between. But he had no allies amongst the devotees of coupled matter and wireless energy. He was trying to tear their world down.

His legs were rubbery, and the stitch in his side was now more than an annoyance. He couldn't get a breath.

Not for the first time, he regretted being 20 kilos over his old track-and-field weight and forgoing that bypass surgery. He stopped running and shifted to an odd high-speed shuffle. He had a good internal map and knew that he was still a half mile from Carondelet, where he might find some aid and comfort.

It was quiet and dark as he shuffled past the entrance to Saint Matthew's Cemetery, and he began to think that he had eluded his pursuer. Then he heard a voice.

"It's no good, Jack. You can't outrun us, and the effort might just kill you. Let us take you back to the College, or maybe to the Moon. Low gravity is good for the heart. They've got everything you need to build your clever machines."

"Not falling for that again, G-man! My work for the Whig masters will never see the light of day! At least out here... " The engineer sank to his knees and gasped for breath. "I can sell my inventions... be my own man... make a new economy... one so powerful that you and all your agents won't be able to stop it!"

"From the way you're gripping your arm, Jack, I'd say your days, or even hours, out here are very limited. Let us help you. We can fix you up and see that you never want for anything again." The G-man stepped closer to the stricken engineer.

"Keep your hands off me!" The engineer groaned and doubled over from the pain. "I'd rather die at here in the open... still my own man... than be a technical monkey in some Whiggish technology zoo, you piece of... " His eyes flickered shut and he rolled onto his side as his labored breathing slowed.

"As you wish, Jack."

The G-man walked slowly into the evening gloom, but he could not grant Jack's wish. An Airborne Triage Unit recovered Jack Kilby within minutes. But the Unit did not take him to any of the hospitals or clinics in Greater Saint Louis. The few reporters who followed the case were never able to determine Kilby's whereabouts, but they did publish dark rumors that another computational savant had run afoul of the Technology Acquisition Office.

Gateway BBQ, The Lemp District, June 1977

Mister B was wiping down the counters in preparation for the end of night shift. His son Frank had the smoker out back started and the kitchen grill was covered with home fries, scrapple, and breaded green tomatoes in anticipation of the usual morning crowd. The first customer of the day walked in right at seven o'clock.

"Good morning, Mr. Perot," Mr. B said, wiping his hands on a worn apron. "It's a bit early for spareribs, but I've got the full morning fare ready, plus some pulled pork, pinto beans, sliced tomatoes, and cucumbers, the breakfast of champions... "

"Just coffee, for now Mr. B," Perot said. "I have no appetite, it's already been a bad day. Jack Kilby's been declared dead, but I don't believe it for a minute. They abducted that poor man, sure as I'm standing here.

"Do say," Mr. B said, leaning his elbow on the counter.

"Yes, I do," said Perot. "He was leaving the Whigs. He was coming back into partnership with me so we could finally build some of the computational machines we were planning back at Texas Instruments. The Technology Acquisition Office had the poor man building integrated circuits for the Whig bastards, just so they could suppress them and keep them off the market."

"You don't say, Mr. P. Sorry to hear about your buddy," Mr. B said, with just enough attentiveness not to seem rude. "No end of troubles for you brainy types. But here's your coffee, and how about we set you up with some scrapple and scrambled eggs, maybe with a little shad roe?"

Perot just nodded. Mr. B yelled over his shoulder, "Frank! Scramble up some eggs and roe, and check the smoker, see if those ribs are ready to turn."

"Yes, Daddy, got 'em on now, then I'll head out to check the ribs."

"Is that your boy back there, Mr. B?" Perot asked. "He was just a stripling last time I saw him, sounds like you've got a full-grown man back there in the kitchen."

"Yes, sir, Frank is my oldest, just turned 16. He's spending summers here with me here at the Gateway, his second home now that his mother and I split. He's got his mom's brains and my brawn, lucky boy... "

A gravity-decoupled Air Cab glided silently down to the curb in front of the BBQ place. A tall man in rumpled clothes stepped out and limped slowly through the front door.

"Mr. Kleinrock! You're here early too. Can I get you the usual?" Mr. B asked, one foot already in the kitchen.

"Many thanks, Mr. B. Cornbread and beans, and a big coffee, black," the tall man said. "Another long night." He turned on Perot, "I don't think we've met before, stranger. I'm Len Kleinrock. Are you a regular denizen here at the Gateway?"

"Ross Perot, Mr. Kleinrock, pleasure to meet you. And yes, I've been pretty partial to Mr. B's BBQ since I started working here in Saint Louis. It's about the only familiar thing here in the Lemp District. Don't care for all the exotic food and machines getting power without wires. And all the remote control, like that Air Cab you just swept in on. A man should drive his own car. And sending all that energy though the air, what's that doing to us?"

"Indeed, Mr. Perot, and I take it from the accent that you're from Texas? North Central?"

"You've got a good ear, Mr. K. I'm a proud Democrat from Dallas. Came to Saint Louis to fight the Whig Hegemony head on, and I've got the machines that will put an end to the Whigs' collective economy and Marxist politics, once and for all."

Mr. K was looking almost as angry as he was intrigued when Mr. B swept back in from the kitchen carrying two large plates which he deposited on the counter in front of the two men.

"Here's your meals, gentlemen. If they're not to your liking, blame the boy," Mr. B said. "I'm going to head out back and help Frank, gotta teach 'em right. Just give me a shout if any more customers walk through the door."

"Much obliged, Mr. B, just what I was needing this morning," Kleinrock said, tucking into his breakfast. "You know, Mr. Perot, I've spent quite a bit of time in Lubbock and El Paso, and I found that the Whigs are pretty popular out in the state of West Texas."

"Now don't you get me started about the Partition of Texas, sir! Zachary Taylor and his Whigs won a dishonorable victory in 1853. The Secession War was a catastrophe for the traditional Democratic vision of individual freedom and personal profit!"

"Easy, Mr. Perot, didn't mean to get you riled up," Kleinrock said. "Please take a seat and let me buy you a cup of coffee. Mr. B doesn't mind if I pour a few myself."

"My apologies, Mr. Kleinrock, I didn't mean to raise my voice." Perot sat back down at the counter and finally started on his breakfast. "West Texas is a subject that gets my back up, and it's another reason the Whigs are so unpopular back home. They partitioned Texas after the Secession War and then imposed their World

Without Wires in the 1880's and 90's before we could get a fully decentralized petroleum economy built up. And we'd have built computation machines and automated all that excess human labor by now if they hadn't locked up Oskar Heil and Bill Shockley in their sealed-off research prisons."

"But Mr. P, what would be the purpose of new computation machines when we have a ready supply of human savants and human computers to do all the cyphering and figuring we need? And I doubt they would consider themselves excess labor."

"Efficiency, Mr. Kleinrock, efficiency!" Perot said. "The machines I'm building will calculate a thousand times faster than the most capable humans and you won't need three layers of checkers and auditors. Companies will be able to save millions in labor costs and book more profits by cutting their staffs and buying more of my machines! It's progress, Mr. K, and you can't stop progress!"

"Odd progress, I would say. Will your new machines buy dry goods, or pay rent, union dues, or taxes, or do volunteer work, or take the family out for dinner and a show?"

"I'm not sure I take your meaning, Mr. K. Computation machines aren't meant to replace human life, they're meant to do human jobs more efficiently and cheaply, so that companies can do more with less and book higher profits. People will have new jobs building and maintaining the machines."

"But to what end, Mr. P?" Kleinrock looked thoughtful. "So, these firms that buy your yet-to-be-invented machines will fire their human workers to make more money for their proprietors and shareholders? The wealthy will become wealthier, and honest, hard-working men and women will be deprived of the ability to provide for their families and make their homes. Why would we want such a world?"

"You sound like a man who would bring back buggy whips and whale oil," Perot said. "America is an experiment in creative destruction, Mr. K, and the jobs lost as old industries are made redundant and irrelevant... " He was interrupted by a quavering siren so loud that the windows vibrated.

"More of that damned racket, what's wrong with a good old steam whistle," said Perot, pushing a finger in his ear as if to dislodge a squealing cicada.

"That's the end of the graveyard shift at Maxim Aerial Navigation. Mr. B is about to have his first rush of the day."

"It's a public nuisance," said Perot."

Kleinrock grinned. "Can't disagree with you there, that fancy new Tesla Acoustic Resonator almost shook the building apart the first time they switched it on. We should clear out in favor of the morning trade, let Mr. B make a living."

"Anything else I can get you gentlemen before the morning rush begins?" Mr. B asked as he rushed in, moving fast and smelling of slow-roasted pork and hot sauce. "More coffee or some toast and preserves? God bless the night shifts, they always come in hungry."

"Nothing more for me, Mr. B, and I believe Mr. Perot is finished as well," Kleinrock said. "Let me cover the tab, Mr. P, in exchange for taking up a bit of your time this morning. I had in mind to walk over to the main yard between Lemp and International Shoe. Thought you might like to see one of our local Southside landmarks."

"A fortunate coincidence Mr. K. I have an appointment later this morning with the CFO at International Shoe about automating their Accounting Department. It's one of the first tasks my new computers will be capable of, even without Jack Kilby's new circuits."

Mr. Kleinrock yelled his goodbyes as he and Mr. Perot walked by Mr. B's fenced backyard, already thick with hickory smoke and the savory smell of the slow-cooking ribs, pork shoulders, and brisket. The Cherokee Caves were several blocks away, but large disk-shaped Runabouts were already floating towards their staging areas, with tour groups from as far away as Kansas City and Chicago. The narrow, dingy caves of twenty years ago had been expanded and widened to miles of lighted underground pathways, linking the natural caves below the Lemp Mansion and Brewery with the Budweiser caves a mile away. Hundreds of tourists were gathering for a day of underground exploration through the maze of tunnels, with frequent breaks for liquid refreshment.

A small gravity-decoupled disk zipped by, so close that Perot had to throw himself against the kiosk of the local kelp-monger to dodge it.

"I will never get used to those infernal things, we simply don't tolerate these unnatural gadgets back home," Perot said, trying to brush himself clean.

"I thought you might approve of Sprite technology, Mr. P. They use union drivers, one can control a dozen gravity-decoupled Sprites, picking up garbage or delivering mail and the like, when not driving an Air Cab," said Kleinrock with a mischievous grin. Mr. Perot was preparing his retort when he saw the wave of hundreds of hungry, tired workers making their way down the street after a long night at Maxim, Lemp, and International Shoe.

"What a mob!" Perot was genuinely surprised by the size of the crowd moving down Lemp Avenue. "They're filling the entire street, Mr. K. Looks like the food cart guys are going to be overrun. Total chaos!"

It was indeed quite a scrum. Scores of carts and vans and stands were strung along Lemp Avenue, selling every manner of food and drink along with a smattering of dry goods and fresh vegetables and breads and fresh meat. The outdoor seats of the local bars and cafes and gaming houses were also filling up rapidly.

"I see something different, Mr. P," Kleinrock observed. "I see men and women walking home with full purses and empty bellies in one of the greatest cities in the Western World. They'll get breakfast and groceries and take-away at joints like the Gateway BBQ. Good people like Mr. B and his son will make their livelihood off this chaos, this mob. All this excess labor buys fresh meat and produce at the Soulard Market. They'll take their kids to the Cherokee Caves, buy dry goods at the Woolworth's and G.C. Murphy's, and pay for music lessons and dental work and theater tickets up on Grand Boulevard. They'll book steamship tickets down at the Arch and cruise the Mississippi for the chance to spend even more of their paychecks on music and dancing in Memphis and New Orleans. They might even throw a few dollars in the offering baskets on Saturday and Sunday, in case they feel a little guilty about the other money they've spent. This mob is the life blood of the city, Mr. Perot, they will make a whole damned country, because they've been given the chance to work hard and enjoy the fruits of their labor. Your computers and machines will never drop a dime on Cherokee Avenue. And for my own part, I will see them never built."

There followed a long silence between the two men, standing only six inches apart, a strange stillness in the midst of the morning rush on Lemp Avenue. Perot, his face a rictus of barely contained rage, peeled off and pushed his way through the crowd toward the International Shoe Administration Building. Kleinrock, a look of regret beginning to cloud his face, cursed under his breath. He'd never lost his temper on an assignment before, much less blown his cover and mission. There was going to be hell to pay back at the Technology Acquisition Office.

A few hours later, Perot emerged from the International Shoe complex, a distinct bounce in his step and a broad grin on his face. He was so pleased that he was thinking of spending a few dollars on a celebration—quite a departure for a man of his parsimonious habits. He was trying to remember if any old friends or family from Texas were in Saint Louis this weekend when he saw Mr. B seated at an outdoor bar on the patio of the Cherokee German House. With no other immediate prospects, Perot made his way over.

"Surprised to see you here, Mr. B, frequenting another eating establishment. Won't you have a lunch crowd dropping in at the Gateway soon?"

"Mr. Perot! Just the man I wanted to see! Pull up a chair and take a load off, and no worries about the barbecue shack. Nothing to serve them anyway, we sold out by 11:30! Best day we've ever had. A tour group from the Cherokee Caves dropped by, bought everything we had but the light fixtures! I put about half the take in Frank's trade-school fund and we decided to blow the rest! He's up to no good down on Grand Boulevard and I was just celebrating with my best regulars, the Koenig brothers, before they headed off to the 3-D Soccer Stadia. They left half a pitcher of Falstaff. Care to join me in a pint of Lemp's finest?"

"A bit early for me, Mr. B. I'm headed back to the workshop."

"Your meeting with International Shoe must have gone well, Mr. Perot. You're looking like the cat that ate the canary."

"Indeed, Mr. B, I just won a big contract with International Shoe. Even without Jack Kilby, we have machines that will completely revolutionize their Accounting Department. A few of them are already operational, and since you appear to free for the day, would you care to take a look at my latest creations?"

"I would be honored, Mr. Perot," said Mr. B, standing up a bit unsteadily, "To see what you've teased out of the ether. Saint Louis is truly the gateway to new worlds and wonders."

Perot was a very gracious host and Mr. B a most engaged and curious guest. They inspected Jack Kilby's first prototype circuit in Perot's office, along with calculational engines in varying degrees of completion, beeping and spitting out ticker tape and punch card data in their respective production bays. The machines were large and unlovely, kludged together with the relatively primitive, but functional, transistors and valves and memory tapes that Perot had been able to scrounge. After a glazed look at the blueprints and advertising copy in the office suite, Mr. B made his excuses and headed back to the Gateway.

A few days later Perot was sitting at his desk, signing the shipping orders for the first International Shoe delivery, when he heard a sizzling sound and smelled the sharp tang of ozone. He immediately threw the fire alarm and ran to the workshop to get his disconcerted staff out of the building. Perot saw the first of the explosions himself. A blinding white light burst from an empty production bay. It radiated enough energy to singe Perot's hair even though he was 100 feet across the workshop floor. The whole staff was assembled on the far side of Jefferson, all accounted for, when a series of blasts blew out all the workshop windows and skylights. Soon smoke was billowing through the roof and everything flammable inside was ablaze. Even with the help of the Aerial Fire Brigade the building and the contents of the workshop were a complete loss.

The Fire Inspectors suspected remote-controlled Tesla thermal bombs—tiny devices, easily overlooked, that could transmit the heat and light from the interior of a blast furnace for a few seconds before they self-immolated. Bombs Without Wires. There must have been a dozen or so scattered all over the workshop. The investigators found that scores of people had routine access to the building, and a very prompt and generous settlement from the insurance company brought all interviews to a halt. International Shoe even paid out, under the Involuntary Separation clause of their contract. And though no one seemed the least bit concerned about the identity of the arsonist, Mr. Perot had his suspicions.

One August morning, after he had packed his few remaining belongings for the long trip back to Texas, Perot walked over to the Gateway BBQ. He found it closed, with a large hand-drawn sign taped to the big plate glass window.

Closed for Expansion—Building a Bigger, Better Gateway!
We'll Never Sell Out Again!
God Bless International Shoe and Lemp and Maxim and Cherokee Caves!

Perot sighed, feeling defeated for the first time in his life and tired of the fight. He returned to Texas, where he made a good living selling Rockefeller petroleum from a chain of Standard Oil stations he bought with his settlement money. He never became a billionaire—no one in Whiggish America ever does. Perot never heard from Jack Kilby again.

Mr. B's son Frank eventually took over the Gateway BBQ and to this day sells the best pulled pork, smoked ribs, fried okra, and cornbread in the bustling heart of Whiggish America.

Southern Truths

Teaching DeSantis a Lesson

Marleen S. Barr

Feminist science fiction theorist par excellence Professor Sondra Lear was excited about beginning the fall term as a visiting scholar at the University of Florida. The gig offered her the chance to be in schmoozing proximity to her New York aunts who had moved to Boca.

She entered her Feminist Science Fiction 101 classroom and began to explain the syllabus. It was well received—especially Joanna Russ' *When It Changed,* in which women happily reside on the lesbian separatist planet Whileaway.

With the exception of a woman with long straight blonde hair who sat in the front row clutching her rosary beads and wearing an oversized anti-abortion button, Sondra thought that all the students looked forward to the class.

Feeling self-satisfied that she had weathered her first class at a new university, Sondra returned to her office to finish unpacking feminist theory books.

There was a knock on the door. A man sporting a long beard and wearing a Florida state trooper uniform entered. "Are you Professor Lear?" asked the trooper.

"Yes, I am Professor Lear the great and powerful feminist science fiction scholar who is also the world's expert on the feminist separatist science fiction planet where women kill men; my specialty is not a plus vis-à-vis husband hunting. No matter. Ayatollah clones are not my type. Who, may I ask, are you?"

"Hello, ma'am. I'm a Florida state trooper assigned to Governor DeSantis' special Textiban Educational Enforcement Unit. Make sure that all your banned books conform to the Book Burka Code; cover them in a black cloth. I can force you to comply because honey, as a member of the Textiban, I am greater and more powerful than you. Based upon an irate student's complaint, I am warning you to cease and desist exposing students to your perverted man-hater philosophy."

"What will happen if I refuse?"

"Little lady," he said while stroking his ayatollah-style beard for emphasis, "the best-case scenario is that I will lock you up. The worst-case scenario is that I will build a fire pit to burn your godless books, add a stake to the fire pit, tie you to the stake, and incinerate you for being a wicked book witch from the north."

"Are you saying that it is impossible for me to teach feminist science fiction at the University of Florida?"

"Dear," he said, "you are an on-the-mark chick. I suggest that you go back to New York where, according to your accent, you came from."

He obliged when she encouraged him to leave.

Sondra decided to assuage her despondency by driving to Cape Kennedy. She entered the Mission

Control room used during projects Mercury, Gemini, and Apollo. While examining the antiquated consoles, she wished that the astronauts had experienced close encounters with benevolent feminist extraterrestrials. Pushing aside this fantasy in order to deal with the migraine the Textiban trooper triggered, she decided to converse with a tweed-skirt-suit-wearing woman of a certain age who was also perusing the consoles. Just as Sondra was about to articulate an introductory locution, she noticed a green tentacle sticking out from under the woman's skirt hem.

"Hello. I'm Sondra Lear. I'm a science fiction scholar. From your tentacle, I see that you're an extraterrestrial."

"You are exactly right, dear. Please excuse the tentacle. I left my spaceship in a hurry this morning. I am Astra from the feminist separatist planet Advil. I have been sent to Earth as an emissary assigned to learn about primitive humanoid spacefaring. I come in peace. Since you are a female Earthling, patriarchal male Earthlings must be giving you a headache. The advanced power of Advil is at your disposal. How can I help?"

During their long walk around the Cape, Sondra explained how DeSantis' onslaught against Florida's educational institutions was stymying her ability to teach feminist science fiction in particular and her colleagues' efforts to convey historical fact in general. While standing in front of the launch pad, Sondra said that the pedagogical headaches DeSantis was causing were beyond even the powers of Advil to solve.

"Be advised that I can handle DeSantis," Astra reassuringly said. "There is no need for me to rely on reinforcement from Advil's neighboring feminist planets. Emissaries Myra from Midol, Edna from

Excedrin, and Tillie from Tylenol can continue to direct their attention to assisting primitive female humanoids such as yourself who inhabit other Earth-like planets. Meanwhile it is time for me to have a word with DeSantis."

Astra raised her hand to snap her fingers. Before she could do so, an alligator ambled along, licking its chops.

"I am new to Florida and not used to murderous reptiles," Sondra said. "Alligators are worse than New York City rats. Please do not feed DeSantis to an alligator. Although he is despicable, he does not deserve to be chomped to death. I hope that you do not share the methods of man-killing feminist science fiction protagonists."

"Not at all dear. I have non-lethal methods for convincing DeSantis to act in a reasonable and democratic manner."

Astra finished snapping her fingers. DeSantis appeared.

"Hello, Governor," Sondra said. "I am University of Florida visiting professor Sondra Lear and this is my new friend, Astra."

DeSantis frowned. "You're that woke educational mob member from New York. I dispatched a Textiban trooper to silence you."

"I am here to empower Professor Lear to rein in your conservative statewide educational agenda," interjected Astra. "Sondra, if you could employ a feminist science fiction text to counter DeSantis and make Florida great for education again, which one would you use?"

"Something Octavia E. Butler authored. I am thinking of *Kindred*. I imagine sending DeSantis back in time to be enslaved on a plantation in the manner of Butler's protagonist Dana. He could then personally experience the history he wishes to erase. Unfortunately, DeSantis is not Black."

"No problem, Sondra," the alien said. "I can transport DeSantis to an alternate history in which Italians as well as Africans were enslaved."

Astra snapped her fingers. DeSantis found himself working in the fields on a plantation in the central part of the Florida panhandle along the Georgia border. Since this is not a horror story, it is unnecessary to describe what DeSantis experienced. Astra and Sondra decided that being enslaved for half a day was enough for DeSantis to endure. After they had a nice lunch and did more sightseeing, Astra again snapped her fingers. DeSantis reappeared.

"Slavery was terrible," he said as he cried and screamed.

"I am not interested in hearing about it," Astra said.

"Slavery was a beneficial experience for you," interjected Sondra. "Slavery enabled you to enjoy a first-person historical perspective."

"So, Ron honey, are you ready to be enslaved for the rest of your life?" inquired Astra.

"No."

"In that case, you must follow Sondra's instructions."

"Ron, sweetie pie, in terms of the title of John Barth's novel *Giles Goat-boy, Or, The Revised New Syllabus*, I want you to reinstate my right to teach feminist science fiction," said Sondra. "In this novel, which depicts the universe being described as a college campus, Barth availed himself of the opportunity satirically to insult everyone. In order to remain living free in the twenty-first century, you must agree to reinstate a revised new syllabus in place of the educational changes you established. In other words, the revised new syllabus I call for is the same as the formerly existing syllabus you nullified. You must allow the conservative version of New College you created to revert back to its liberal initial iteration. You must agree once again to allow educators to teach race, class, and sex. You must learn critical race theory. You must make the University of Florida a safe place to teach feminist science fiction. Last but not least, you must abolish the Textiban.

"I surrender. I agree to everything," DeSantis said.

DeSantis returned to Tallahassee and rescinded his conservative educational agenda. Astra bid adieu to Sondra, hovered in her spaceship on top of the Cape Kennedy launching pad, and blasted off back to Advil. Sondra, after visiting her aunts Myra, Edna, and Tillie in their Boca condos, went back to enjoying teaching her feminist science fiction class. Her blonde student, newly married to the now clean-shaven trooper Sondra had closely encountered, decided to open her mind to feminist science fiction. Sondra gave her term paper on Russ' *The Female Man* an "A."

Note: This story is dedicated to the memory of my beloved dissertation director Norman N. Holland who was the Marston-Milbauer Eminent Scholar in English at the University of Florida.

We Owe It to You

Maroula Blades

For Rosa Parks

It takes a movement to bring about change in dry infinity or, some may say, the lack of one. Your tired legs could stand no longer. In "no man's land" you sat, clasping painkillers on your lap. A colourless rider stood in the aisle. The bus driver's coarse voice punched the air with, "All right, you niggers. I want those seats." Your quiet "No," a distended cloud, rained on Montgomery, Alabama 1955, where the eyes of whiteness stalked the streets. Phantoms with spike tongues ran, flaunting coshes to thrash "darkies' flesh." The Jim Crow law marched without a curfew.

A paper chase settled on the lawn of the Supreme Court. The puzzle of names screamed as they came together, counted. Even the ghosts cut their nooses from budding Memorial Trees, faces with crooked lips, gouged-out eyes and abysses where their manhood should be, rallied. The wind morphed battered features, floating on the Mississippi River, a painful exhibit of fathers, brothers, and youths. Snagged, waterlogged bodies defiantly rose from the river root, some with bobby socks and plaits, and others who had once the form of gazelles faced the sun, anaemic and bloated. Black peeled itself away from the backs of mirrors, a transparent happening. No excuses not to see through the window. It took 382 days. The mandate: Alabama's bus segregation laws unconstitutional.

You became our planet, the sun for Black folk to turn to. Swarthy necks grew out from your orbit, gravitating towards freedom's light. "Onward Christian Soldiers," armed with a protest, a pillar of Blackness with an aim as sharp as a pickaxe. Soulful voices echoed for miles out of the ghettos, over moonscapes and down through the tree-lined suburbs. A future ran straight into our hearts, designed like a main road.

The stone which fell is still falling, your word freed it, but it still feels the burn of repression in the freefall. Your titanium smile is etched in the core, a fire of light in the dark, a flickering universe of hope that tomorrow will be brighter, wiser, and full of release.

The Last Day on Earth

Heinrich von Wolfcastle

Lines of cars stretch for miles into the horizon and theirs is just one in a seeming infinity. Waves of heat curve the air above the hood.

"I don't think we're going to make it," Julie says.

"There's nothing to make," Chris replies.

They keep their voices down to avoid waking their son, his face wedged between his car seat and his Ninja Turtle-themed pillow.

"I just mean—" Julie begins. She looks around at the cars packed to her left and right. "I don't think we're going to make it," she repeats. She plunges her thumb into the plastic wrapping of their first and only case of bottled water.

"Look, we have the strongest military in the world— " Chris stops himself and shakes his head. After a pregnant pause, he starts again, "We just don't even know enough to worry."

"You really believe this is a war thing?" she asks. "What, like some terrorist attack?"

"I don't know that it's a war thing," he replies.

Chris wants to be gentler than he is. This is their first private moment since they woke up to the big bang at four this morning, and Chris recognizes that it's his chance to get Julie thinking a bit more rationally about the situation.

"You just won't see the alternative," she says.

"Will you stop it with that nonsense?" he replies.

"You and I can take Jacob out of the car right now and just start walking off this highway. We don't have to sit here like this."

"You're crazy. What about all of our things?"

"Our things will do us no good when we die sitting in this stupid car on this stupid highway!" she yells in a whisper. Noticing the rising tone of her voice, she rolls her volume back and continues, "We can just get out and leave it all here."

"And go where?" Chris asks.

Julie waves towards the trees lining the freeway. "The forest."

"The forest? What are we going to do, scavenge for food?"

"Look, I don't know," she says. "I just know that this is not how I want to die—cooking inside a car in the middle of goddamn Georgia in July!"

"You've always hated it here."

"Listen to me, we can do this. We just leave the car here. This is bad. I can feel it," she persists.

"Maybe that's the problem. You *feel* too much."

"Look around you, Chris! You think I'm a nut because I insisted we leave? You heard the explosion! It fucking broke the living room window. If I'm a nut, then so are the million-and-a-half cars full of people around you! This is not going to work. We're not moving." Julie slams her hands down on her thighs.

Chris responds with silence. There is nothing to say any more. He takes his foot off the brake and moves them a few inches closer to the car in front of them. By instinct, he turns the radio on but is reminded by static that something about today's argument might not end like all the others.

They sit in their parked car—their four-door sedan that Julie insisted they buy to replace the two-door coupe Chris owned when she got pregnant. The Car Talk was perhaps Chris's greatest display of semantic talent. But, in the end, Julie held the power in the relationship and he still resented her for it.

"You're so goddamned stubborn!" he says.

Another wave of honking moves through the string of cars.

"Mommy, where are we?" Jacob's voice chimes in from the back.

"Still driving, honey. We'll be there soon," she reassures him.

"Go back to sleep, Jakey," Chris says.

"But I'm hungry."

Julie hands back a small bag full of cereal. "Here you go, honey, but then you have to try to go back to sleep, okay?"

"But I want to play!"

"Just eat your snack and we can talk after that," Chris negotiates.

"Okay." Jacob reaches for the bag of cereal.

Julie turns back to Chris and mutters, "Just for once in your life, listen to me."

Julie rubs her eyes and sits up in her seat. "How long was I out for?" she asks with sleep caught in her throat.

"About two hours," Chris says.

She reaches for the knob to adjust the air conditioning before realizing the car is turned off. "Jesus! Turn the car on," she says while fanning herself.

"Just saving gas," Chris says under his breath. He restarts the car. "It's going to get a lot hotter before we get anywhere."

Julie groans. "Did we even move at all?"

"About half a mile, maybe."

Julie sees that the scenery is about the same as before—endless lines of trees. The sky that had been slow to wake up is fully lit and already blasting summer heat. She peers into the passenger-side rearview mirror and sees pockets of individuals outside their cars. Some are adjusting luggage strapped to their roofs, others are off and peering further up the road. Two young men engage in a shoving match.

"Natives are getting restless," she says.

On cue, the car to her right slams on its horn.

"Any news?" Julie pulls the sun visor down and opens the mirror to see if she appears as tired as she feels. She does.

"Radio is still out. Still no phone service. No internet," Chris says.

Julie peers into the distance and sees a car at the side of the road with shattered windows. "This is a nightmare," she says. "How's he been?" Julie motions to Jacob in his car seat.

Jacob has a set of headphones on and is watching a show on the family laptop. Julie turns around and waves to him. It's easier for her to find a fake smile than she expected, but Jacob doesn't notice her anyway.

"We have to be careful on gas."

"Right. So, what's our plan here?" Julie asks. "I mean, we won't even have enough gas to make it to the next station at this rate."

"Right now, even if we saw an exit for gas, I doubt we could get there. Just too many cars."

"So, let's leave the car and hoof it," Julie starts again. "Stuck in this traffic and running the AC will kill the car anyway."

"And do what once we're on foot?" he asks.

"I don't know." Julie breaks from her thought as a man in a brown beanie cap walks past her window holding a homemade sign indicating the end of times. The man spins around and yells to the cars around him as he makes his way up the aisle.

Julie moves her ear closer to the open window to hear the man.

"Look around you, sheep!" he yells. "The lord God is your shepherd! He opened the sky, and through it, his demons came to cleanse the earth of nonbelievers. Repent your sin! The end of times is here! In Jesus Christ's name, amen. Amen, sisters and brothers!"

Chris turns the radio on again—with purpose this time. A blast of static shakes their ears before Julie turns the volume down.

"I don't know, Chris. What we're doing right now, this is giving up."

He hears her, but there is nothing to say. He takes his wedding ring off and traces the inside of it with his right forefinger, feeling the inscription printed on the inside.

"Look," Chris nods towards a man gesturing and posturing at the hood of another car.

"What's he doing?" Julie asks.

"I don't know, but he's not happy about something."

Julie hears their volume but cannot gather much from their words. The man waves his hands in the air while the car driver honks his horn in return.

"Should we do something?" Julie asks.

"No," Chris says, shaking his head.

"But what if this turns into a fight?"

"It's their business. Besides, the guy could have a gun for all we know."

The man slams his hands down on the hood and spurs the driver to blare his horn continuously. The man kicks at the car's headlight but fails to do any damage.

"I don't like where this is going," Julie says. Before she can continue, the car they're watching lurches forward, slamming into the man and pinning him against his own car. He flails his arms in the air and screams upon seeing his legs crushed between the two cars. When the car reverses, the man crumples to the ground.

"Oh God!" Julie covers her mouth and turns to Chris who's looking on blankly. She turns back to Jacob; he's focused on a movie playing from the laptop.

"You have to help him," Julie urges.

"What? I'm a lawyer, not a medic," he replies.

"Well, we have to do something," she says. "We have our first aid kit in the trunk!"

"I think he's going to need more than a Band-Aid." Chris moves the gear shift to drive and lets the car creep up about another foot before putting it into Park again. "Just go back to sleep, babe," he suggests, as the man writhes in pain on the ground. His screams fade into hoarse groans

~~~

"Hey, wake up," Chris whispers.

"I'm awake. Just thinking," she responds with her eyes closed.

A sudden knocking on Julie's window startles Chris. A Black man in a white T-shirt stands outside the car and motions with urgency for Julie to roll down her window. Chris shakes his head "no" to the man outside, but Julie is already lowering the window.

"What's going on?" Julie asks.

"I don't know, but it's something bad," the man replies. "I'm parked a few miles back. We started to smell some smoke off in the distance coming from behind us, and then there was some strange sounds and some hollering going on." The man pauses to catch his breath before continuing. "Couple of guys were even saying they saw these things moving around in the forest or something." He reads Julie and Chris's expressions to see if they understand the message. "Look," he goes on, "I don't know what's happening here, but a few of us got out of our cars and thought we'd start spreading word up this way. Maybe get out of your car and leave it here. No one's moving anyway."

"*Things* in the forest, or something?" Chris scoffs.

"Look man, you do you. I'm just spreading the word. God be with you," the man says. He slaps the car door as he runs off to start knocking on windows again.

"Things in the forest," Chris repeats with a chuckle. "High as a kite, that guy," Chris nods to Julie for consensus.

"I believe him. I've been telling you, something strange is going on. We're just sitting ducks here." Julie follows the man with her eyes and notices a line of abandoned cars in the grass just off the highway.

"You are—" Chris hesitates, changing the direction of his thought. He purses his lips and points his finger to hold his place in the conversation. "If you know, then you tell me. What has you so riled up on this?"

"What has me so riled up on this?" Exasperated, Julie gestures to the miles of cars around them. "It makes sense. You believe the bullshit they feed you on the news? It's all diversion is what it is."

"Diversion from what?" Chris asks in his formal, dismissive way.

"It's like I was trying to explain to you yesterday. There's some guys at work who were talking about the unexpected effects of climate change," Julie starts. Jacob rustles in his car seat, reminding Julie to return to a whisper.

"Oh, so you're just mad that we don't have long winters anymore?" Chris says with raised eyebrows.

"Just shut up for a second, Chris." Julie says.

"Mommy, are you and Dad fighting?" Jacob asks.

"We're not fighting, honey," Chris says. He reaches a hand back to pat Jacob's leg but misses and knocks the boy's stuffed tiger to the floor before taunting Julie further, "So what does this have to do with climate change? Enlighten me."

Julie sighs and starts again, "They were saying that with all of the Arctic defrosting, we might have released ancient viruses or something. It makes sense. Think about what benefits most from all the extreme rain and heat and humidity—the mosquitoes. Maybe what's happening—"

"Money has always been in oil and coal and a lot of wealthy people stay in power by pulling back our resources from researching global warming," Chris begins, speaking over Julie..

"Maybe it's a super-powered resistant-bacteria or a super-virus." Julie's voice trails off as she notices a group of men crossing over the median. One of them discards an empty beer bottle, it shatters across the pavement. Another spike in honking follows.

In a pause between horns blaring, Julie's voice is louder than she intends, "We're a cancer on this planet, and maybe She's shaking us off."

"Why can't it just be a bomb?" Chris challenges. "Why does it have to be something magical?"

"It could be a bomb! It could be a damn big bomb. There could be more bombs coming! It could be biological, chemical, nuclear—who knows?! It could be terrorism or a military invasion. It could even be our own country!" Julie yells.

A loud popping sound interrupts their argument. To their right, three men in camouflage and overalls emerge from the forest. They're toting rifles and handguns.

"Who are they?" Julie asks.

"I don't know," Chris says with an edge of sincere fear that frightens Julie.

"Are they bad guys, Mom?" Jacob asks.

"No, honey." Julie answers without taking her eyes off the group of men. "You don't need to worry about them. I want you to watch your movie."

"Can you do that?" Chris joins in.

"You've been so good, and I know this trip has been hard, but we're going to start moving really soon," Julie says.

Further up the road, the three men surround a pickup truck pulling off the highway. The door opens to a cluster of popping sounds like firecrackers and the driver falls to the ground clutching his stomach.

"Oh, God," Julie whispers.

"What was that sound, Mom?" Jacob asks.

A bearded white man surprises them by tapping on Chris's window with a metal pipe. He looks to be in his fifties and wears an old army jacket and bandana. He raps on the glass again.

"Roll down your window," he bellows.

"I can hear you like this," Chris yells back.

"Who is that, Mommy?" Jacob asks.

"Just a friend of Daddy's," Julie says. "What do you think he wants?" she murmurs to Chris.

"More handouts."

"He looks mean," Jacob says.

"Roll down the window," the man wearing the army jacket implores.

Chris obliges.

"Listen, man, you gotta get your family outta here. This clusterfuck—excuse my French—is turning bad real big and real fast," he says. It is difficult to see his mouth move under his beard.

"I appreciate it, but I can take care of my family." Chris dismisses the man and raises his window again.

"Suit yourself! But if you want an escort, you let me know," the man offers. He walks off, the back of his jacket showcasing a collage of patches dedicated to fallen soldiers. As he moves on, he looks through the windows of several cars around him. Again, he picks one out from the crowd and taps on the driver's window with his pipe.

To the right, a man rides up on a motorcycle and passes their car. He revs his engine as he passes idle cars until a driver opens his door. The bike rips the door from the vehicle and sends the rider to the ground, his contorted body folded over itself.

"Look at this. I think he's right, Chris. It's time for us to go. We're just not safe here anymore," Julie says.

"We're safe in this car!" Chris shouts.

A tall and thin man crosses in front of their car and over to the median to their left. He carries a megaphone. Looking past him, they see a group of men yelling into a blue car in the distance.

"The whole world going crazy," Chris says.

The man with the megaphone stands on the median divider beside their car and yells into his megaphone, "Aliens have landed! The noise you heard was their ship falling to Earth!" His proclamations are met with honking from the cars around him. "The aliens have landed! I repeat, the aliens have landed!"

"Shut up, buddy!" a driver calls out.

"The explosion you heard was the beginning of our mass extinction!" the man goes on.

"Get down from there!" other drivers shout.

Fueled by their protests, Chris lowers his window and joins the yelling. "Shut up!"

Julie looks at Chris in disbelief and slaps him across the arm. "That doesn't help!" she hisses.

"Mom, why did you hit Daddy?"

"I didn't, Jake. Just watch your show!"

The man with the megaphone goes on, "They froze our communication! They froze our emergency services! They will divide us and kill us!" He turns to face the other side of the highway to continue his warning. Unbeknownst to him, a glass bottle is flying through the air and towards his head. "The aliens—" he starts again when the bottle strikes him behind the ear and sends him to the concrete road beside Chris and Julie's sedan. Cheers erupt from a car full of college kids in the adjacent lane.

Julie flings open her car door and runs to the man.

"Julie, get back here! It's not safe!" Chris calls from the car. He looks around, considering getting out himself, when he notices the gang of camouflaged hillbillies in their stolen truck. The driver has his gun perched on the window.

Julie crouches next to the injured man. "Are you OK?" she asks. Blood gathers under his head. He is awake but unable to make eye contact with her. Further down the aisle to her left, she notices the body of a woman on the ground. "Oh, God," she mutters. Another tragedy, one she had not witnessed.

A few car lengths away, the man in the army jacket fights with the driver of another car.

Chris turns the radio on and blasts the volume to let static drown the chaos around them like a white noise machine. "Julie, you get your ass back in this car right this second!" He shouts through the open window. But she can't hear him over the radio.

Julie remains crouched next to the fallen man outside their car. Chris reaches through the window to grab her when another glass bottle crashes across the top of their car. Chris traces the arc of the bottle back to the college kids a few cars over. "Goddamned motherfuckers," he mutters. Chris throws his car door open and nearly hits Julie in the head.

Chris walks towards the college kids' car and kicks at the driver's door. "You think it's funny to throw bottles at my wife?!" He punctuates his words with his strikes.

The driver attempts to get out, but every time he goes to open the door, Chris kicks it closed again. "Funny, huh!?" Chris taunts. He expects his foot to ache or throb but finds the sensation of the door giving way to be gratifying.

Behind Chris, a man wearing a fisherman's hat gets out of another car and pulls Chris away from the college kids' car.

"Hey, hey, you can't do that! Cool it!" The fisherman attempts to restrain Chris and pulls him backwards.

Chris spins around in the man's grip, "Get your fucking hands off of me before I have you so tied up in litigation that you and your next ten generations live off of welfare."

While Chris is in the man's grasp, five young men exit the car that Chris had been kicking.

"Look what you did to my car, faggot," the driver exclaims. He has Greek letters tattooed across his arm. The driver pulls an arm back and punches Chris in the gut while the fisherman continues to restrain him.

"Who are you gonna sue now?" the fisherman asks as he drops Chris to the ground.

"Pick him up," one of the college kids commands. A lanky young man grabs Chris by the hair and lifts him to his feet.

Chris, still unable to find his air to speak, whimpers as the frat boy slaps him across the face. Chris turns his cheek. He wishes Julie could help him but is too ashamed to call for her, lest she see him beaten by the group of young men.

The frat boy grabs Chris by the face as another one of his friends holds Chris on his feet and restrains him. "Look at me, faggot," the frat boy commands. "You're going to pay for my door."

Chris looks past the frat boy and makes eye contact with the driver of another car who averts his eyes, refusing to watch as Chris takes a fist to his jaw.

"About the price of your car, I think," the frat boy taunts.

Chris groans and whimpers again, feeling a tooth fall from his mouth. A warm trickle of blood trails from his nose.

The frat boy takes Chris's face again. Chris shuts his eyes and waits for impact but is met with a plunking sound and the sensation of warm liquid splattering over his face. He winces at the imaginary strike and opens his eyes to see the man in the army jacket standing over the frat boy. His metal pipe is bloodied.

The other frat boys shrink back in horror at the sight of their friend's deformed head. Chris wipes the boy's blood off of his face while the man in the army jacket kicks at the frat boy's body on the ground.

From behind him, Chris hears a clicking sound that makes him sick to his stomach. The fisherman points a gun at the man in the army jacket. Time freezes and the men spend an eternity calculating their positions.

The sound of an explosion unfreezes the men. Chris falls forward onto the hood of the frat boys' car, deafened by the gun's eruption. The man in the army jacket dies, a look of disbelief frozen on his face as he falls to his knees before collapsing onto the concrete.

The sound of gunfire encourages the hillbillies to fire several shots into the air along with a series of catcalls. Chris pushes himself off the frat boys' car and is met by the fisherman's gun.

The fisherman's eyes are cold and stern, his face expressionless. Strangely, in that moment, Chris notices that the man's outfit is well-coordinated with khaki shorts and a plaid top, worn under a tactical vest matching the color and style of his hat. Chris wonders what kind of man shops for matching outfits and also fires a gun so readily. The answer doesn't matter, he supposes—nothing does anymore, really.

The frat boys pull some golf clubs from the trunk of their car and hold these weapons over their shoulders. Chris feels them approaching from behind. Past the fisherman, empty cars litter the highway, many of them with broken windows where they have been looted.

Chris's car sits with its doors open. His car will be emptied and looted like the others before long, he thinks. In the distance, he sees Julie with Jacob in her arms running across the highway median. She never once looks back—never hesitates to leave him there with the fisherman's gun aimed at his forehead and covered in a stranger's blood.

Chris leans his head back and turns his attention away from the car horns and pauses, waiting for the small explosion that will signal the end. In that eternal waiting room, he hears an old sound so familiar and so wanted that it startles him. The static blaring from his radio ends, just like the sound an old record player makes when its needle finds the vinyl groove.

~~~

"...And further south, 75 has become a literal parking lot where people have abandoned their cars on both sides of the highway. Again, it is believed that the fire was started by the heat wave we've been experiencing, which burned some high-voltage equipment, sparking

several small explosions. Grid operators report that they cut power while emergency services attended to the fire. Utility workers are expected to work into the night to restore power to the area. Again, we encourage you to stay cool and, most importantly, remember, there's no need to panic."

Southern Truths

The Chatham County Blood Shower of 1884

Anya Leigh Josephs

Today

Chapel Hill, North Carolina, is a place particularly and peculiarly resistant to haunting.

Certainly it has some of the prerequisites for a good Southern Gothic story. On any day from May to October it has that eldritch kind of heat. When the humidity hits your skin, as viscous as snot, when you're trying to breathe in and the air is drowning you, you have the instinctive sense that something evil is lurking. There is certainly a rich enough legacy of misery to summon a few ghosts: a few hundred years of slavery, lynchings, and wife-beating, and a few dozen churches that have extolled the need for such violence.

But this is background noise to what Chapel Hill is today. You don't step out in the humid air. You don't sit on the porch with a glass of lemonade and think about the past. You go from air-conditioned car to air-conditioned shopping mall, the air cold and bleached clean.

You don't learn about the terrible things that used to happen. You drive down the town's main street and look at murals celebrating the home of Southern progressivism. At the center of campus, the most recent graduating class has raised funds for an installation honoring the enslaved workers who built the university. Hundreds of tiny figures hold up a slab of marble. You can see their struggle, their confinement, their suffering. Students mostly consider this monument a great place to sit and grab lunch, laying their takeout sandwiches on the marble, carelessly ignorant of who and what holds them up, less an honoring, and more of a continuation.

Less than a hundred yards away is Silent Sam, the monumental bronze statue of a Confederate soldier. It stands at the doorway to the university, on every postcard, with the gun he never fires. He is, the University insists at the frequent protests that arise, a purely historical curiosity.

The past in Chapel Hill has been not just forgotten, but built over. The natural world has been paved and cooled into a perfect habitat. There is nothing left that can cause a feeling so pure and sharp as fear.

And yet there is plenty of pain.

Most of it comes from the town's children. It's a hard time to be a teenager, everyone says, and maybe nowhere harder than this university town, where the symbol of success looms over and limits you. In Chapel Hill, there are rainbow flags in every window. But two miles down the road and Confederate flags replace them. You are trapped, they remind you. You are a prisoner within yourself.

There is nowhere for all that pain to go. There is no evil to fight, no villain to conquer. There is only the pulsing internal despair, in this unhaunted town.

Girls grow up. Some of them get away. Some find wives or adopt puppies. Some get apartments in the city or doctorates in geology.

But most stay. They have girls of their own. They sit by the pool and watch these daughters swim, watch them tug down their swimsuit bottoms to try to hide the neat cuts they've carved into their thighs. The mothers dole out one slice of pizza per girl (you're getting a little chubby, bless your heart). At a certain point in time they will, without word or explanation, hand out crinkling cylinders with a tampon inside, which will be inexpertly applied by trembling 11-year-old hands. Sex will occur, with all the entailing fluids. New children will be born, blood-smeared and shrieking, as if they somehow know what lies ahead.

No, there is nothing haunting Chapel Hill, North Carolina. But all the same, there is plenty of blood.

Yesterday

Down around here, the weather's nearly always mild, even on a February day like today. Mrs. Kit Laseter is, nonetheless, dressed: shift, stays, two good petticoats, a fine dress in a midnight-blue wool, flounces at the sleeves her only concession to the present fashion for decoration. She is, after all, an ordinary sort of woman, plain dressed and plain spoken.

There is, nonetheless, a pleasant dignity in being the sort of woman that Mrs. Kit Laseter is. Her father was a preacher, but not a Revivalist or some sort of big-tent showman. Just an ordinary small-town preacher. Her mother bore six children and died in childbed and a pool of blood when Kit was four. When Kit was sixteen, her father introduced her to Mr. Stephen Laseter, who owned eight acres not too far from the center of town and who was only ten years her senior. This, she recognized at once, made him an agreeable match, and they were married on her seventeenth birthday.

Men were in short supply in those years after the war, and she knows she is lucky to have one at all, much less a man like Stephen: a good God-fearing man, and neither too old nor too unpleasant to look at. She expected she would come to love him in time, and so she has, more or less. Certainly she loves the life they have together.

She is now the happy mother of three children: two girls and a boy. The farm is doing well enough for them to keep a maid, but not well enough for a whole staff. She cooks and does most of the tidying and minds the children herself.

Twenty years ago, before the war, it would have been different, but those days are gone. There's no sense in longing for what is past, as fools at the public house do when they're in their cups. Though times are hard throughout the South, the Laseters are doing well enough.

Mrs. Kit Laseter knows herself to be a fortunate woman indeed, as she sets out to walk her property line on this February day. Even though the task has fallen to her, and not to a farmhand or (as it would have when she was a girl) to a slave, she tells herself she doesn't mind. She laces up her working boots and wraps a shawl around her shoulders and sets forth to walk the property line.

Today

Karen Barrington-Harris is seventeen years old. She's a pretty girl, long blond hair, long tan limbs.

The boys like her. Maybe, some whisper, the boys like her too much. Her dad isn't in the picture, mom works long hours. At lunch hour, her next-door neighbor sometimes peeks through the window and sees Karen with a boy. Not always the same boy. So it's hardly a surprise to Karen when she realizes she's pregnant.

What is she going to do? She can't have a baby. She's a nice girl, from a good family. Plenty of girls graduate Chapel Hill High pregnant, but they do so from trailer parks or apartment buildings off 15-501, not from behind the gates of the Logan Farms subdivision.

But Karen, contrary to the assumptions people make when they see her, is a smart girl. She does her research. She takes her mom's old minivan and leaves a note on the counter ("Gone to Stephanie's to study!") and drives to the clinic, where she is informed, sympathetically, but definitively, that, here in this bastion of liberalism, the doctor still must follow state law, and state law says she needs a parent's permission for an abortion.

So instead, she logs onto her parents' heavy desktop computer and does some research, goes to the hippie grocery store in the next town and buys a dozen kinds of herbs, and steeps them according to instructions.

She feels a bit magical for the first time in her life as she brews the abortifacient. It's new and thrilling. Maybe, she thinks, it's time to stop fooling around with boys. Maybe her mom is right, and she should make something of herself. Go to medical school like her mom did, or at least show up for fifth period algebra sometimes. Maybe she has a future ahead of her, after all.

Karen Barrington-Harris dies gasping in a pool of blood in the spotless bathroom of her mother's 6,000-square-foot house. The neighbors are told it was cancer, that she was so brave she didn't want anyone to know that she was sick. She is buried in a white dress in a closed casket.

No one believes this, of course, but no one is rude enough to question it, either.

Yesterday

A little cool, the air is, and thick with rain that won't fall. The earth has congealed into sticky mud. The trees that line the outside of the property are bare fingers in the slate-gray sky.

It's a pretty landscape, really, barren though it may be. And not everything is gray and dead. North Carolina is famous for its pines, and there are a few among the leafless trees that dot the edge of her land. Their sage-green needles are especially lovely in the face of that bleak sky.

Kit wonders if the rain will come later tonight. She hopes so. It will do the crops good.

The Laseters are lucky to have land that has held up well enough, that's still healthy and productive, but it's been a dry winter. No snowfall, only a little rain. The earth gets thirsty at a time like this, just before growing season. She and her family have enough, but she's seen enough of their neighbors going hungry in recent years to shrug off the threat of drought.

So she walks, and she watches the sky, and she hopes. What else can a woman do, in this land where all the battles have been fought and lost?

Today

Like six hundred and fifteen other Black children, three hundred and seven of them Black girls like her, May Simpson goes to Chapel Hill High School. Unlike the six hundred and fifteen other Black children, and three hundred and seven other Black girls, May Simpson is in three advanced placement and two honors classes. She maintains a perfect grade-point average and is shooting for a full scholarship at the University of North Carolina.

May does not want to be a trailblazer, a defier of stereotypes, an inspiration. After fifteen years of being told by every teacher that she doesn't need to push so hard, and wouldn't she be more comfortable in the regular classes, and Advanced Placement is really for, you know, college-bound kids, she'd like to let all those words sink in and stop her.

She is acutely conscious that she isn't, in fact, particularly special. Sure, she's smart. There are lots of other smart Black girls, too. She's not better than any of the kids who had their potential denied because of the color of their skin, not back when Chapel Hill High was segregated and her parents had to attend classes all the way across town in a windowless building that's now the district administrative office, and not now when the "honors" class might as well come right out and call itself the "white" class, enshrining separate-but-officially-not-equal into the laws of the town where she lives.

What May has is a mother who will not let her give up. Her mother always says, "Do you know what we went through so that you could get an education? You're going to get every second of it you can, and I don't care if those little white girls hurt your feelings."

And they do hurt her feelings. Not just the little white girls, who are relentlessly staring at her body (which they find to be too big and too Black), who touch her hair from the seat behind her in Mrs. Stevenson's sixth period English class. But also the little white boys, who kick her desk, who trip into her and squeeze her ass, only half-bothering to pretend it's an accident, and the white men and women, the teachers who assume she's come to the wrong classroom, and the parents who ask if she's sure she doesn't want to focus on sports instead of doing speech and debate.

She feels like she ought to be hardened to these things. As her mother says, she comes from a long line of people who've endured a lot worse than funny looks and unwanted touches.

Thinking of it that way doesn't help a bit, as it turns out. Certainly not when the college acceptance letters start coming in, and hers pile up on her desk: UNC. Duke. Howard. Vanderbilt. Emory.

She'd keep it to herself, but the school newspaper prints an article about the scholarship she received. May can feel the white anger simmering around her, the dangerous heat of the entitled.

She expects the violence before it erupts. Some of them wait for her outside the cafeteria after lunch. This is barely about her, and it's not the first time.

They twist her arm and kick her shins and break her nose. She cleans up the blood in her car and doesn't tell anyone, not even her mother. She doesn't care to see the look of guilt, nor of resignation.

It's all healed by graduation, anyway, and if she enjoys the green, sick looks on their faces when she's named valedictorian, well, that's her own business.

Yesterday

Kit's children are playing in the field nearest the house. She's not sure what the game is—some sort of complicated maneuver including the tossing of rocks and a good deal of running about like wild beasts—but they're laughing madly. She shouts at them to make sure their chores are done, and they ignore her.

They're good children, though, really. Elisabeth, the oldest at eleven, is an angel, obedient and quiet, quick with a needle and always happy to mind her siblings. She's not a pretty girl, is the only trouble, but she's a good one. She'll be all right, Kit tells herself. In a few years, they'll find a nice, steady fellow for her, perhaps an older man with the sense to not worry too much about looks.

Stevie, named for his father, is a rambunctious eight-year-old. He gets in as much trouble as he can, but she keeps an eye on him. Nothing too bad can happen to a child with a watchful mother. Myrtle, her baby, is only three, toddling furiously after her siblings.

They'll grow up in a time of peace, and that's the important thing. A good, Christian home, and no fear of the country breaking in two again, the way it had when Kit herself was a girl. They'll have good lives ahead. And she'll leave them this land she's walking on, to give them a start.

It's not much, but it's the best she can do for them.

Today

Zabitha Stoker is only nine years old. This sort of thing (the doctors call it premature puberty) happens more and more these days. Her grandmother, who is an old Carrboro hippie, says it's hormones in the milk. Her mother, who got really into Jesus when Zabitha was a baby, thinks it's the sinfulness of the world.

Either way, Zabitha Stoker is nine years old. She has a Moana backpack of which she is enormously proud, which she takes to third grade with her every day. She has sneakers that light up. She has never had a thought about kissing a boy, other than to conclude that it would be disgusting.

What she does have is her period.

She doesn't know it's called that. In Chapel Hill, sex education doesn't start until the fifth grade. It consists of children being bussed to a nondescript brick building called "The Poe Center," where boys and girls are separated and they are taught the basic biological mechanics of puberty. (When that day comes, fourteen months after Zabitha begins to menstruate, her mother will not sign the permission form for her to go. She will say her daughter can learn anything she needs to know about "all that" at home.)

At nine, Zabitha knows nothing. She doesn't know what those parts of her body are called, much less why there is blood pouring out of them. She tries to staunch it with toilet paper, with old underwear, with paper torn out of magazines. She wakes up in the middle of the night to wash her sheets in the sink. At school, she stands up from her desk and finds a pool of red where she had sat, tries to scrub it up with the sweater she now always wears knotted around her waist.

Eventually, her mother catches on. She finds the piles of blood-stained clothes hidden in the garbage. She tells Zabitha off (wasteful, filthy, can't you control yourself) and hands her a box of pads. No further instruction is provided.

"Congratulations," her mother says tonelessly to her the next morning. "You're a woman now."

But she isn't a woman. She's a nine-year-old girl. She doesn't understand why she should be glad to be told she's something that she's not. She doesn't understand why men, grown-up men, are starting to look at her now, at the parts of her chest that are changing shape and that are sore all the time. She doesn't understand why she would want to be a woman.

She doesn't understand why her body is bleeding. She doesn't understand why the bleeding keeps coming, every month.

Yesterday

Everything looks well enough around the property line, Kit thinks to herself, with no small measure of satisfaction. There was some sign of fox tracks the other day, but, though she searches carefully for them, they are no longer there. That's reassuring.

They can scarce afford to lose the chickens. They'll go hungry without the eggs.

She spots a few places where the fence could use some mending. She'll tell Stephen to do it when he gets back to the house tonight. Winter is a good time for such things. It's a lot of work, keeping a farm running. But in winter, when none of the cash crops are growing, that's when you get a chance to look at a break in a picket fence, a stone that needs to be hewn out of a field, a creaky stair to the porch. It's a quiet time, a peaceful one.

It's a quiet, peaceful life that Mrs. Kit Laseter enjoys, whatever the time of year. Even in high summer, when the farm is buzzing with hired hands and she's got her hands full keeping the children out from underfoot while she tries to keep all the men fed.

Has she ever wished for something else? Maybe. Maybe when she was a girl, there was a part of her that longed for adventure and excitement, that thought she might fall in love, or cut her hair short and go for a soldier, or never marry and become a maiden poetess. Something like that.

But never seriously. Never more than in a passing fancy, and it's easy enough to let those pass.

Today

Maureen McDonagh has educated, sophisticated parents who teach at the university, so they haul her off to the psychiatrist when she starts cutting herself. They believe in science, and that mental illness is a disease, and that it can be cured with the correct doses of talk therapy and psychotropic medication.

The psychiatrist is a cheerful, chubby woman in her late forties who lines the walls of her office with brightly illustrated books about self-acceptance. She introduces herself as Susan. She teaches cognitive behavioral therapy techniques. She asks questions about Maureen's parents. She prescribes a succession of pills with ridiculous names.

Maureen doesn't even try to tell her the truth. She wouldn't have the words for it if she did. No, she says, no one picks on her at school. (No one looks at her at all. Last week, she tried to sit with some of the neighborhood girls at lunch, and they didn't even look at her. They just laughed, and laughed, and laughed, until she got up and took her tray to a table where she ate alone). Yes, she feels safe at home. (She got a B+ on a math test and her dad spent all week making jokes about disowning her. He was just joking. She knows this because he said it, *I'm just joking,* again and again, while she stared blankly down at the 91 on top of the paper that was the best that she could do). No, she doesn't know what's wrong. (Her skin doesn't fit on her body right. Sometimes it feels like the razor could cut it loose again, and she could put herself back together right).

Maureen's mother makes her roll up her sleeves and hold out her arms before school every day. She checks the cuts, makes sure they're healing, monitors carefully for new ones. She purses her lips as she does this. Maureen can tell that she's angry. (When she is older, she will recognize that it was fear, not disgust, in her mother's eyes. At fifteen, she sees only the anger.

Eventually, Maureen solves her own problem. She walks to an art supply store and buys special, very sharp blades for the purpose. She tapes them to the inside cover of her favorite novel, *Dune,* and places it carefully on the shelf until they're needed. She starts cutting only on her inner thigh, up high, close to the groin. It's more dangerous and less satisfying than cutting on the arms, but it's also invisible. The pain bubbles out alongside the blood. She doesn't tell the therapist, or her parents. She smiles and tells them that she's doing better. She tells her friends that her parents are so annoying, that they just can't possibly understand what it's like to *feel* the way Maureen feels, the deep agony of being fifteen.

She doesn't tell anyone: *I wish you would catch me, even though I'm doing the best I can to hide this. I wish you would help me, even though I push you away. I wish you would staunch the bleeding.*

Yesterday

It's right around four o'clock when the rain starts. In the summer, it thunderstorms at this time near every night, but winter rains are rarer, usually longer. It's getting dark, so Kit's most of the way back to the house, but she stops and takes shelter under a tree. Lord knows she has walked these acres enough times that she'll find her way back well enough in the dark.

Her back against the cold trunk of the winter pine, Kit watches the rain fall. There's something strange about it. She notices the texture of it first. It looks thicker than rain ought to be, heavier. Around here, it snows maybe two or three times a year, not more, but it's not unusual to get a little hail.

She doesn't worry 'til she sees the color of it. She thinks it's a trick of the light. Something to do with the sunset, even though the sky is gray, tinting the rain a color it shouldn't be.

But it isn't. She looks to where it's starting to puddle, right around the post of the fence that needs fixing.

The red, *red* puddle.

Today

Does it need to be said—the other reason that girls bleed? Sometimes it's wonderful. Sarah-Alice Jones, 17, in the back of her boyfriend's truck, right after the prom. Leanne McHale, 15, behind the bleachers. Doreen Yu, on her eighteenth birthday, because her girlfriend didn't know to clip her fingernails short first. Rosie Saperstein, 19, who *likes* it like that, rough and quick on the blue mattress of her dorm bed.

Sometimes it's not. Haeyun Kim, 15, with her boyfriend, also in the back of his car, but saying, then screaming, no, stop, I'm not ready. Marlena Perez, 17, during cross-country practice, when she went off-trail with six runners from the boys team. Dorie Peters, age 7. Rylie Somers, 16, who goes home and slits her wrists afterwards.

More often it's somewhere in between. Girls who say no, who say wait. Do they say no because they're not supposed to want, or do they say yes because it's not polite to say no? Often, even they do not know.

Either way, they bleed.

From *The North Carolinian* Newspaper

On February 25, 1884, Mrs. Kit Lasater, "noted for truthfulness," was walking near her home in the New Hope township of Chatham County when she heard what she thought was a hard rain fall. Glancing up she saw only clear sky but when she glanced down she saw what appeared to be the aftermath of a "shower of pure blood."

None of the liquid had fallen on her but it had drenched the ground and surrounding trees for some 60 feet (some accounts say yards) in circumference from the spot where she stood. Upon hearing her story, neighbors rushed to see for themselves and, when later interviewed, confirmed the story as related by Mrs. Lasater.

Samples were collected and sent to Dr. F. P. Venable, a professor at UNC, for evaluation. By mid-April he addressed the topic to the Mitchell Scientific Society. In every test performed except one, the conclusion was the same. The samples appeared to be blood. Venable could offer no explanation beyond the results of the tests...

Southern Truths

Watching Public TV in the South

Gary Bloom

I'm in a prefabricated tinfoil motel
channel surfing in this reliably right-wing Southern state
landing on the local public station
hoping for a respite from NASCAR
and Crimson Tide
but finding a woman in military camouflage
holding up the antlers of a deer
so the deer's eyes can meet the camera
and her smile is as broad as the deer's rack
while a few camouflaged men snap pictures
of this proud moment—
a dead deer,
a woman with a rifle,
blood everywhere.

Southern Truths

In the Darkness, Defending the Wall

Allan Dyen-Shapiro

The scraggly-haired thirtysomething claiming to be the boy's mom pushed her ID through the intake window. Sure, it looked real, as best Stacey Whitman could tell with most of the fluorescent light bulbs out or flickering, but Stacey wasn't taking crap from anyone. If the youngster wasn't responsible enough to carry his Greater Orlando ID card, the mom should have him chipped. She looked past the mom at the dirty brown kid. God only knew what diseases the kid carried. It didn't matter, no card, no admittance.

Yet, like a rash on a hot day, the pushy pain-in-the-behind woman refused to go away. "Please, Miss. He left his card at his dad's house. We're divorced. He's been coughing up yellow gunk and running a fever all week— "

"So, you thought you'd bring him here and infect our doctors and nurses?" *The nerve of this bitch.* Stacey sat up straight in her chair and adjusted her white pleated scrub top to maneuver the badge with her job title into the woman's line of sight. "How do I even know for real you are the mom?"

Even if the kid got his skin color from his father, you'd expect a few of Mom's features. These two didn't look at all alike. "I'll bet he's an illegal." She fixed her gaze on the "mom." "You a coyote?"

The dirt on their jeans might have come from crawling through a tunnel dug underneath The Wall into one of the hard-to-patrol, forested areas of Greater Orlando. It would explain the unwashed pair's pine-needle-and-animal-droppings odor.

Now, the woman was sniffling, and her body shook. *What an actress.* Obviously, someone had paid this *starlet* to smuggle a Tampa refugee into Orlando.

Stacey didn't hate the urchin because he was dark-skinned—she was more liberal than the other intake nurses. It wasn't his fault a hurricane had destroyed San Juan, that the destruction of municipal sewer systems had infected most of the kids with cholera and overwhelmed Tampa with displaced PRs. Nor was it his fault the Gulf had kept rising and collapsed Tampa's dikes.

Illegals snuck over and under The Wall into Orlando during the city's blackouts. Not enough money to maintain the grid, the mayor had said. Any one of them who got through could cause an outbreak that would kill Stacey, her mom and dad, and her neighbors. Public health workers like Stacey were the city's last line of defense.

"I'm an Orlando resident." The lady grasped the counter with both hands and gulped a few breaths. "Born right here. I had a job with Disney as an industrial engineer before the parks closed. Now, I'm a librarian. Look at my card—all there."

A glance at her screen sufficed to verify these statements.

"My ex-husband repairs air conditioners—he has his own business. This is our son." She placed a hand on his shoulder.

They'd let a few browns stay in Orlando. Somebody had to fix stuff. The story was plausible. "So, he ain't been outside The Wall?"

The woman shook her head. "And his symptoms aren't the ones you'd see with a virus. The fever is too high. And with most of the viruses, you cough up blood. The yellow mucus makes me think it's bacterial pneumonia."

It would still be breaking the law to admit the kid without his ID card. Stacey was reaching for the button to call security to escort them out when the runt's scream stole her attention.

"Mama," he yelled in a Puerto Rican accent. His gaze focused not on the librarian, but on a different woman, whom a guard was frog-marching across the lobby toward the security wing. That lady's skin was even darker than the boy's.

Just as Stacey had suspected. She returned her eyes to the coyote. "I thought you said *you* was his momma."

The scraggly-haired woman didn't respond.

They could have forced Stacey's head into a vise and tightened the screw, and it wouldn't have triggered any worse of a headache than the brat's high-pitched screaming did. He made such a racket that the rent-a-cop brought his prisoner over to Stacey's window and let her hug her offspring.

After the boy calmed down, the woman who'd been talking to Stacey gazed into the other one's eyes. It was only for a moment, but Stacey understood what *the look* meant. The surprised expression on the guard's face told Stacey he, too, now knew the pair's secret.

"You know that sort of thing is illegal," Stacey whispered.

The fake mother spoke in a hushed tone. "I'm sick of hiding. I lied to you about a husband—this is my wife. Pedro is our son. So, if you want to turn us in, go ahead, but please let Pedro see a doctor."

They'd exiled the gays. Forced them outside The Wall. At least it's what had happened to Stacey's older sister. Mom and Dad had turned Donna in, telling Donna she was no longer their daughter. Stacey had never said anything about it, but she'd thought they were wrong. Every once in a while, Stacey posted an old family photo to Facebook, secretly hoping Donna would see it and know she was still loved.

The cop pulled a radio from his belt and barked into it. "False alarm. The suspect hiding in the bushes was avoiding her husband. She isn't an illegal." When he received an acknowledgment from the dispatcher, he returned the device to his belt. "My brother was gay. A mob beat him to death."

The cop turned to Stacey. "Willing to let this go? You'll avoid a lot of paperwork."

Stacey nodded and admitted the child without entering anything into the computer. The women held hands as a nurse led them to the other end of the ER and pulled a privacy curtain closed around them.

Stacey's heart raced. She'd never defied the law before, and man, did it feel good. Too bad she couldn't tell anyone. Too bad she couldn't tell Donna.

But darn it, if she ever saw folks treated unfairly again, she'd help them too.

A few hours later, the family of three left with a prescription for antibiotics.

The rest of the evening got dull. Stacey savored the sweetness of her once-a-shift, employer-provided diet soda—a pricey perk allowed to anyone who had worked at the hospital for more than five years. She found herself watching the network news program on the big screen in the empty waiting room. The guy they were interviewing talked about how to spot coyotes who snuck illegals into Orlando to use the taxpayer-funded city services. He said the coyotes studied folks' social media and found secrets. Artificial intelligence (whatever that was) discovered the best way to trick unsuspecting, loyal citizens by playing on their sympathies.

Sure as heck wouldn't happen on my watch. Stacey gritted her teeth. She was always on guard, always looking out for anyone different. You can't be too careful about folks who aren't like you.

An hour before the end of her shift, the power went out. Stacey sat alone in the darkness.

Southern Truths

The Prodigal Sin

Tom Howard

Tim drove through Virginia's countryside, searching for a small-town hotel to spend the night. He was in no hurry to rejoin his trophy wife in Richmond. After finishing an aggressive court case, he often wandered, lusting for something he couldn't explain to his therapist. The big paycheck, the mansion, the beauty queen, and the hot mistress should have been enough, but it didn't satisfy him. It never did.

He entered the village of Serenity, identified by a faded sign and composed of several rundown houses and a trailer park. He stopped and pumped gas at the combined service station and store. He didn't know how these places stayed open selling gas, worms, and packaged muffins.

A cherry-red pickup with giant tires and a blaring stereo pulled in behind him, and a brunette wearing a halter top and cutoffs jiggled from the passenger side into the store. Her boyfriend, a tall, lanky lad in a dirty baseball cap, pumped his gas and stared at Tim.

Entering the store, Tim encountered shelves containing hardware and canned goods. A pot-bellied man at the counter conversed with the girl in the abbreviated outfit, his eyes never rising above her collarbones.

"Need help finding anything?" an old woman asked. She stopped stocking bags of chips.

"Bathroom, a sandwich, and a drink," he said, "and to pay for the gas."

"Restrooms are outside. Sandwiches in the last case. Skip the tuna fish."

She shouted at the front, "Pa! Tell the Whore of Babylon to pay for her cigarettes like everyone else."

"Yes, Ma." He smiled at the girl. "Sorry. You heard the boss."

The young woman pulled soggy bills from her top, picked up the pack of cigarettes, and left.

"She paid, Ma." Pa wiped his brow with a dirty handkerchief.

"Great. Her boyfriend just drove off without paying for his gas again."

Tim chose a ham sandwich and a soda and carried them to the counter. "And twenty dollars in gas," he said.

Pa stared out the door with a vacant look as if the Babylonian would return and grace him with more cleavage.

"Oh, yeah," Pa said. "She's something, isn't she?"

"She is," Tim agreed, sure he didn't mean Ma.

"You old perv." She tossed an empty cardboard box at her husband. "Sooner or later, the sheriff is going to lock you up."

"Double D Danvers can lock me up anytime," Pa said. "I'll put the kid's gas on his dad's tab. The mayor likes his high and mighty image and always pays."

Ma turned to Tim. "Are you visiting someone in Serenity?"

Pa chortled. "Ma's the worst gossip in town. If you spend any time here, mister, she'll know all about you. What she can't find out, she'll make up."

"I'll give folks plenty to talk about if you don't keep it in your pants, old man," she began but stopped when the bell above the door jingled.

The young woman in a white sundress who entered looked as out of place as a rose in a dandelion patch. The blonde, her hair down and feet bare, brightened the room when she entered.

"Afternoon, Miss Hope," Ma said.

"Afternoon." Hope smiled at Tim. "Hello."

"Hello." He took his change from Pa, trying not to stare. Hope looked pretty in a young, unvarnished way with flawless skin, vivid blue eyes, and full lips. Not his type.

"Pickle relish," she said, "and plums if you have any. Today is P Day." She giggled, and Tim wondered at her mental age. She brushed by with a wicker basket on her arm. Ma scurried after her as if Hope were royalty, helping her find things that started with P.

"Is she all right?" Tim asked.

"Oh yeah." Pa placed the purchases in a bag. "Her mother, Dora Price, owns most of Serenity."

Tim could've bought a bigger town with only one of his offshore accounts.

"Is there somewhere in town I can stay tonight?" Tim asked. He hadn't planned on stopping, but it would be dark soon, and he wasn't in a hurry.

While Pa gave him directions to the rental cabins at the edge of town, Ma returned to the front counter.

"It's a shame." She shook her head. "Dora works Hope like a slave while she sits up there with her binoculars, watching everything we do. If the mailman has a nip between rounds, Dora complains to the post office. Heaven help us if anyone cusses on the Sabbath."

Pa chuckled and handed Tim the bag. "Better leave while you still can, stranger. Soon Ma will be talking about you like she does the other lost souls in this town. And don't let Mrs. Stevens overcharge you for the cabin."

"Stevenses?" Ma asked. "There's a marriage made in hell. Blanche has the first dollar she ever made renting out those cabins, and Billy hasn't moved from in front of the television for forty years. Avarice and Sloth, those two."

"Thank you." Tim headed for the door.

When he left the bathroom, a tall man in a black trench coat stood across the street and glowered at him. Part of his jaw was missing. A former smoker? As Tim drove away, he recalled the cigarette companies he'd defended and how much they'd paid him.

He spotted a picnic area at a small lake and stopped to unpack his dinner at a concrete table. The nearby trashcan over-flowed with beer bottles.

The calm lake shined like a mirror in the late afternoon sun. An old house, gray and solitary, crouched on a hill across the lake. Hope's mother must watch the town from there. He'd forgotten her name. Dinah? No, Dora. Dora Price.

He ate his ham sandwich, contemplating the strange town and the colorful occupants he'd seen so far.

Something crunched on the gravel behind him. He jumped, frightened that the man with the damaged face had followed him. Instead, Hope appeared through a gap in the hedge, carrying her wicker basket. "I call it Lake Lethe."

She sat on the table. "It's not the real Lethe, of course. Do you know the tale?"

"The river where people go to lose their memories? Or is it the one where you had to pay the ferryman to cross?"

She giggled. "The first one. That's not the entire legend, you know. Whoever lost their memories always returned for them. Even if they didn't know they'd lost them."

Interesting. "Are you heading home?" he asked.

"Yes. Mother will want to know all about you." She smiled. "Do you like my teeth?"

"Sorry?" he asked.

"My teeth. My mother says they're okay, but I think they could be straighter."

"They look fine."

"You're from the city, aren't you? I want to go, but Mother says I'm too young." She laughed as if she'd said something funny.

"It's a rat race," he said. "I escape from it occasionally to clear my head." His therapist said part of him was missing, and he searched for it.

"Mother says she can't leave, but maybe someday I can. After they all come back. They have to, you know. They can't help themselves."

"Who?" A cool breeze made him shiver.

"Did you know Pandora's box wasn't a box?" she asked.

"I didn't know that." He found following the young woman's erratic train of thought a challenge.

"The translator got it wrong. He thought the word *pyxis* meant box, but it means jar."

"You're well educated," Tim said. "And your name is Hope, like the last spirit left in the box, I mean, jar."

"Yes," she said. "They got that right."

"I'm a lawyer. My name is Tim Gore."

"Gore?" she asked. "Like blood and gore? I asked mother to take me to see Mr. Evers when a truck hit him, but she wouldn't."

"The funeral director wouldn't be a tall man with a scarred face?" he asked. "I think I saw him in town."

"Oh no," Hope said. "That's Mr. Evers. Would you like to walk around the lake with me?"

"No, thank you. I'd like to reach Stevenses' cabins before dark." He packed his half-eaten sandwich and unopened soda into the bag.

"You must join me and my mother tomorrow for lunch." Hope placed the basket on her arm. "She'll be happy to see you again."

He felt a sudden urge to flee this strange town and its odd occupants, but he didn't know why. The next town couldn't be far.

Hope hopped off the table. "Welcome to Serenity, Mr. Gore." She held out her hand.

He shook it. "Thank you, Miss Price."

"Don't worry. You can't help yourselves. You have to come back."

The picnic area had turned dark and cold. "I'd better be going."

"Yes. Tomorrow is Q Day. It's always hard to buy things that begin with Q. See you at lunch."

"I hadn't planned to stay here another day," he said. "I should be getting home. My wife will be worried." He lied. Her personal trainer occupied most of her time.

"We'll see. Don't let Mrs. Stevens charge you for extra towels."

As a dark cloud blotted the last of the sun's rays, she disappeared through the hedge.

Taking his bag, he returned to his car. Serenity seemed more ominous in the darkness.

~~~

In the morning, Tim needed caffeine, perhaps a complete transfusion. When he'd left the picnic area the evening before, he'd considered driving to the next town and finding a posh hotel, but the individual Stevenses' cabins with their windows of amber light looked inviting.

Mrs. Stevens had handled his credit card as if she smelled week-old fish, but the cabin had a good rate. He didn't pay for the extra towels. The cabin held a big bed, and he threw himself into it.

He slept fitfully, and in his dreams, various Serenity citizens pursued him around the room. First, Hope tried to coax him into a bronze jar, then Mr. Evers appeared and attempted to give Tim leprosy. If he hadn't tripped over stacks of Tim's money while chasing him, Tim would've woken up diseased or dead.

Then, Ma and Pa took turns pulling him into a giant sausage grinder. He woke often and felt like a victim in a bad horror movie. He wrestled with sweaty blankets until the sun came up.

He took a long hot shower, and his skin glowed red when he stepped out. He expected to find leper's scabs and wished he'd gotten extra towels. The room had no coffee maker, so he checked out on his way back to Pa and Ma's.

Mrs. Stevens gave him his receipt with the phone in her ear. She talked to Ma about how Tim had spent the night alone as if he weren't listening.

Ma had called the Stevenses Avarice and Sloth. Considering Ma and Pa personified Gossip and Lust, how could she throw stones?

Outside, he breathed deep to clear his head. Lack of sleep left him feeling fuzzy. Who would he meet in Serenity today? Gus, the Sadistic Dentist? Edith, the Homicidal Housewife? Wait, being sadistic wasn't a vice, but murdering someone was a crime.

Pulling up at Pa's, he nodded at creepy Mr. Evers across the street and entered the store.

"Morning, Mr. Gore," Pa said. "Did you have a good night?"

"Coffee," he muttered. "Strong and hot."

"Against the back wall. I just made a fresh pot. Bed not comfortable?"

"It was fine." He found the largest Styrofoam cup in the stack and filled it to the rim. It smelled wonderful.

Ma appeared from the back. "Hope has already been in this morning. She said you'd been invited to lunch at the big house."

"Better be careful," Pa said with a leer. "The old lady's a widow. You might not make it back to the big city."

Tim stared out the window at Mr. Evers' shadowy figure. He'd moved from across the street to the gas pumps. "What's with Mr. Evers? He's been staring at me since I arrived."

Ma joined him. "He's not been right since a truck hit him. Knocked him fifty feet off the road."

"And he lived?"

"We're tough around here," she said. "Sugar?"

"No, thanks." He blew on his coffee. "Why is he staring at me?"

"He doesn't like strangers," Pa said from the counter. "He's looking for whoever hit him."

Tim shook his head. "Do you have cinnamon rolls? Mrs. Stevens doesn't serve breakfast."

"Over here," Ma said, "but don't eat too much. Hope has been cooking all morning."

"About that," he said. "I think I'm heading home before lunch. I've stayed longer than I intended already."

"Hope will be so disappointed," Ma said. She didn't seem sad or surprised by his news. "Cream?"

"No, black is fine." He selected a packet of cellophane-wrapped cinnamon rolls and didn't look at the expiration date. Although Ma hadn't been upset that he was leaving, he hated disappointing Hope.

The bell rang, and for a minute, Tim thought Hope had returned, but a rotund man in a dirty lab coat entered. His smock showed streaks of dried blood. The neighborhood butcher?

"Doc!" Pa shouted. "How's it hanging?"

Tim would never have pegged the unhealthy-looking man with glasses and a comb-over as Serenity's doctor.

"Mr. Gore." Doc extended his hand. "I heard you were in town." With Ma as the town's public-address system, everyone probably knew Tim had put on clean underwear this morning.

He shook a puffy hand. "Doctor?"

"Walters." He pumped Tim's hand for too long. "Eugene Walters. Pleased to meet you."

"Thank you." He pulled his hand away and refrained from wiping it on his pant leg.

"Very pleased," Dr. Walters said. "You know, Mr. Gore, we've got an empty storefront beside my office with a nice apartment in the back. Make a good bachelor pad."

"Thank you," he said, surprised by his offer. Tim owned the largest law firm in Richmond. Did Serenity need a lawyer? "I'm heading home today."

"Right after he has lunch with Dora," Ma said.

"Very nice." Doc turned to Pa. "I came in for my daily pick-me-up."

"Got it right here." Pa pulled a brown paper bag from behind the counter. "I'll put it on your tab."

"Thanks. See you later, Mr. Gore." The doctor scurried from the store, unscrewing the bottle as he went. Tim understood now why Mr. Evers face looked like a freshly dug garden.

Ma shook her head. "He's a quack."

"I don't know," Pa said. "Maybe everyone doesn't need anesthesia."

"Yes, they do," Ma said.

Tim agreed with her. He paid for the coffee and rolls. "How do I get to the big house on the hill?"

Pa smiled. "Go back to the cabins and take the first left around the lake. It's the only house on the road."

"Thanks." He didn't know why he'd decided to visit Dora Price after all. A guy had to eat. Since he didn't need gas, he sat in the car and ate one of the rolls and chased it with coffee so hot it burned his tongue. At least creepy Mr. Evers had disappeared.

Tim should have left Serenity yesterday, but for some reason, he lounged around like he lay on the French Riviera. Tim considered buying the town just to bulldoze it.

After spending the morning sitting at the park reading yesterday's paper, he drove to the Price house. He'd tell Hope hello, have a quick lunch, and get back on the road. Not normally soft-hearted, lack of sleep and Serenity's strangeness had affected him.

"Mr. Gore!" Hope opened the frosted-glass door. He'd parked on the gravel drive, impressed by the Victorian house atop the hill. Although it looked unpainted from town, standing on the wraparound porch revealed a house painted battleship gray.

She wore the same sundress she'd worn the day before. "Please come in. I hope you like chicken."

"I thought this was Q Day," he said. "I expected quiche."

Her face fell. "I can start again."

"No. I love chicken."

The foyer opened into a formal parlor. Dark walnut paneling lined the walls. A woman in a wheelchair sat in the middle of the room, backlit by windows.

"Mr. Gore," Hope said, "I'd like you to meet my mother, Pandora Price."

"Pleased to meet you," he said. "Thank you for inviting me to lunch."

The old woman rolled forward. "You are welcome here, Mr. Gore." Her eyes appeared large behind her thick spectacles. Her hair, steel-gray, lay coiled in a tight bun atop her head. She reminded Tim of the woman on the Old Maid cards he'd played with as a child.

"If you'll push me into the dining room, Mr. Gore, we'll enjoy what Hope has prepared."

Lunch sat on the table. He placed the old woman at the table's head and sat opposite Hope. Neither woman said grace, and they served themselves.

"Delicious," he said after taking a bite. "Excellent roast chicken and vegetables, Hope."

She smiled. "If you give a person long enough, they can become an expert at anything, even cooking, Mr. Gore."

"You can't have been cooking that long." He took a sip of the burgundy. "You're too young."

Both women laughed.

"We age well in our family," Mrs. Price said. "Mr. Gore, what do you think of our little town?"

"It's very interesting," he said.

"You haven't met half of them," Hope said. "Some only come out at night."

Mrs. Price laughed again. "Don't scare him, dear. Give him time to adjust."

He'd only had one drink of the excellent burgundy, but he felt lightheaded. Perhaps his fatigue made him groggy. The ladies hadn't touched their drinks. He needed a long nap and a massage, far away from here.

"Pandora," he said. "That's an interesting name. Your daughter told me Pandora's box was really a jar."

"Yes," the old woman said. "Would you like to see it?"

Before he could answer, Hope rose and lifted a bronze jar from the nearby buffet. It glowed in the sunlight coming through the windows. Inlaid with orange and black underglazes, an intricate design encircled the container. From his seat, and in his muddle-headed condition, the pictographs appeared to be writhing bodies, not all of them human.

Hope caressed it. "Pretty, isn't it? Very old. Mother used to polish it with her blood. These days, I prefer wax. Would you like to touch it?"

The jar and the young woman's reverence toward it repulsed him. The image of her mother dripping her blood on it made the object even more surreal and unsettling.

He'd leave Serenity after lunch.

"You're smart, Mr. Gore," Pandora said. "Put the pieces together. A small town where everyone wears their vices like a hairshirt. You know what a hairshirt is, don't you?"

He nodded. One wore a rough animal hairshirt as a penance for their sins. "You believe you're the original Pandora and Hope from the Greek legend?"

"It's difficult to understand, Mr. Gore," Pandora said. "But in your heart, you know it's true."

"Don't you see?" Hope sat on the arm of his chair. "You're one of us."

He shook his head. "You can't be the Hope that Pandora found in the box after the vices and evils had escaped."

She removed the lid from the jar. Looking at it filled him with dread.

"Don't worry." She revealed the empty interior. "When you all return, it will be filled again."

Tim's head spun. These women were insane. Slowly, their words sank into his head: his desire for profit, his search for fulfillment always beyond his reach, his disappointment with life.

"We'll be free when everyone returns," Pandora said. "I'll have paid for my original sin of curiosity. Don't fret, Mr. Gore. You're stuck here with Disease, Strife, and Pain until all the other sins arrive."

"In the meantime," Hope said, "we'll have raspberries and radishes tomorrow."

If he could get up from the chair, he'd leave Serenity, but he couldn't move. He cleared his throat. "Who am I supposed to be in your psychotic game?"

Pandora stood from her wheelchair. "Greed, of course. Eternal, insatiable Greed. You'll fit right in here in Serenity. Won't he, Hope?"

Hope nodded. "He will. Mr. Gore, have I shown you my teeth?"

Southern Truths

The Southern Whyfors

JW Guthridge

George Bernard Shaw, the great Irish playwright, once observed that the English and the Americans are two peoples divided by a common language.

As someone born and raised in Arkansas, I have experienced this reality throughout my life. Language is the key to deciphering Southern culture. You cannot understand one without understanding the other.

For example, "Bless Your Heart" is probably the best recognized multipurpose Southernism. Don't believe me? Bless your pea-pickin' heart!

On its face it is a literal blessing given in recognition. It also gets used in a more condescending fashion, or worse, a subtle and dismissive assertion that one is not the sharpest tool in the shed. The intent of the speaker makes the difference. "God Bless you" or even "Bless you" are used in exactly the same way but are not heard as often.

Why do we express ourselves like this? It comes down to the rules of conduct we have set for ourselves. Someone who has manners yet chooses to use them to offend has weaponized their manners. This makes the un-ironic condescending use of "Bless your heart" understandable. It takes on the power of the more universal "Yes, dear," without implying intimacy.

More than just a means to cause offense, Southern manners is a set of rules to live by. One must overtly ignore the social lapses of others, as well as things one would prefer not to be true. That allows one to project a desire to avoid the scrutiny of one's own failings.

It is that in particular that strikes me as odd when it comes to the way Southern folks have treated and mistreated those who love differently. Gay culture in the South has its own set of rules, and the two sets are mostly congruent with each other. Only when the two sides struggle against each other that differences manifest. Until then, the polite refusal to acknowledge that which offends is the status quo. This is as Southern as pecan pie, but it is not confined to this topic.

~~~

Our love of food is not unique. Take a look at Canada's signature dish, poutine. The way in which we apply food to every problem is. Consider the Southern wake, where everyone brings something stuffed full of sugar, fat, and/or grease. These surplus calories are all but forced on everyone as if the food could fill the void in one's life left by the departed. It never does, but that does not stop us from trying!

So many things to talk about when it comes to food. It really lets the South's farming roots shine, pun intended. Smokehouse barbecue, deep-fat-fried everything, the blessing that is butter, and dishes that look at home at either the State Fairs or Fear Factor— the South is full of flavor.

Corn is a good example to study. Corn-on-the-cob, whole-kernel corn, creamed corn, popcorn, corn chips, hominy, grits, cornbread, and of course Karo. If you don't recognize the last one, it's a brand of shelf-stable high fructose corn syrup and is the magical secret ingredient that makes the body of pecan pie so gooey and sweet! Now, that's nowhere near a full list of what Southerners have done with corn as it's something of a wonder crop.

Legumes of all sorts are another staple. Most famous are the classic black-eyed peas, though baked navy beans with BBQ will give them a run for the top spot. Add bacon to a pot of black-eyed peas and you have a perennial favorite. Ever eat black-eyed peas and hog jowl on New Year's Day for good luck? I'm told this Southern superstition has made it out of the South in recent years.

There can be a social aspect to shelling beans or hulling nuts. A recurring memory of my youth was for several adults to sit around big brown paper grocery bags full of green pea pods or purple hulled pea pods, "cutting up and holding court" as the expression goes. It is mindless work done with the hands while talking, singing, or listening to others. Reach into the bag, grab a pod, crack or split the hull open and extract the peas within, discard the now empty husk, deposit the peas in a pot or basket. Rinse and repeat.

Pecan hulling is similar, everyone grabs a nutcracker and starts breaking open the hulls to extract the nut-fruits within. Oddly enough, not all the extracted pecans end up in the collection basket for some reason, and no I ain't talking with food in my mouth thank-you-very-much.

Too hot in the house to cook? Grab the cooler and fill it with soda and beer, and head for the creek. Pick up a watermelon on the way, and you have got a good start for a party. Watch the kids go nuts in the water, maybe even join them. As the afternoon yields to evening, listen as the symphony of nature plays its magnum opus as you dine. If the skeeters haven't driven you indoors yet, enjoy the stars coming out and later stories and songs around a fire.

Southerners feed people to be social, eat with others to be social, and feel our social best when we have a full belly while around others with full bellies. It is a part of our agrarian heritage. Food is wealth to a Southerner, it is the means by which we feel secure in our future. We will share our wealth without the slightest provocation. So think of this the next time you are at a Southern-style potluck, but remember, if you leave hungry it's your own dang fault!

~ ~ ~

Much of the South's history has been marred by concepts considered unspeakable today. The elephant in the room is racism. It is a pernicious cancer that resists being excised. The racism seen today is neither as brutal nor as overt as it was during Jim Crow, but it persists. Maybe in another generation we can finally put this stain on our history away for good.

I got to learn about this history first-hand when I entered the Little Rock school system for seventh grade in 1985. I was assigned to Horace Mann Junior High, the campus noteworthy for having been the Black high school in 1957 and was the specific school the Little Rock Nine fought successfully to avoid.

During my three years there, I suffered, more than half of my classes in classrooms not air-conditioned. Sitting in vintage school desks, sweating buckets in the heat, while trying to hear the teacher over the drone of box fans... I found it rather easy to sympathize with those who sought escape from a system of "separate but equal." The inequity of such seemingly innocuous policies has stuck with me.

Southern Truths

~~~

How is the Southern way different from other regional cultures? Curating our perceptions and cherry-picking our darling details. That is not uniquely Southern, the troublesome things we ignore and the darling details we do pick are. We suffer a tendency to refuse the truths that are our history, and this buttressed by our social traditions to overly ignore faux pas has combined to make healing difficult.

Today most Southerners find it too uncomfortable to look back at Jim Crow because they think it leaves them no path forward. Most agree it was wrong, few agree on how to fix it, and the ones that lived through that era are dwindling in number every day. Making things worse, revisionists make a living by keeping the topic too hot to be addressed intellectually.

We simply need to open our eyes and hearts to discover the power of justice and honesty. That will empower the South to rise again, spreading wings to fly away and leave behind the soiled nest of past crimes and hatred.

My father often told me that "mistakes are experience in disguise," so how can we learn from our failures if we ignore them? I fear that the South will repeat the doom of our past if we cannot.

We can soar without need of hate to lift us. The distinct flavor of Southern culture can survive. If we clean up our messes, acknowledge our mistakes, and learn from them we can keep on Whistling "Dixie"—figuratively, of course—into the bright future in store for us all, no matter where we are from. Bless your heart for listening, but if y'all will excuse me, I hear a cinnamon roll calling my name.

Southern Truths

Lot of Desert Between Us

Bill Parks

I leaned back and adjusted my boots on the porch railing. The shade and my sunglasses dimmed the summer sun just enough to make staring out into the desert bearable. I could see a plume of dust down the state route, but that's relatively normal for the middle of the day. Condensation wetted the sides of my faded red, white, and blue Koozie, and little rivulets streaked the gold star on the Lone Star can.

The car pulled into view around the bend. I sighed, took one last long sip, and set the beer into the cup holder on my blue camp chair. As the car approached, I stood up and watched my shadow spill into the dirt driveway.

The car pulled into the lonely driveway quickly, its tires losing traction for a fraction of a second. Several coats of dirt muted the silver paint and the windshield was a wiper-blade shaped peephole. I stood up and waved at the car furiously, stomping my foot as it stopped right in the open. The driver's door opened and I let out a frustrated shout.

"'Round back!" I stomped back up the stairs and grabbed my beer. I took another sip before I came unglued. The car door shut and the driver pulled behind the house in a puff of loose dirt. I banged my fist on the railing and felt it crack a little. *They're gonna get us all killed.*

The young woman driving the Civic turned the car off and dropped her face on her steering wheel. Her green sun dress was wrinkled and her mascara was running just a touch at the corners of her eyes. She was petite with dark hair cut short. Two women in the back, dressed in matching gray athletic gear, sat in silence. I watched them for a moment and then motioned for them to get out of the car.

"Well, I guess this is it?" the driver said to her two passengers. They waited silently.

"Good afternoon! Sorry for the theatrics outside, y'all, it's been a long day already and it ain't even noon." I used my best welcoming voice after I took a few calming breaths. "Please, bring your bags inside and we'll talk." The driver grabbed her purse and the two passengers grabbed matching black duffel bags. As the passengers moved into the light, I watched them quietly. *They match the photos; good. Not all of them had.*

"So... " the driver began and then trailed off as the three of them walked into my house's old living room. One beige sofa, a green recliner, and an old cathode-tube television pressed up against the wall greeted them. I plopped down in my recliner and inclined my hand toward the sofa. They sat. The two young women in gray huddled close together.

"So. How was the drive?"

"It wasn't what I was expecting, that's for sure," the driver replied quickly.

"How so? Were you stopped?"

"Three times!"

"Oh, good. OK. That's normal. Haven't run the route often, have ya?"

"No... sir."

"Please don't call me sir. I'm Jason and you're my guests. Did you get any questions that aren't on the list?"

"No, no we didn't. Oh, and I'm Stacey." Stacey settled back into her seat on the sofa, her tension easing visibly. The two women in gray looked at each other and then looked back at me.

"Please don't introduce yourselves, you two. That *is* what we provide, after all." I turned back to Stacey. "Were you questioned when you were stopped?"

"One officer asked what I was doing with them. I gave the third answer from the sheet and it sufficed," Stacey replied quickly.

"Third answer?" I sat forward in my chair and tried to hide my concern.

"Yeah, why?"

"Hmm. Just making sure. For tracking. Did you plan to go home today, Stacey?"

"I don't think I can make the drive again. I know it's just a couple hours, but... "

"That's fine. Please take the two manikins in the entry, put them in your back seat, and go about three miles back up the road, the way you came. Second house you'll come to, same side as mine, much bigger though. Stay in the car until you get in Jack's garage. Oh, and make sure to turn on the heaters in the manikins before you leave."

"Heaters?"

"Surveillance is getting tight. Bring 'em up to body temp in about 60 seconds, give your car the same signature as when y'all pulled in." I shrugged my sunburned shoulders and the lighter, unburned flesh peeked out from under my gray tank top as I moved. Stacey left and followed my directions mechanically. I sighed with relief as the car pulled out of the tiny semi-hidden spot behind my house.

"What... happens now?" one of the young women asked.

"Well, we can't leave 'til after dark. That's several hours and I'm guessing you wanna sleep?" I paused and waited for them to nod. "Well, you can make your way to the back room," I pointed to the visible door. "It ain't much, but it has a couple of beds and an attached bathroom. You're free to shower, sleep, or both, but please be dressed in the clothes provided by 8."

"Is that when we'll leave?"

"That's when I'll ask you to come back out so I can look you over." The women exchanged furtive glances. "To make sure that you'll be safe for the next leg. Don't worry, I'm the only one here until your ride comes, and I'll be out on the porch." They both let out their breath and darted to the back room.

I grabbed my laptop off the kitchen counter and went back out on the porch. I replaced my empty beer with another from the small fridge next to my chair and took a long drink. I logged into my VPN and tested the connection. *Perfect.*

I typed rapidly and sent a brief message: "mongoose." In seconds I received a reply: "cobra." I cracked my back and neck and disconnected the laptop. I put it away before settling into my camp chair.

Hours passed as I read my newspapers, starting with the *Houston Chronicle* and working through *The Washington Post, The Wall Street Journal,* and *The New York Times.* I grabbed another beer after a bit, but I wasn't in a hurry to finish it. After a while, I heard a whirring sound and pulled my shotgun closer to my chair, my hand resting on it lightly.

Light reflected off a silver orb as it zipped into view. I picked up the shotgun, made sure it was loaded, and put it on my lap. I pulled the *Times* back up to my face while I waited. The orb slowed as it approached the house, flitting to a stop at eye level just off the porch.

"Good morning, Mister."

"Just call me Jason. And you are?"

"Rico13020213, but you can call me Thirteen, Mr. Jason." I sighed loudly enough for it to hear me. "May I ask you a few questions?"

"That depends. Right now, you're trespassing."

"I'm here to make inquiries of the resident. I believe that this is an exception to trespassing laws."

"Then inquire, Thirteen."

"I'm employed by Rico & Sons to provide information regarding illicit behavior."

"That's not a question."

"Did you have visitors to your residence earlier today?"

"I did."

"What for?"

"They were lost and dehydrated. I let them cool off and sent them on their way."

"All of them?"

"Yes."

"Do you know any of their names?"

"Hmm. Nope, I didn't ask and they didn't offer. It's been... " I made a point to check the clock hanging above the fridge. "Four hours now?" I waved a calloused hand at the clock, hoping to emphasize my point, and kept staring at the orb from behind my sunglasses.

"Where were they headed?"

"Well, I sent them up the road to the Shell for directions. I wasn't quite certain where they're headed."

"Up the road? East or West?"

"The only Shell is East." I paused. "I've answered your questions, now it would be in your best interests to get off my property." I cocked the shotgun. The orb moved back toward the road. I cleared the shotgun, reloaded it, and returned it to its spot next to the fridge and sat back down. Another beer and a printed copy of *BBC News* passed the next hour. The sun set over the interminable desert, silhouetting the cacti and setting the hills aglow in brilliant reds and golds. An owl hooted as it woke up. I stretched and grabbed a bottle of water instead of beer.

Two black motorcycles zipped into the driveway, both hard to see in the growing dark. I waved as they parked behind the house. Doors slammed and boots tapped along the hardwood floors as I made my way to cook breakfast. Well, dinner, but it was the start of our real day. The house filled up with the smell of bacon, eggs, and coffee. I cooked quickly, humming along to "Gunpowder & Lead."

"Smells good, Jason," a tall woman, her skin dark against her black motorcycle jacket, commented, inhaling deeply.

"Lin, y'all know I can't send ya out there without somethin' ta eat!" I replied, turning the music down with my free hand.

"Mongoose? You sure about tonight?" Lin asked, obviously a little worried.

"Yeah. Mongoose. Got "cobra" back from the handlers, though."

"What in the hell... "

"We don't make that call. Where's Deb?" As if summoned, the second motorcycle rider walked into the kitchen, her boots conspicuously missing. "Ah, yes, no shoes in the house."

"No shoes in any house, Jason! So, I trust you, but gotta know. Mongoose? Cobra? What's going on?"

"Delivery got stopped three times. Nothing abnormal, but... she was prompted by the algo to give answer number three to "What are you doing?" It has popped six times in eight deliveries. That's got less than one percent probability. Maybe the algo is messing with the cops, maybe it knows something I don't, but maybe... "

"Maybe there's something there," Lin finished for him, comfortably.

"Yeah. I also got visited by a Rico AI drone. Not exactly out of pattern, but it was a bit testier than usual. Usually I'd chalk it up to commissions drying up, but... well, I've been drinking water for a while, just in case."

"Let's get them up soon. I said 8, but they should eat. They'll be happy when they smell bacon, I reckon," I chuckled as Lin poured five cups of coffee and then opened the door to the back room.

"Good evening, I'm one of your drivers, no need to be alarmed... but Jason's cooked up dinner. Or breakfast. Well, both for us," Lin laughed at her own joke. The two women walked out quickly. *They're both dressed already. Dossiers are correct, very easy lift tonight.* Everyone sat at the faded, light-colored dining table, scratched across its surface in several places. I heaped food onto all the plates and put the rest in the middle of the table.

"Lin... I think you should stop in Jal, and Deb runs Hobbs through Eunice."

"Why's that? Jal's clinic..."

"Just to the safe house in Jal. No time to switch clinics, anyway. Just get out of sight for a bit, long enough for Deb to get into Hobbs, and then you run to Hobbs."

"If you say so... "

"You're having me run Hobbs through Eunice? Why?"

"Split you up and still get you outta Texas quick."

"They spooked you good, eh, Jason?" Lin puts her hand on his back.

"Yeah. I'd rather run it myself in the truck, but I don't know if that'll do."

"We scurry, finish dinner, and scram. I'd rather stay together, though." I nodded at Deb as she continued. "Maybe you lead and we follow you together? That way you trip any traps. We ride behind you."

"You OK? Ain't like you to be rattled, J," Lin whispered.

"I'm fine. I just don't like having you and Deb both out there. Definitely not together."

"We've got this."

"But your son... "

"We're both coming back."

"Of course. Well, if anything happens, Uncle Jason... " Lin waved me silent. She strode into the living room and looked her passenger up and down. Satisfied, she depressed little buttons on all of their suits.

"What?" one of the passengers asked.

"Cooling. Against drone heat sensors. It'll last 'til we get across the line, at least." Lin jammed helmets on the two women, put her own on, and gave Deb's a little tap. Deb laced her boots with lightning dexterity and moments later we were ready. I popped my water bottle and coffee cup in the console and sped off into the night, Deb and Lin following well behind me. *Give us speed and silence to the border.*

The desert was quiet, and the small towns were mostly asleep. I was careful not to run any red lights or trip any speed sensors in the towns. I started to get comfortable as the dark enveloped my truck again. I drove unnoticed and alone through the desert. Suddenly, 18N lit up in red and blue *behind* me. *Shit.* I slammed to a stop.

Deb

I squeezed on my brakes and watched a couple of police drones descend to eye level. Lin slowed and stopped more gracefully. The patrol cars slid onto the highway from the scruffy brush on the side of the road, and a couple of deputies popped out of their cars. The sheriff himself popped out of the last car. I'd seen him on campaign flyers just last year.

"Good evening, ma'am," the sheriff said calmly as he approached Lin. "Where are you going?"

"On a ride, sheriff."

"Yes, yes, I see that. With a young woman. Well, a young fugitive."

"Fugitive?"

"Ah, yes, she's pregnant and we've been tipped off that both these women have an appointment at a clinic in Hobbs tomorrow morning. You aren't going to Hobbs, are you?" Lin didn't reply. The sheriff clicked his tongue and pulled Lin and her passenger off her motorcycle. "Well, you're under arrest."

"For what?"

He answered by pulling me and my passenger off my bike. I tripped over his boot and stumbled on the pavement.

"We'll read you the full charges at the station. For now, just remain silent, it'll be easier that way." He chuckled as he eased me into the waiting backseat of his patrol car.

I froze and watched Deb and Lin through my rearview mirror. I kept telling myself to breathe as I pulled my cell phone out of my dash. "Ackbar," I typed furiously into the message bar, and hit Send. The signal was weak, and I watched the spinning wheel attempt to send the message for what felt like forever. That's when

I heard the whirring. My truck's tires squealed as I hit the gas and raced down the desert highway. I heard the whirring over the engine, but I couldn't see a damn thing in my mirrors. *Where are they?* Suddenly, a soft thud caused my truck to swerve. I regained control by braking and wrenching the steering wheel wildly, but another thud as I rounded the next curve sent me flying off the road into a ditch. Everything went black.

A drone descended on the crash. A protrusion with a needle slid into my arm, stinging, and I could just barely read the drone's screen as it checked my blood alcohol content. The readout stopped at 0.04. I sighed. Then another needle slid into my arm. I shivered reflexively, painfully, as the reading ticked up, stopping at .21. My vision blurred.

"Dispatch, this is PD 614. We have a fatal crash, DWI, BAC .21 at time of crash. Subject DOA."

"Roger that, 614. DOA. Dispatching an ambulance to confirm."

"Bastards," I whispered as a third needle entered my arm.

Greater Expectations

Manny Frishberg and Edd Vick

The Candidate sat in his bed, considering ways he could further screw the snowflakes. He'd done so much when he was a governor: built walls, shipped migrants north, challenged voters, signed bills gerrymandering the hell out of his state. His campaign's mailing to registered Democrats with the wrong election date had been a classic. The memory cheered him up a little.

A sound came, waxing and waning, scratchy sounds of rustling newsprint, and magnetic tape being run through a recorder. The bedroom door flew open, and he heard the noise coming up the stairs, then straight toward his door. His face paled when a figure entered the room. Before his eyes was a translucent Richard Milhous Nixon.

"Hello, my fellow American," said the face.

"Who the hell are you?" said the Candidate. He glanced over at his wife, obliviously sleeping through the encounter. He glared at the specter. "I mean, I see who you're supposed to be. Is this some kind of virtual reality humbuggery?"

"Why do you doubt your senses?"

"Because," said the Candidate, "I've seen what Artificial Intelligence can do. I bet you're fake. Or I ate something past its sell-by date. There's more hologram than horror about you, whatever you are!"

He chuckled at his own wit, disappointed that the Nixon figure did not. Voters would have eaten it up. Then he noticed the long train of newspaper clippings and recording tape wrapped around the ex-President's wrists and ankles.

"Impressive, huh?" the specter said, rustling the chain. "I made it. Clipping by clipping, tape by tape. I'm here to let you know you can have one just like it."

"I can?"

"Sure. Just keep it up and you'll be where I am now." Nixon's face was sweating, little runnels sliding down and dripping onto the Candidate's duvet. "Anyway, let me get through this. You're going to be visited by three spirits."

"Wait, isn't that the plot of some old movie?"

"You will be haunted," insisted Nixon's ghost, "by three spirits. Expect the first tomorrow when the bell tolls one. Expect the second on the next night at the same hour. The third, upon the next night when the last stroke of twelve has ceased to vibrate!"

"I've got a state dinner tonight. Could we postpone? Or maybe I could take them on all at once? I have an opening at 8 p.m. next Tuesday." The Candidate picked up his date book, pencil at the ready. When he looked back up, Nixon was gone.

~~~

The following night, the Candidate remembered that Nixon had warned him of a visitation at one o'clock. When the appointed time arrived, there came the sound of hoofbeats outside the house, then a heavy tread. The

Candidate, starting up into a half-recumbent attitude, found himself face to face with his unearthly visitor.

"Are you the Spirit whose coming was foretold?" the Candidate asked.

"You bet your boots I am!" said Ronald Reagan. "I am the Ghost of Elections Past. Rise and walk with me!" He took the Candidate's hand. "Giddy-up!"

As the words were spoken, they passed through the wall and stood on an open interstate highway leading up a hill to a city. This was no ordinary city. All its buildings were gleaming white, reflecting the sunlight.

"I—I've dreamed of this," said the Candidate, squinting at its brilliance. "The Shining City on the Hill! America, the light and hope of the world."

"Yep." Reagan had donned a pair of aviator sunglasses. "Fantastic speech fodder, really gets the pulses racing." He gave his familiar folksy grin. Without taking a step, they glided along the highway to the city. Around them were people of all colors, working and playing together.

"Ah, here we are."

In front of them stood two twenty-somethings, a man and a woman. He was the Candidate and she his first girlfriend.

"I remember this," whispered the Candidate.

"You love another," said the girl.

"When have I said that?" said the Candidate-to-be.

"You didn't have to say it. It's there in a thousand signs. That Bible you carry everywhere. The public prayers. Going to church three times a week."

"Well, what of it? I'm supposed to love God."

The Candidate turned to the ex-President. "No, please. Take me away before she says it." But the Gipper waved him off. He was eating popcorn a piece at a time from a bag he'd picked off a nearby cart.

"There's no room left in your heart for me," said the girl. "You're too busy showing off your religion."

"Oh, so very cinematic." The popcorn having suddenly disappeared, the Gipper held his hands up in two L-shapes, framing the image of the girl walking away as with a movie camera. "Cut!"

The ex-President took his arm. The world whipped past them, until the Candidate found himself quite alone, sitting up in bed as the clock struck two.

~~~

Waking himself with an unusually loud snore, the Candidate did not have to consult his alarm clock to know it was 1 a.m. Taking care not to wake his devoted wife, he swung his feet to the floor and stood. He stared at the blackness through the windows of his governor's mansion, ready for whatever form the second spirit would inhabit.

He noticed a light coming from under the closed door. He crept to the door with trepidation, but from the other side, he heard children's voices and, when he opened the door, he was startled by bright lights and colorful paper creations festooning a public library's walls. A group of children sat cross-legged in a circle and a figure in a glittering ball gown sat on a half-size chair, a large picture book on her knee, showing it around the circle before reading a page.

Her eyelids were coated with a thick layer of sky-blue shadow, and she had comically long, black eyelashes. Above her eyes, her brows glittered silver; she had wide, cherry-red lips. The dense mask of flesh-pink concealer coating her cheeks and chin didn't quite hide dark stubble. She started to read, then stopped and looked over at the Candidate. *No, not* she! he realized in a flash. *This volunteer—or specter, or apparition—is a* MAN!

"I am Ruby Bridges," the figure read. "My work will be precious. I will bridge the 'gap' between black and white... and hopefully all people!"

"Wait," the Candidate cried out as the reader displayed the next pages, "Just what's that book about?"

"It's the autobiography of the six-year-old girl who desegregated the Louisiana schools in 1960," the reader explained.

"That's not allowed! It might make some *other* children think their parents and grandparents weren't perfect. Colored children... I mean the children of color had their own schools, ones that were closer to their homes, too. And some learned useful skills."

The reader stopped reading. From the folds of her festive dress, she drew two white children: well-fed and haughty. The pair stood at the reader's feet and clung to the sparkling garment.

"Spirit! Are they yours?" the Candidate demanded, one well-drawn eyebrow raised. "Are you sure you haven't met them? I'm certain their parents have taken them to some of your rallies. This boy is Hatred. The girl is Privilege."

"Must be the products of a good charter school," said the Candidate.

The reader just shook her head. "Clearly," she said, as she steered the Candidate back through the doorway into darkness, "you're not going to learn anything from *me* tonight."

"Groomer," the Candidate shouted. "You're sexualizing these poor innocents. Do you even have their parents' signed permission slips to be here reading to them?"

"Your loss, sweetie." The reader brushed her lips against the Candidate's, leaving a vermilion trail on his gaping mouth.

~~~

The Candidate shuddered as he awoke and shuddered repeatedly through the day as he remembered that stubble, those lips. He watched both the black-and-white and Technicolor versions of *A Christmas Carol,* and then *Scrooged* for good measure, trying to figure out the point.

Scrooge had turned into a Woke Socialist, giving away geese and stuff. Was *he* supposed to learn something of the sort from these encounters?

Surely not. His was the righteous way. Nixon had said he was doing a great job, and Reagan had praised his crusade. At least he was pretty sure that was what they'd done. But that woke crossdresser! He'd be damned if he had anything to learn from that thing! What he'd learned was that the sooner their kind was outlawed, the better.

Maybe they were all tests, sent by the Devil. If ghosts existed, then maybe God and his Nemesis did as well.

The Candidate drank coffee after 5 p.m. so he'd be plenty awake for the third spirit. According to the Dickens, this one was going to show him the future.

Sure enough, at the last stroke of midnight, the Candidate's room faded away. Before him in the gloom stood a tall figure in a long cloak, its face not visible.

"Am I in the presence of the Ghost of Elections Yet to Come?" the Candidate demanded.

The spirit said nothing still, but swung its cloak around, engulfing the Candidate in its darkness. Then the room dissolved into another scene: a different room, cavernous and gloomy, illuminated only by the Exit lights atop the doorways. Confetti and half-deflated balloons had been swept into piles and the hotel linens piled into laundry carts.

A lone figure sat at the table on the stage at the far end of the room, his head cradled between his elbows.

Even his wife and closest advisers had left him to face the rest of the night alone. On a giant screen behind the podium, a man in a white shirt and khaki pants was pointing to numbers beside pictures of the Candidate and his archrival.

"Spirit, I'm confused," the Candidate admitted. "Is that poor guy at the table me? Is this the future that *will* be, or only the shadow of what *might* be?"

The spirit just pointed at the scene playing out before them.

"... has won Ohio," the man in the khaki pants was saying. "And, with that, the Fox News Decision Desk has concluded that Malia Obama has been elected America's forty-eighth President."

The Candidate gasped and clutched at the spirit's robe. "Please, I can change," he said, giving his most photogenic smile. "I'll get better."

Hell yes, he could improve. He saw it so clearly, now. He could pass laws outlawing all those abominations, make sure children were brought up by married women—married to men, he amended. He could make all their great country's borders secure. "God bless *us!*" he shouted. "Everyone!"

The spirit guide standing beside him shook its head, slowly, hopelessly.

Faintly, there came a sound very much like a thousand TV pundits pontificating. The Candidate looked down to see a chain made of concertina wire and rejected ballots reaching for his leg.

Neighborhood Watch

Mike Wilson

It's the day after Thanksgiving in the time of COVID. Larry and Samantha are wrapping Christmas presents with CNN on in the background when they hear a knock. Larry looks at Samantha. She's puzzled, too.

"I'm expecting something from Amazon but it's not due for a couple of days."

Larry puts down the scissors, hauls himself up from the living room floor, and walks to the foyer. No Amazon truck, no package on the porch, but there's a flyer stuck inside the storm door.

Tonight! Rosemont Hills Neighborhood Watch Meeting. Rosemont Hills Clubhouse. Save the United States and the Constitution. Open Carry Invited. There's a picture of a soldier in riot gear that looks like Darth Vader. Larry returns to the living room where Samantha's writing a grandchild's name on a To-From tag.

"What was it?"

Larry hands her the flyer.

"'Open carry invited?' Is that like 'bring your own bottle?'"

"I think it means bring your own gun," he says.

They've read in the news how Trump supporters attend public events visibly armed, surround the houses of people Trump doesn't like, and shout threats. But it's unnerving to see such angry fire stirring in the mostly-white, liberal suburban neighborhood of Rosemont Hills.

"What's the purpose of this meeting?" Samantha asks.

"I don't know."

As if on cue, CNN launches into a story about right-wing militia storming a state capital, angry men threatening to kidnap the governor. Larry watches the footage, men chanting, some with rifles. He doesn't see police in the picture stopping them.

Larry returns to the front door, checks the lock. He's never done this before in the middle of the day. *Open Carry Invited.* Larry doesn't own a gun. He doesn't like guns. He wonders how many of his neighbors do. He decides to find out.

~ ~ ~

The meeting is in the Rosemont Hills community room, customarily the site of events like the neighborhood fair, where kids get their faces painted and play games, or storytelling hour for the toddlers, or the neighborhood Christmas party. But tonight, the room is filled with men as tense as juveniles at basketball tryouts. There's nary an African-American, Asian, or Latinx person in the room. Presumably these men live in Rosemont Hills, but Larry doesn't know any of them. Some stand in groups with acquaintances, sharing conversation occasionally punctuated with angry laughter. Others, like Larry, are alone, looking lost, or sitting in the metal folding chairs lined up in front of the lectern. Though it's the middle of the COVID pandemic and infections are skyrocketing, only Larry and one older man are wearing masks, and the older man quickly takes his off—the effect of peer pressure. Some folks wear Trump shirts or MAGA hats, but most are wearing drab colors—olive-green, gray, tan—or camouflage, or some kind of pseudo-uniform. Some have flag patches sewed on the shoulder, as many of them Confederate as American. About half have guns visible, everything from assault rifles to pistols holstered on the side or shoulder. Larry notices men checking out what their neighbors are carrying to see how their own weapons compare.

"Okay, let's get this show on the road!"

A tall man, fortyish, reddish brown hair and beard, is standing behind the lectern. His shoulders are broad and he has a large nose with a bump halfway down the bridge. He's wearing a black shirt with sleeves rolled up to display his tattooed muscular forearms.

The buzz of conversation dies. Larry takes a seat in the back, at the end of the aisle, with an empty chair between him and the guy next to him. He's worried to be in an enclosed space with so many unmasked people. The meeting probably violates COVID guidelines, but Larry, glancing at the AK-47 in the lap of the guy next to him, isn't going to report it. Once everyone is seated, the speaker scans the room quietly, taking the measure of his audience. He smiles.

"It's good to see so many patriots who care about their country and have the weapons to defend it. I'm Ron Peterson, president of Kentucky People's Militia. I'm passing a sheet around. You'll see there are places for your name, address, phone, and email. There's also a place to list whether you've ever been convicted of a felony. You don't have to say if you don't want to, but the reason I'm asking is it may matter if, at some point, the Justice Department or the Sheriff wants to deputize us."

Deputize?

"That'll never happen," someone in the audience shouts. "The Democrats won."

"Maybe they did and maybe they didn't," Ron says, still smiling. "Things aren't always what they seem. And when the civil war starts, even Democrats will whistle a different tune. Either way, we have friends in law enforcement who see things the way we see them. The way I think *you* see them."

Has Larry stepped into the Twilight Zone? He's not unfamiliar with the alternate universe cultivated in the petri dishes of Fox News, The 700 Club, and social media trolls, but to see it embodied in flesh and blood, ensouled with human agency, is like hiking through the woods, turning the corner, and seeing Bigfoot twenty feet away. He never knew people like this were in his neighborhood. Like Ron Peterson says, things aren't always what they seem.

"Anyway," Peterson says, "our neighborhood needs security no matter who claims to be the government. The Deep State is just that, deep. That's why President Trump was robbed in a fraudulent election. He was making America great again, but the Deep State didn't like that, and the Deep State is deep."

Ron generates a presence when he speaks, a testosterone-infused aura of authority. And he's intelligent. Probably the higher-ups of the Nazi Storm Troopers were intelligent, too. Larry looks at faces around him: rapt, serious, believing. Probably the Storm Troopers were good citizens who loved their children. The thing that strikes Larry about everyone in the room is that they all are human beings, no different than Larry. Except they have guns and an urge to shoot them at other people.

"Different things can happen," Peterson says. "For example, our neighborhood needs protecting from Antifa and Black Lives Matter."

"Assholes on my street have Black Lives Matters signs," says someone on the audience, indignantly, "and most of them are white, for Chrissakes!"

Peterson nods, expressing his disgust and his solidarity with the speaker. Then he squares his jaw and looks at the audience.

"Just remember that Donald John Trump is still our President. When he calls us, when we are chosen, like the disciples of Jesus, we'll enforce the Constitution by all means necessary, even it means giving our lives for our country."

The audience breaks into applause. At that moment, the guy next to Larry hands him Ron's clipboard with the information sheet. Larry takes it and nods but has no intention of entering any information. He turns his face back to Peterson, as if filling out the information sheet might cause him to miss an urgent directive Peterson is about to give.

"Should we steal Black Lives Matter signs?" someone asks.

"Up to you. Technically, that's trespassing and theft, so don't get caught. But everyone should keep a list of people on your street who are suspicious."

Larry, the only person in the room wearing a COVID mask, is certain he's one of those people. But what will these patriots do with their "list"? Ron talks for a while about how the election is stolen, ticking off and trashing, one-by-one, all the bad guys—Chuck Schumer, Nancy Pelosi, Hunter Biden, Hillary Clinton, and most of all, Barack Obama, whose election, evidently, was the moment America went to hell in a handbasket. Finally, as the meeting draws to a close,

Ron circles back to the suspicious people in Rosemont Hills

"I'll send a password to the email you enter on the information sheet that will allow you to join Kentucky People's Militia on our website. In the members-only section, you'll have access to our reporting form. You should submit a report on suspicious people who live near you every day, even if you don't have a lot to report. What information are we looking for? First, why are they suspicious? Look for things like rainbow Pride flags or Biden signs. Maybe they're gay or race-mixing. Maybe you know their politics from what they post on social media."

Larry and Samantha's Facebook pages make them poster children for the kind of folks Ron wants dossiers on.

"Second, what kind of security system do they have—cameras, motion detectors? Dogs? Guns? Third, what are their movements? Where do they work, when do they leave, when do they return—both adults and children. What are their travel patterns? What are their vacation plans? This intelligence will be invaluable when the shooting starts. Kristallnacht was a success because the Nazis carefully collected and compiled this kind of intelligence in advance."

Kristallnacht?

Ron ends the meeting with a call to prayer. As all the men bow their heads, pledging to follow Jesus into Armageddon, Larry slides out of his chair and tiptoes out of the room. Out of eyeshot, he quick-walks to the door, opens it, and escapes into the night.

Streetlights shine pools of light on the road. It's spitting rain, almost cold enough to snow. He sets off for home at a brisk pace, looking over his shoulder once or twice, making a mental note to pull up the Black Lives Matter sign from his front yard.

~ ~ ~

Southern Truths

Rachel Maddow is describing the strategies Trump's legal team are using in lawsuits demanding that the vote in states Trump lost be declared fraudulent. Trump's proof of fraud is the fact that he lost, which he contends was impossible without fraud. But Larry is only half-listening to the TV. He's on his laptop, visiting the Kentucky People's Militia website. There's not much there, just a vague paragraph of QAnon gibberish. Larry figures the good stuff is in the members-only section. He wonders whether the FBI is monitoring it.

Since the meeting, Larry has watched for signs of harassment of the Black family that lives a few doors down. He's unaware of any so far, but a couple times he's noticed a guy in a MAGA hat walking down one side of the street and back up the other. Larry knows the dog walkers in the neighborhood—the lesbian couple with six dogs trotting together like a bouquet of flowers on leashes, the old lady whose little white Maltese looks like a Swiffer sweeping the sidewalk, the senior hippie with the old Collie-Shepherd mix that can barely walk. Larry knows the joggers, the power walkers with hand weights, the Black husband and wife one street over who sometimes pass by hand-in-hand, but not so much now that it's cold.

But this guy in the MAGA hat is unfamiliar. He seems to be studying the houses, slowing down to stare, as if he might pull out a notebook and jot notes. But maybe Larry's imagining things. Things aren't always the way they seem. Larry is startled from his reverie when Samantha taps him on shoulder.

"I got a message that my package from Amazon has been delivered, but there's nothing on the porch." She shows him the screen of her phone like it's a smoking gun.

"Did you contact Amazon?"

"I will. But what if somebody just stole it off our porch?" Her point is the intrusion, not the financial loss.

"Tis the season," he says, but porch theft has never happened to them before. They don't have one of those doorbells with a camera, so there's really no way to know. Larry decides to check neighborhood porch thefts on *Rosemont Hills Neighbors*, a website maintained by fellow liberal do-gooders reporting lost pets, garage sales, swaps of goods and services, and local petty crime. Larry sees there have been reports of porch thefts, but more seriously, reports of burglaries. Larry looks at addresses. The burglaries are not just in the section of the neighborhood dedicated to low-rent apartment buildings, nor the main drag where duplexes and fourplexes have front yards the size of prison cells.

"There was a burglary on our street," he says to Samantha.

"On Happy Trails?"

"Yeah, and on Dumpling Court." Dumpling Court is where the six-dog lesbians live.

"I guess the neighborhood watch group you went to isn't protecting us from burglars."

"No, they're protecting us from Joe Biden."

"I thought you said they were getting ready for civil war."

"That, too." Larry hasn't told Samantha that he sent an anonymous tip to the FBI about Kentucky People's Militia, even though the internet says no tip is anonymous if the police want to find you. Larry didn't allege crimes had been committed, only that Peterson mentioned civil war. That probably didn't merit an investigation—people on Truth Social are calling for civil war and Trumper politicians are dropping hints that if it happens, it will be understandable because "people are angry."

"Look!" Samantha says over his shoulder, pointing at the screen. "Rosemont Hills Neighbors is sponsoring a Black Lives Matters march!"

Ron studies the notice. The march will be the afternoon of New Year's Eve to celebrate the upcoming "New Year of Change!"

"Let's march with them, okay?"

"Sure," Larry says. What better way to ensure that he and Samantha are invited to Ron's *Kristallnacht*?

~~~

December 31, 2020, is a sunny afternoon, mid-40s. Larry and Samantha bundle up, put on COVID masks, and walk to Dumpling Court where marchers are assembling. Everyone is wearing masks, even the gal with the megaphone organizing everything. Larry and Samantha wave to various neighbors, then walk over to Joey and Karen.

"Trump is talking martial law again," Joey says. "He says he can declare the election illegal under the Insurrection Act because it's treason."

Larry nods and looks at the ground, not in the mood to plumb the depths of Trump's insanity. But Joey isn't finished.

"Actually, I hear that the Nashville bombing outside the AT&T building Christmas Day was a right-wing militia operation."

"They say it was suicide," Larry says.

"Yes, that's what they say, but things aren't always the way they seem. Trumpers say the bombing was to destroy data on AT&T servers that proves election fraud."

"Why would right-wing militia do that? They *want* to prove there was election fraud, right?"

"Right, but they can't, because there was no fraud. So they blow up AT&T servers they claim would have proved it, then spread rumors that Biden ordered the bombing to cover up theft of the election, which justifies declaring martial law and dissolving Congress, which means the electors can't report the results of the election and Biden can't take office."

Larry can't wrap his head around what Joey is telling him, but that's a daily experience during the Trump era. Fortunately, it's time to march.

"One household per line," the megaphone gal says, "or at least socially distance."

The crowd begins to form lines behind two Black women, six feet apart, holding poles that support a large Black Lives Matter banner. Row after row they fill the road, marching down Dumpling Court like orderly ants. When it's Larry and Samantha's turn, Joey and Karen join their row at a distance of six feet that quickly shrinks to three feet as Samantha and Karen move closer to talk.

The column slows as they near the intersection with Happy Trails. Larry looks over his shoulder and sees most of the marchers are white. The Black women in front carrying the BLM banner take a right turn, lift up their megaphones, and begin the chant.

"Black Lives Matter! Black Lives Matter!"

Marching this way down his own street in Rosemont Hills startles Larry's sensibilities. Unlike protests downtown on streets lined with businesses and government buildings, this crowd is shouting twenty or thirty feet from living rooms and bedrooms in a safe suburban neighborhood. Some yards they pass have *We Support the Police* and *Blue Lives Matter* signs. How do occupants of those homes feel about this protest? Do they think Antifa is invading?

Larry feels swept up by the force of voices amplifying each other exponentially, and for a moment it feels like the group has power—but power to do what? They're mostly just a bunch of white liberals protesting in their own neighborhood against a wrong that rarely touches them directly and mainstream media has all but forgotten amid the tsunami of COVID news and Trump's daily tweet tantrums. Larry is ashamed to admit that only after the chanting started did he recall George Floyd and the others and remember what's being protested. In the distance Larry hears a flurry of explosions—*bam-bam-bam-bam-bam!* And for a moment, he thinks it's gunfire, then realizes people are celebrating New Year's Eve early.

When they pass the crest of the hill, Larry sees vehicles parked crossways in the street at the end of Happy Trails, where it opens to the highway. At first he thinks BLM organizers have sealed off the end of Happy Trails so automobile traffic will not interfere with the march, but as the marchers close the distance, Larry sees that the vehicles are pickups and standing in the beds are men with guns. As the front of the parade draws near, the men in the trucks jeer and shout obscenities. One of them holds up a noose. The Black women holding the banner pivot to the left, down a side street, without breaking stride, as if the turn was planned. As marchers reach the pivot point, they shake their fists at the armed and bearded men, but keep shouting "Black Lives Matter! Black Lives Matter!" When Larry and Samantha reach the pivot point, Larry spots Ron Peterson, a pistol in his hand, staring at him.

~~~

Thanks to camera phones, the protest makes local news and social media. So do the men in the trucks, denominated a "counterprotest" sponsored by the Kentucky People's Militia. Larry and Samantha are liking and sharing posts about the protest when the doorbell rings. Larry goes to the door. A man in a tan overcoat, open in front, dark pants, white shirt, and red tie, unfolds his wallet, displaying a badge.

"I'm Detective Doug Burns with the LPD Bureau of Investigation. I'm investigating the protest. Do you have time to answer a few questions?"

Larry lets him in, takes his coat, drapes it over a chair in the dining room, and escorts him to the living room. Samantha looks alarmed by this intrusion of a stranger.

"This is Detective Burns," Larry says. "He has questions about the protest."

"I'm Samantha."

"I know," Burns says. "Larry and Samantha." The detective knows who they are. Why? He places his phone on the coffee table, tells them he's going to record the interview, and pulls out a notebook and pen.

"You were in the march, right? Who else do you know who was there?" Larry and Samantha tick off names of neighbors and Burns writes them down.

"What about the counter-protesters?"

"You mean the men in the pickup trucks who were making threats?" Samantha asks.

"What kind of threats were they making?" Burns asks. Samantha gives an account of what she heard and mentions the noose.

"Did either of you recognize the men in the truck?" Burns said *either of you* but he's looking directly at Larry.

"I know the name of one of them," Larry says. "Ron Peterson."

"What do you know about Peterson?"

"He's the leader of a militia group. They have a website."

"How do you know about this website? Are you a member of this group?"

"No, I'm not. Someone put a flyer in our door about a neighborhood watch meeting and I went. Peterson spoke at the meeting."

Burns is expressionless, neither confirming nor denying he believes Larry. Then he says, "You're on the side of Black Lives Matter. When you went to that meeting, were you spying on the Kentucky People's Militia?"

There is something very deliberate about the way Burns asks. Larry panics, remembers Peterson said he has friends in law enforcement, remembers Peterson staring at him from the struck bed, remembers the anonymous tip he made. Did Burns trace it to Larry? Is Burns a militia sympathizer?

"No, when I realized it was a militia group, I left."

This isn't exactly true. Burns stares at Larry. Then he says, "I guess things aren't always the way they seem."

Burns has more questions. Does Larry know other members of the militia or anything about their activities? Larry doesn't. Has he communicated with Peterson or other members of the militia by phone, email, text, in-person, or otherwise, either before or after the protest? Larry hasn't.

"Officer," Samantha says, "what exactly are you investigating?"

"I'm not at liberty to say." Burns switches off his recorder, closes his notebook, stands, and thanks them for their time.

~~~

During the next two days, Larry gives himself over to paranoia. Is Burns investigating the protestors? Larry looks up the crimes of riot, disorderly conduct, and unlawful assembly. They require violent conduct or danger. The protest, insofar as Larry knows, was peaceful. Is Burns investigating the militia? Larry hopes so, but Burns hadn't asked for details on Peterson's willingness to engage in insurrection. Is Burns a militia sympathizer investigating Larry? If so, why hadn't he asked if Larry had reported the militia to law enforcement? Larry is pacing back and forth in the living room when Samantha says, "I need an avocado."

"What?"

"An avocado for the salad. Can you run to Kroger? And pick up a bottle of wine."

Larry backs the car out of the driveway and turns on NPR. Trump is tweeting that he will punish fashion magazines for never putting Melania on their covers. Republicans are claiming the Georgia Senate runoff is fraudulent, though it hasn't taken place yet. Larry turns off the radio.

Kroger's lot is packed. Larry parks some distance from the store and is about halfway to the entrance when he spots Ron Peterson coming toward him. Peterson is carrying a plastic bag of groceries. When he sees Larry, he scowls, then paces quickly toward Larry, forcing a fake smile.

"You were at the meeting, weren't you?" he says, shifting the grocery bag to his left hand as he puts his right hand on the gun holstered at his waist. At that moment, two uniformed police officers appear on either side of Peterson and grab him by the arms.

"You're under arrest," one of them says. The officers force Peterson face down over the hood of a parked car. They remove his gun from its holster, cuff him, and walk him to a police cruiser.

~~~

"The good guys win!" Larry opens a second bottle of wine.

"Slow down," Samantha says. She's right, he's had too much, but not every day does Larry prevent civil war. He wonders if he'll get a medal or an interview on *60 Minutes*. He can hear Lesley Stahl saying "What would you do if you knew an armed militia planned to overthrow the government? Tonight, we'll talk with a man who may have saved our democracy."

Samantha switches from CNN to the eleven o'clock news. After a couple of commercials, Ron Peterson's mug shot appears on the screen.

"Tonight, police arrested the alleged leader of a burglary ring that has been terrorizing Central Kentucky."

Burglary?

"Ron Peterson, leader of the Kentucky People's Militia, was taken into custody this afternoon and charged in connection with a series of burglaries over the past six weeks. Authorities say Peterson used his position in the militia to gather information about the security systems and travel patterns of burglary victims, ensuring the burglaries could be accomplished when the victims were not home. Peterson also is implicated in a rash of porch thefts. Police say members of the militia gathered information used to accomplish the burglaries and gave it to Peterson, believing it would be used in a civil war to restore Donald Trump to the presidency. Peterson has a previous record for crimes involving theft and deception."

There will be no interview with *60 Minutes.* Larry's anonymous tip didn't mean diddly. He looks at Samantha. She takes his glass, pours, hands it back to him, grins.

"I guess things aren't always what they seem to be."

Southern Truths

Rapture

E.E. King

Priscilla sat next to her husband Hewn. The road on either side of them stretched ahead, endless, flat, and arid. They had a long drive before them. It was hundreds of miles from their home in Lynchburg, Tennessee, to Salvation, Oklahoma. There she and Hewn would join hands and hearts with 100,000 or more brethren under the big white tent. There they would raise their voices in prayer, giving thanks together under the watchful eyes of God and Jesus.

The wind blew, dusting the trees and flowers gray. The land was colorless. Priscilla's hands moved back and forth, forth and back, knitting a pair of blue wool booties for Hewn. He already had more than twenty pair, but she liked to keep occupied.

"Idle hands are the devil's tools," she sighed.

The view ahead was blocked by a huge semi. "Jesus bless this journey," Priscilla muttered. "Jesus bless the loneliness of the long-distance trucker and keep him company."

Suddenly, as if in answer to her supplication, the doors of the semi flew open. A dozen figures rose out of the truck—up, up, up, lighter than prayer, higher than the notes of Sister Jessie Fargo's soprano solos.

"It's the Rapture!" cried Priscilla, "Jesus, take me too. Jesus, don't leave me here, poor miserable sinner though I am."

She fumbled with the car door handle, struggling to release her seat belt and unlock the door. The bodies soared above her, disappearing like lost hope. It seemed forever before she managed to open the door.

She cast herself out, gazing expectantly into the heavens. She did not rise into the air like the floating bodies. She did not ascend to meet Jesus in the sky. She didn't even get a good look at the flawless, female forms vanishing like prayers into the clouds. They were unicolored, these figures, toothless pink mouths wide open in a silent scream.

No, instead the pavement rose to meet her, harder than disbelief, final as endings A second semi raced over her, flattening her flesh and faith across two lanes. She never knew that the truck ahead of her belonged to a blow-up doll manufacturer who had forgotten to latch his doors.

The Sword and The Trowel

Lancelot Schaubert

It'd started with a dark joke offered to a heart surgeon. Not over golf—golf wasn't exactly Rex's thing. Nah, they were in the backyard of this more-money-than-sense heart surgeon trying to distill pine sap into turpentine in order to make a survival recipe accelerant.

Pine sap'll burn in rain, it's crazy stuff. Guy was a billionaire, the heart surgeon. Sort of an over-paid doctor who buys up gobs of local real estate and stock and corn futures and obscure books and lithographs and then simply lets his money make money.

They'd been at the surgeon's house working that pine sap over. Not at the house, actually—they were in what Rex had nicknamed "the catacombs" on the nice days and "the bunker" on the bleak ones. Suppose he could have flipped the names, either way. The man was bragging about his gun stock.

Dr. Courtenay had dug tunnels all over his property and filled them with Glocks and AK-47s. He could, if he'd wanted, have started a small revolt. A man like him had tried in Illinois once, they'd even had a tank before the Feds came and shut them down. The sort of man who reads stories like *The Most Dangerous Game* and thinks, "I want a hunting story like *that*."

Dr. Courtenay asked, point-blank, what Rex would do if there was an active shooter situation at their megachurch. I won't mention the name here, but it's the church you've passed on your commute. You know the one.

Rex said simply, "Get as many people as I can to the exit. That's my job."

"What?" Dr. Courtenay asked, indignant. "No, I meant as someone so obviously skilled with a pistol."

Rex eyed him almost angrily. "Get as many people as I can to the exit."

Dr. Courtenay eyed him, both eyes, one squinted, while sipping his Manhattan. "But you've surely been held up before. Mugged?"

"In those situations, I use a matchbox with a twenty-dollar bill rubber-banded around; it does more good. Most folks just want money."

"But we're talking about an active shooter, a mass shooter."

"Yes."

"So he doesn't want money, but revenge. Or some twisted glory. What then?"

"Get as many people—"

"To the exit, sure. But why? Why, Rex? When you could take them out yourself in a handful of quick shots?"

Rex took a sip of his beer and swallowed, thinking of how he could explain years of de-escalation training, of the awful, awful things in war you think, as a boy, that you want to experience—until you do. Then he took another sip. Then swallowed, breathed in deeply, and said, "Because I know of no church more heavily armed. And I know of no group of people with that many firearms that knows so very little about basic gun safety. If there's an active shooter in that building, you'll have hundreds of guns whipped out. And it's not like in the cowboy movies where it's all bandits and no-name redshirts."

"Redshirts?"

"No-name disposable characters who don't matter to you."

"Why they called redshirts?"

"It's a Star Trek thing."

"You're a Trekkie?"

"Never mind, Court. Point is these are real, innocent people. Or an innocent as idiots with guns can be. Redshirts and bandits would be nice, but in a crowd full of heavily armed untrained idiots, people will get hurt."

Dr. Courtenay sat and thought. The frown lines showed that wasn't what he'd wanted to hear. "Solution?"

"Teach them safety. De-escalation."

"Would you do it?"

"Oh sure, if I had the place. I don't have the place. Takes too much money to build a firing range. Then to build a business. Then to run the damn thing."

Dr. Courtenay smiled. Clearly *that* was what he wanted to hear. "I'll fund it. Fund everything else in this town, why not that?"

Rex had not expected that. "Uh." He'd come to teach the man to distill pine sap. Seemed he'd failed in that regard.

~~~

But start it they did, you see. They picked a plot of land just outside city limits to avoid city taxes and the city building code that had gotten so much more complicated since the disaster. They built a long warehouse, multiple compartments in it, multiple types of firing ranges—mobile, static, battle, hunting.

They hung a sign over the door with a Bible verse from Nehemiah 4:15-23:

When our enemies heard that we knew their scheme and that God had frustrated it, every one of us returned to his own work on the wall. From that day on, half of my men did the work while the other half held spears, shields, bows, and armor. The officers supported all the people of Judah, who were rebuilding the wall. The laborers who carried the loads worked with one hand and held a weapon with the other.

... and they told everyone they'd build the church with one hand and defend her with the other. But only wisely. Only wisely. They named the shooting range The Sword and The Trowel.

The parishioners came in droves to learn firing etiquette, technique—mostly how not to shoot themselves or their friend in the process. Every once in a while, someone would pull off a specific caliber shot— most often one of the .32 pistols or .45s—and Rex was back in the truck on the .40 cal, blowing holes through the walls of the *mudhif*, the ones made of swamp reeds— which was little more than large-scale mowing. He'd only learn later that the local village had used the *mudhif* as a wedding venue. And a guest house.

The *sheikh* had hosted American soldiers there. But what did Marsh Arabs know about hospitality? Rex would shake his head and be back there, trying to decide whether to keep teaching or to burn the whole place down and take the insurance money. In the end, he'd been right: they needed more, not less, folks in town to know how to take a hot and dangerous situation and turn it into something far, far gentler.

It did bother him, though, that parents brought their seven-year-olds. Legally, he couldn't keep them from doing it. He could turn them away as a business owner, but the culture here was so gung-ho gun go that he worried word would get out and then he wouldn't have any customers. Businesses, after all, are just glorified beggars. The difference between a missionary or an artist who asks for patronage and a business is that the businessman thinks he built it himself, not his patrons. So if he turned down too many kids... teach the young, he figured. Might work out okay, raising up the next generation to think differently about this than their parents did.

Many of them wanted him to tell war stories. They had *M*A*S*H* and *We Were Soldiers* in mind. They didn't realize what it's like to be forced to eat an MRE while brain tissue drips from the mud ceiling 'cause your commander needed you at rendezvous at five o'clock so he could take the rest of the day off. This your commander requested from the safety of the embassy. No need to belabor the horrors. They'd told him that the number of things he'd seen was fit for a Delta Force agent. He was just a regular. But the deployment, redeployment, promotions: the things he'd seen—all of this had taken its toll.

So now he just said, "No thanks," to the sixty-year-old blue-haired accountant from the missionary forwarding agency.

"Hold your palm under the grip like this." Weeks and weeks he worked. They made a lot of money on memberships, target sales, and bullet-proof vests.

It didn't matter.

~~~

The active shooter came into the back dressed like a bit character from *The Matrix*. Not Goth, so much, as military blacks with pads. It was around that time that the hymn started up:

The day of resurrection!
Earth, tell it out abroad;

The shooter lifted his assault rifle. A single scream came from one of the ushers right before the guy shot the minister. The singing stopped, but the words remained on the screen:

the Passover of gladness,
the Passover of God.

As the shooter turned on the crowd in the section to his left, five men pulled out pistols.

A cop came running.

The shooter fired on the crowd, splitting the skulls and chests of the homeschooling co-op.

From death to life eternal,
from earth unto the sky,

The five men opened fire on the guy. Four were terrible shots and hit the crowd in the balcony. They killed Mr. Heiber, who'd planted all of those beautiful pear trees. Trimmed them so they didn't turn into sails that cracked or uprooted. The Barnabas ministry often turned those pears into tarts for the old grandmas pinochle group.

Their stray shots also hit Miss Gyzander, who'd taught most of the children in the building how to play piano, how to sing, how to play chimes for the chime choir.

Another volley hit Mr. and Mrs. Thompson, a couple of insurance tycoons. That took out one of the largest donations to keep the church going, particularly because the Thompsons had yet to revise their will: They'd kept procrastinating about it and the most recent version left everything to the ASPCA in memory of their nasty fifteen-year-old miniature poodle Frenchie who'd kicked the bucket in the middle of his seventh surgery.

The balcony crowd—and many others by this point—thought it was a terrorist attack. Multiple shooters. They weren't wrong. They just didn't consider themselves terrorists.

> our Christ hath brought us over,
> with hymns of victory.

Verse two, also on the screen, read:

> Our hearts be pure from evil,
> that we may see aright

Rex, in the middle of this, was doing what he'd always said he would do: getting as many of the parishioners to the exits as possible. He probably could have pulled his firearm and laid low many of the shooters, as Dr. Courtenay had suggested. But that was the part Rex hadn't really spelled out for the heart surgeon: then he'd be shooting his friends again.

Speaking of which, some other parishioner with a grudge had taken the fray as an opportunity to shoot Dr. Courtenay in the femoral artery. Dr. Courtenay, in his rage, shot back. Both would bleed out before the ambulance and cops arrived.

The active shooter, by the way, had long since died. He was simply the catalyst that set off the chain reaction.

A philosophy professor in the corner lay in the fetal position, muttering and rocking. His hands covered his ears as he muttered, bug-eyed, "Apparently the solution to guns *wasn't* more guns. Apparently the necessary and sufficient cause of a mass shooting *was* a gun. Apparently if you *remove* the gun, you remove the *necessary and sufficient cause.*" The muttering went on and on and on, not half so disturbing as that full body rocking.

No one could hear him over the gunfire. Rex got more of them out of the building than you would have expected. He saved probably a thousand lives between his quick work and his delegation to some brave young students of his own: not the football team, but the Dungeons and Dragons crew. Rex hadn't known folks played D&D at his church, but he didn't mind.

He'd played.

He at least knew what a redshirt was and, he thought darkly, plenty of them were dying today. That's the sort of PTSD-thought he couldn't tell old ladies.

Turns out that D&D crew had spent a lot of time mentally preparing for this situation and being situationally aware. Also, frankly, a couple of the seven-year-olds he'd taught: they did the best. They'd taken Rex's training seriously.

The cops showed up. SWAT. A bunch of armored and armed men surrounding the gladiatorial arena with assault rifles, shouting, "EVERYONE, PUT DOWN YOUR ARMS."

Well, some of those pulled off shots too. And then it was more or less civil war. Right to bear arms and all.

Rex had long since reached the parking lot, muttering to himself, "They don't really believe it. They don't really believe they'll rise. If they did, they wouldn't worry about dying and wouldn't need *the protection*." Then, the seizure came on strong.

Folks he'd helped ran back to try and keep him from biting off his own tongue by shoving their foul-tasting wallets in his mouth.

~ ~ ~

The medicine was helping, mostly. The dog was helping a ton and often as he'd had to put down a dog, this one... this one he probably couldn't. This one... well, as far as his experience went, it hurt the dog just as much to have someone murder it as it would to walk it through a natural death. How could he know? He wasn't the dog. So he softened because of that one. Perpetua, he named her.

Later that week, Rex spray-painted the word *into* over the shooting range sign. The Sword *into* The Trowel. Then he sat in the middle of the empty firing range with a hammer and a forge he'd bought off his new buddy. One of the Dungeons and Dragons crew, a LARPer who'd done most of the medieval armor for that movie they'd shot locally. Rex worked with that guy to pound superheated pistols and assault rifles into shovels and spades, plowshares, and pruning hooks. *Community service*, he thought with each blow of the hammer on the anvil. *Community service*, that was the phrase his therapist had refused to use. They'd hung a new sign, a new Bible verse, over the old one from Nehemiah. This one read:

Many peoples shall come and say, "Come, let us go up to the mountain of the Lord, to the house of the God of Jacob; that he may teach us his ways and that we may walk in his paths." For out of Zion shall go forth instruction, and the word of the Lord from Jerusalem. He shall arbitrate for many peoples; they shall beat their swords into plowshares, and their spears into pruning hooks; nation shall not lift up sword against nation, neither shall they learn war any more.
—Isaiah 2:3–4

~~~

In the background, the national news was alternating clips. They'd show a live clip. Then they'd show a one-liner from a comedy bit. Over and over and over again. New live interview, same old clip from the same old sketch.

The first clip would show a live interview of a congressman saying, "Now is not the time to talk about gun control. You can't change the second amendment."

Then an old Jim Jeffries sketch. Jim said, "Sure you can: it's called an amendment."

Over and over and over they did this: live interview, clip, live, clip.

The locals watched it all like some sick reality-horror show.

It didn't stick.

But the ads for baked beans, cruises, Super Bowl, social media, and summer movies did.

Are you gonna go see the one about that action hero? Looks really good, really good. I hear he does all his own fight scenes. Anyways, see you later, I gotta go get my nails done.

Leave Hospitality at the Door

Brianna Malotke

First came the initial banning of everything
And anything that dared be different.

Children's books went first with pages
Bursting forth with a kaleidoscope
Of differences—showing how beautiful
Being a unique soul can be.

As if taking an *a, e,* or *i* could make
The children *owe you* in the future

The South shields, like an unwanted
Shade, snuffing out the growth
Of these young sunflowers,
Arms desperately reaching out
towards the sky, blindly seeking.

Southern Truths

The next generation, the kind souls
Who just want to read and learn,
Instead fester, growing in anger,
As more and more bans are placed
These young adults' fates intertwine.

The poison that seeps from the roots
In the South forces kids to find a way
To bloom and spread, like clover
Overtaking poison ivy, and they do.

Prayers and thoughts mean nothing
When children are being buried,
Age-appropriate only matters with
Words in a book, nothing else.

As book bans continue, as gun reform
Is pushed aside for words scare more
Than tiny dead bodies, our future
Demolished with each book labeled
Too much, too different, too graphic.

Southern hospitality ends when
You take a stand for a future
Free of hate and full of acceptance.

Delia's Legacy

Alma Emil

Clint Seeger spotted the three gravesites for sale on PlotsAreUs.biz and thought, *Perfect.* The listing read:

Three adjoining plots in the Gracious Redeemer section at Magnolia Grove Memorial Park, just off Main Street in historic Sherville. Family-owned since 1944. An exclusive setting that has been sold out for many years. $10,000.

Of course, Delia would need only one of the spaces, but he thought it best to have some insulation from other graves. At least for the time being.

As soon as he received the Certificates of Ownership from Magnolia Grove, Clint drove out to the old Sherville stone yard to order Delia's headstone.

"Sorry, Clint." Neville Parker, the Black man who owned the stone yard, shook his head. "You see, we don't do much in the way of headstones anymore. It's mostly boulders and pavers for those landscape designers down in Miami." He waved one arm in the direction of a huge granite boulder being loaded onto a flatbed truck. "I still do some engraving for family, but you'll get a much better price if you go with one of the big companies out of state. You pick a design from their online catalog and they ship your headstone direct to the cemetery. Sorry you drove out all this way. Should've called."

Clint listened, then shook his head. "Neville," he said, "This is a real special stone, and I need you to do it. Delia's ill, likely to go in the next few months. I promised her she could see the stone beforehand, make sure it's exactly what she wants."

"Sorry to hear about that," Parker said. He paused, sighed, and stepped one of his dusty workbooks up on a slab of black marble. "Well, how about you folks write up what you want to see on the stone, and I'll get you an estimate. Artwork—you know, angels, trees, and such—those'll be extra."

"Money's not an issue," Clint said. "And we can skip the angels. I brought the inscription with me." He reached into his worn sports coat and pulled out a folded sheet of white paper. "See what you think."

Parker took the paper, fished reading glasses from the pocket of his blue work shirt, and walked slowly over to the shade of the building. He unfolded the paper and read the few typed lines. Then he read it again. He looked over at Clint and raised a bushy eyebrow. "Just where you planning to put this stone, man?"

"Magnolia Grove Memorial Park. Gracious Redeemer section."

Both of Parker's eyebrows went up. "Heh. You don't say. Well, I can get you a real good price on this one. I'd say you're going to find out just how Gracious those Redeemers are."

The two shook hands and Clint strode back to his car. Behind him, he could hear the stonemason chuckling, "Magnolia Grove. Gracious Redeemer section. We'll see."

Delia died peacefully three months later—far more peacefully than she'd lived, Clint reflected. He received the usual round of effusive condolences that were *de rigueur* in a small Southern town. Many friends and neighbors, most of them elderly, attended the funeral. For all that Delia had rabble-roused her way through life, she and Clint were still from one of Sherville's oldest and most respected families. Their ancestors dated back to the bad old days of the antebellum South. Especially as they'd grown older, their liberal opinions and progressive politics had been dismissed as quaint and harmless. One neighbor, seeing a "Biden for President" sign in their front yard, had remarked to her minister that both of the Seegers must have dementia.

After a quiet graveside ceremony, Delia Seeger was left to rest in peace for six months. Then, after the grave dirt had settled properly, her headstone arrived and was "placed" by the groundskeepers. All hell broke loose the following morning.

Clint was not surprised to get a call from Magnolia Grove.

"Mr. Seeger," the cemetery manager began.

Clint grinned. The man's tone, usually unctuous, was for once truly mournful. "Yes?" Clint said.

"Mr. Seeger, I'm afraid that your wife's headstone... well, it's in violation of the cemetery's regulations," the manager said.

"Really? You'll have to show me which ones. My attorney and I went over your regulations in detail, and he assured me my dear wife's headstone is entirely acceptable."

The cemetery manager spluttered like a panful of fried green tomatoes. Meanwhile, reporters began knocking at Clint's front door. He was prepared, with printouts about Delia's distinguished career in law, journalism, and politics ready in a stack by the front door.

Late that night, while everyone else in town was busy watching Sherville's mayor trying to explain the headstone situation on the 11 o'clock news, Clint clipped a bouquet of white blossoms from Delia's favorite lilac bush. Then he strolled the ten blocks over to Magnolia Grove Memorial Park. The elaborate wrought-iron gates of the cemetery were locked for the night, but Clint knew about a gap in the magnolia hedge out by the caretaker's shed. It was conveniently near the Gracious Redeemer section.

He strolled to Delia's grave, knelt, and blinked back his tears. "You're still giving them hell, dear," he said. "I love you."

He set the bouquet of lilacs down in front of a handsome granite headstone bearing the epitaph:

Here lies
Delia Jefferson Seeger
Lifelong activist, feminist,
and crusader for human rights
Born December 4, 1953
Died of embarrassment
November 6, 2024
At the hands of the Republican Party

About the Authors

Marleen S. Barr, who is known for her pioneering work in feminist science fiction theory, taught English at the City University of New York. She received the Science Fiction Research Association Award for Lifetime Contributions to SF Scholarship.

Barr is the author of the novels *Oy Pioneer!* and *Oy Feminist Planets: A Fake Memoir.* Her B Cubed Press volume, *When Trump Changed: The Feminist Science Fiction Justice League Quashes the Orange Outrage Pussy Grabber* is the first single-authored Trump short story collection. It is followed by *This Former President: Science Fiction as Retrospective Retrorocket Jettisons Trumpism.*

Maroula Blades is an interdisciplinary artist living in Berlin. She received 2nd place for her interdisciplinary project, 'Stones in Symphony', at the German 2023 Amadeu Antonio Prize. In June 2023, the UK Society of Authors Foundation awarded her a novella-in-progress grant. The Academy of Arts in Berlin selected her for the 2021 INITIAL Special Grant. In 2020, Chapeltown Books released her flash fiction collection, 'The World in an Eye'. Her works appeared in *The Caribbean Writer, Thrice Fiction, The Decolonial Passage, Ake Review, Abridged Magazine, The London Reader,* and *Midnight & Indigo,* among other publications. Ms. Blades gives bilingual (in English and German) poetry and prose workshops in Berlin schools and high schools. She presents her multimedia projects at many international literary festivals in Germany, such as the Berlin International Poetry Festival, Humboldt University, Brecht House, and Lit-Cologne.

Gary Bloom was born in Minneapolis and attended what is now Minnesota State University, Mankato, where he studied sociology. He has been a teaching assistant in a psychiatric hospital, a driving instructor for spinal cord injury patients, and a computer programmer. His articles, photography, and poetry have been published in newspapers, magazines and websites, including *Kaleidoscope, Milwaukee Magazine, The Buffalo News, The Grand Rapids Press*, and *Black Diaspora*. He is retired and lives in Mississippi.

Zachary Taylor Branch is the pen name of a semi-retired scientist and consultant, enjoying the good life with his wife Nancy in Lorena, TX. "The Gray Horizon" was his first professional fiction sale, his short story "The Nerine Seven" has been published in *Alien Dimensions* Issue #26, *Alien Dimensions Space Fiction Short Stories Anthology Series*, and "Doctor Decon" received an Honorable Mention in *Allegory*'s Fall 2023 issue. His fiction writings are profiled on his blog, https://zacharytaylorbranch.com/ where you can also inquire about his real life, non-fiction writing. His family has deep roots in Virginia, the basis of his fictional New Elisia, and his children David and Elise are too far away in Saint Louis and Houston, pursuing careers in counseling and medicine.

Alan Brickman writes short stories and flash fiction. In his day job, he consults to nonprofit organizations on strategy and organizational development. Raised in New York, educated in Massachusetts, he now lives in New Orleans and can't imagine living anywhere else. Alan's fiction has appeared in the *Ekphrastic Review*, *SPANK the CARP*, *Sisyphus Magazine*, and *Deep Overstock*, among others. He can be reached on his email at alanbrickman13@gmail.com.

Adam-Troy Castro is a science fiction, fantasy, and horror writer living in Florida. His fiction has been nominated for the Hugo, Nebula, Stoker, and World Fantasy awards and he is a winner of the Philip K. Dick Award for *Emissaries from the Dead*. His more than 100 publications include four Spider-Man novels (including the Sinister Six trilogy) and stories with the characters Andrea Cort, Ernst Vossoff, and Karl Nimmitz.

Castro is also widely known for his Gustav Gloom series of middle-school novels and has authored a reference book on *The Amazing Race*.

Allan Dyen-Shapiro is a Ph.D. biochemist, currently working as an educator in Southwest Florida. He has sold short fiction to venues including *Flash Fiction Online* (where he is currently a first reader), *Dark Matter Magazine, Grantville Gazette (Baen's Annex), Small Wonders, Translunar Travelers Lounge*, and numerous anthologies. He also co-edited an anthology of speculative fiction set in the Middle East. He is an active member of SFWA and Codex.

He blogs about issues of interest to his readers at allandyenshapiro.com, where you'll also find links to his stories.

Find him on Facebook (@allandyenshapiro.author) and follow him on Xitter (@Allan_author_SF), Mastodon (@Allan_author_SF@wandering.shop), and Bluesky Social (@allandyenshapiro.bsky.social).

Alma Emil is a pen name for a speculative fiction author raised in the Southeast who loves setting short stories, especially political short stories, in small towns. The gossip! The intrigue! The generations-long feuds!

Stories under another of her pen names, K.G. Anderson, have appeared in *Galaxy's Edge*, *Space and Time Magazine*, *Metaphorosis*, and, of course, B Cubed Press anthologies. For more: http://writerway.com/fiction

Ronald D. Ferguson taught college mathematics for many years and published 4 mathematics textbooks. An active member of the Science Fiction and Fantasy Writers Association, he now writes full-time, both fiction and non-fiction. His short fiction has appeared in numerous venues, most recently "Cylinders" in Flame Tree Publishing's *International Anthology Adventures in Space* and "Druid Days, Dragon Knights" in *NewMyths.com*. He also writes Young Adult fiction using the pen name R D Ferguson. He, his wife, and their rescue dog live near the shadow of the Alamo. Other credits at: www.RonaldDFerguson.com.

Manny Frishberg has been writing stories since he could hold a pencil, and selling them since 2010. He does developmental editing for independent authors and small press publishers, and the bidding of two cats.

David Gerrold is the author of more than 50 books, hundreds of articles and columns, and more than a dozen television episodes. He is a classic sci-fi writer who has created some of the genre's most popular and definitive scripts, books, and short stories. His novels include *When HARLIE Was One*, *The Man Who Folded Himself*, *The War Against The Chtorr* septology, *The Star Wolf* trilogy, *The Dingilliad* young adult trilogy, and the *Trackers* duology. His short story "Night Train to Paris" won the Bram Stoker Award. The autobiographical tale of his son's adoption, *The Martian Child*, won the Hugo and Nebula awards for Best Novelette and was the basis for the film *Martian Child*.

If trucks are the lifeblood of the American way then **JW Guthridge** is an American red-blood cell, carrying foodstuffs throughout the vascular system of Highways and Byways to feed the nation. He is based in Arkansas with his family, including a rather mischievous feline that keeps trying to stow away. Mostly a writer of speculative fiction and fantasies, he also pens travelogues about his journeys. Follow along with his travels at https://www.patreon.com/JW Guthridge

Kay Hanifen was born on a Friday the 13th and once lived for three months in a haunted castle. So, obviously, she had to become a horror writer. Her work has appeared in over fifty anthologies and magazines. When she's not consuming pop culture with the voraciousness of a vampire at a 24-hour blood bank, you can usually find her with her black cats or at https://kayhanifenauthor.wordpress.com
Twitter: https://twitter.com/TheUnicornComi1
Instagram: https://www.instagram.com/katharine hanifen/

Alexander Hay is a writer who currently dwells in North West England, which isn't the Deep South at all, but the beaches are nice, and there is more than enough strangeness to be found. His previous credits include *Nature's Futures, Apex Publishing, Utopia Science Fiction* and *Leading Edge Magazine*. He is presently writing a novel—but then, who isn't?

Larry Hodges, of Germantown, MD, has over 210 short story sales and four SF novels. He's a graduate of the Odyssey and Taos Toolbox writers workshops, a member of Codex Writers, and a ping-pong aficionado. As a professional writer, he has 21 books and over 2200 published articles in 190+ different publications. As an amateur presidential historian he spends much of his free time waving his arms in frustration at those who don't know which president had a pet raccoon, which one is in the Wrestling Hall of Fame, and all the misinformation that comes out during presidential elections. He's also a member of the USA Table Tennis Hall of Fame, and claims to be the best table tennis player in Science Fiction & Fantasy Writers Association, and the best science fiction writer in USA Table Tennis! Visit him at www.larryhodges.com.

Liam Hogan is an award-winning short story writer, with stories in *Best of British Science Fiction* and in *Best of British Fantasy* (NewCon Press). He helps host live literary event Liars' League and volunteers at the creative writing charity Ministry of Stories. More details at http://happyendingnotguaranteed.blogspot.co.uk

Tom Howard is a science fiction and fantasy short story writer living in Little Rock, Arkansas. Inspiration for "Prodigal Sin" was the Pandora's Box myth and what would happen if the vices all lived in one town.

Anya Leigh Josephs is a North Carolina-raised, New York City-based writer of speculative fiction. Their work can be found in venues like *The Deadlands, The Deeps, The Magazine of Science Fiction and Fantasy* (forthcoming), and *Fantasy Magazine.* Anya's debut novel, *Queen of All,* a queer fantasy adventure for young adult readers, is available now. When not writing, Anya works as a psychotherapist, sees an awful lot of theatre, reads voraciously, and worships their cat, Sycorax.

E.E. King is an award-winning painter, performer, writer, and naturalist. She'll do anything that won't pay the bills, especially if it involves animals. Ray Bradbury called her stories, "marvelously inventive, wildly funny and deeply thought-provoking. I cannot recommend them highly enough." She's been published in over 200 magazines and anthologies, including *Clarkesworld, Daily Science Fiction, Chicken Soup for the Soul, Short Edition, Daily Science Fiction,* and *Flametree.* Her newest novel, *Gods & Monsters* is currently being serialized on *MetaStellar*: https://www.metastellar.com/books/gods-and-monsters-by-e-e-king/

Check out her paintings, writing, musings, and books at www.elizabetheveking.com and at https://www.amazon.com/author/eeking

Brianna Malotke is a writer based in the Pacific Northwest. In addition to being a member and on the Social Media team for the Horror Writers Association, she's also co-chair of the Seattle Chapter. Her most recent horror work can be found in *Dark Town, Lost Souls,* and *The Nottingham Horror Collective.* She has horrifying poems and short stories in the anthologies *Beautiful Tragedies 2 and 3, The Dire Circle, Out of Time, Their Ghoulish Reputation, Holiday Leftovers, HorrorScope: A Zodiac Anthology* and *Under Her Skin.* In August 2023, her debut horror poetry collection, *Fashion Trends, Deadly Ends*, was released by Green Avenue Books. Her romance novella series, *Sugar & Steam,* will have its third book released February 2024 and is written under the pen name of Tori Fields. During October 2023 she was a Writer in Residence at the Chateau d'Orquevaux in France. For more: malotkewrites.com

Elisabeth Murawski is the author of *Heiress, Zorba's Daughter* (May Swenson Poetry Award), *Moon and Mercury,* and three chapbooks. *Still Life with Timex*

won the Robert Phillips Poetry Chapbook Prize. A native of Chicago, she currently lives in Alexandria, Va.

Bill Parks lives with his wife and four kids in the Maryland suburbs where they are active in community academic and athletic activities. His writing has appeared in *Green Ink* and *Viridian Door*, among other places, and he's starting an adventitious foray into podcasting by launching Glossed Over, which you can find on all major hosting platforms.

Lancelot Schaubert

Well Bob wanted a bio,
Lance wanted to lie—oh
the trouble's he's garnered at cons.
Cause he tells all the staff he's a live xylograph
dipped in elf blood (post-coated in bronze).
But Bob wants you to know Lance is primed for this show—
New Haven Review bought his work,
as did dear old *McSweeney's* and TOR.com's theses
on power in Brand's wonderwork.
Lance produced photonovels and films on the fossils
that turned into sludge in Alaska.
Then following Buffett, invested his profit,
so blame his career on Nebraska.
There's junk in his home: swords, a Martin in foam
A typewriter, signet, and classics.
Some think it's eccentric—you know we're concentric
in fantasy's own demographics.

Leanne Van Valkenburgh is a Florida-based educator with eighteen years of experience teaching English and social studies to at-risk secondary students. A proud mother of one, she finds inspiration in her travels across the globe, with Norway and Finland as particular favorites. Her adventures have also taken her through Europe and China.

Edd Vick writes stories with stars and ghosts, with dinosaurs and lost children, with worlds both altered and familiar. His first short story collection, *Truer Love and Other Lies*, is available from Fairwood Press.

Heinrich von Wolfcastle is an affiliate member of the Horror Writers Association and a member of the Great Lakes Association of Horror Writers. His work has appeared in multiple anthologies and magazines. Though he lives the life of a recluse, he has been known to emerge from the shadows for trick-or-treaters on Halloween night.

Sara Wiley is a senior at the University of Missouri, studying Theatre with an emphasis in writing for performance. Her play "Spring Cleaning" was a finalist at the Gary Garrison 10-Minute Play Festival in 2024. This is her first written work to be published. Sara aspires to continue writing and hone her craft in graduate school.

Mike Wilson's work has appeared in magazines including *The Pettigru Review, Fiction Southeast, Mud Season Review, The Saturday Evening Post, Deep South Magazine, Still: The Journal, Barely South Review,* and *Anthology of Appalachian Writers Vol. X*. He's author of *Arranging Deck Chairs on the Titanic* (Rabbit House Press 2020) and resides in Lexington, Kentucky.

Cliff Winnig's work appears on the *Escape Pod* podcast; in anthologies such as *Many Worlds, High Noon on Proxima B,* and *Scott's Planet*; and elsewhere. He is a graduate of the Clarion writing program and has taught writing workshops at local science fiction conventions. He hosts the SF in SF reading series and third Sundays for the B Cubed Sunday Morning podcast. When not writing, he plays sitar, studies aikido and tai chi, and sings bass in a local choral ensemble. Though originally from Memphis, he currently lives with his family in Silicon Valley, which frequently causes him to think about the future. He would like to thank Mike Tarkington for the use of the name Degenerates Against Memphis.

Jim Wright is a retired US military intelligence officer and freelance writer. He lived longer in Alaska than anywhere else and misses it terribly. He now lives in the fetid Panhandle of Florida in an ancient Cold War bunker of a house surrounded by alligators and rednecks. Find his Stonekettle Station blog at https://www.stonekettle.com or follow him as Stonekettle on Facebook.

Publishing Southern Truths has been
a profound plunge into a peculiar culture
that is not readily defined nor easily
understood.
We've tried, though.
I can only hope all y'all enjoy this
anthology.
Thank you, Karen, for walking this
road with me.

Bob B.

About B Cubed Press

B Cubed Press is a small press that publishes big books about things that matter.

A percentage of every book we publish is donated to charity—usually the ACLU. We are approaching $6,000 dollars in donations. Note this includes monies from authors who donated their royalties or payment for stories.

We can be reached at Kionadad@aol.com

We're on Facebook as B Cubed Press and our writers gather regularly on the B Cubed Press Project page on Facebook. We can also be found online at https://bcubedpress.wordpress.com

Made in United States
North Haven, CT
15 November 2024

59876991R00178